WORTH FORGIVING

VI KEELAND

Worth Forgiving
ISBN-13: 9781682304242
Edited by: Caitlin Alexander, Warneke Reading
Cover art: ©RomCon ® www.romcon.com
Cover model: Jamie Dominic, www.facebook.com/OfficialJamieDominic
Photographer: Jamie Dominic Photography
Interior layout: Deena Rae @ E-BookBuilders www.e-bookbuilders.com

"When people show you who they are, believe them."
—*Maya Angelou*

This book is dedicated to the man that inspires the words, yet never reads them.

Table of Contents

Chapter 1

Jax

Back in my hotel suite, I let the pulsating stream of hot water in the shower pound my aching muscles. Taking two weeks off from training might as well have been a year for all the screaming my muscles are doing as I finally get my ass back to a gym. Although my body may be pissed at me for more than just taking a few weeks off.

The last couple of months I've abused it. Trying to avoid the circus that my family's life became over the last six months, I've spent half my recent days ducking from reporters and the other half drinking myself into oblivion. It was the reporters that finally got to me. The assholes are relentless, pretending to be joggers while I ran my usual path around Arlington Cemetery, only to jump in front of me and snap pictures. The more pissed off they made me, the more money they'd likely get for their shots.

I've switched hotels twice in the last two weeks, yet the reporters always find me within a day. I'm the cheese to these damn rats and they seem to sniff out where I am before I can even unpack. People in D.C. know who I am, know who my father is. All it takes is a hundred dollar tip to the bellman and the rats are at the door of my suite pretending to be housekeeping. If I can get to the airport without being followed tomorrow, I might finally get some peace in New York. Nobody will care who I am there. The news moves faster, the pictures from the latest story that ran in the New York Times and Wall Street Journal two weeks ago are hopefully long forgotten.

Drying off after my shower, I make the mistake of turning on the flat screen in my bathroom suite, hoping to catch the day's market report. I wipe the steam from the foggy mirror and, just as it clears, a picture of dear ole Dad reflects back from the TV behind me. Unable to stand the sight of his groveling, pathetic face anymore, I flip it off quickly, saving myself the pain of hearing some speech a twenty–two-year-old Harvard grad likely prepared. A speech prepared using results from a poll on what could be done to save his ailing career, I'm sure.

Turns out my father, a once upstanding pillar of the community, public servant extraordinaire, Senator Preston Knight, is the opposite of everything he preaches. The man that I grew up admiring, looking up to for his honesty and hard work, is a complete fraud. A fake. A liar. The opposite of everything he supposedly stood for.

Too in awe of the persona that was my father to see things right in front of my eyes, I justified everything I'd seen over the last decade – him not coming home, interns a little too friendly, even the smell of perfume on his suit as he'd quietly slip in through the back door in the morning, still wearing last night's clothes. I told myself everyone wanted a piece of him, to bask in his light, be near the righteous churchgoing Senator. In reality, it was him that wanted a piece of everyone. Every woman, that is.

Christian values my ass. Six months ago I found out I had a brother. One that is only a matter of weeks younger than me.

The love child of a rising Senator and a drug addict stripper. And the best part? My half-brother, the other spawn of Satan himself, is a fighter that just took the middleweight championship. Something I dreamed about when I was a kid, only to be told repeatedly it wasn't a respectable career by my father. Irony's a bitch sometimes.

I only wish that's where the story ended. It seems that once the news of my father's infidelity broke, there was an endless stream of women who couldn't wait to share their story. Torrid stories of them and my father. The sick shit he was into, things a kid should never know about their parent, regardless of their age. And the adultery wasn't even the worst part. Once he was done with the affairs, he discarded the jaded women like trash, yielding his power and clout to threaten them into submission. A liar, cheat, *and* an abuser.

Lucky me. I look just like him.

Wrapping a towel around my waist, I walk to my ringing cell and answer it, even though I'd rather not.

"Mother," I answer sternly.

"Jackson, where are you?" She's done nothing wrong, yet I can't help but feel resentment toward her. Why is she still standing by his side?

"I'm leaving town for a while. I'm fine." Intentionally, I fail to mention exactly where I'm going. Who knows if she'd tell him, even if I told her not to.

"Your father and I have been worried sick about you." Whatever tension the heated shower helped to uncoil quickly ravels its way back through my muscles at the mere mention of Daddy Dearest.

"Maybe he should have thought about us before he decided to screw half the women from D.C. to California."

"That's not fair, Jackson." Really? I thought I was being nicer than even *he* deserves. I toned down my true feelings out of respect for her.

"I need to go."

"When are you coming back?"

"I don't know."

Mom's quiet for a minute. For a split second I wonder if, maybe, she finally realizes it's not just all about Dad. It's about us, too. The woman has spent her whole life worrying about *his* career. *His* reputation. *His* success. Sometimes I think she's lost who *she* is.

"Your father needs us, Jackson. He needs our support now more than ever," she pauses before going in for the kill. "And the media needs to see us forgive him, if he has any chance of the world forgiving him, too."

"Goodbye, Mother." I don't give her a chance to say anything else before I press end, tossing the phone back on the nightstand.

Feeling more pity than anger after hanging up, I pack my suitcases and don't bother putting clothes on, or pulling the covers back, before crashing on the big soft bed. Tomorrow I move forward. On my terms. With my *own* plans. No looking back at the life I once thought I wanted. Because I never really wanted it, *he* just talked me into believing I did. And you know what? *Fuck him.*

After the best night's sleep I've had in weeks and a flight that actually lands early, I'm eager to get to the new gym. On the way, I make a few calls, checking in with my CFO and assistant. Lucky for me, I have Brady Carlson. He's not just my CFO, he's also my oldest friend. The last few weeks he's been juggling more than just my once thriving investment firm. Reporters stake out our building, nervous clients call hourly needing reassurance that my family's bad publicity won't affect them. It seems my father's stink has made its way into my business to stay for good. I can hear the stress in his voice. He probably hasn't slept in a week. I'm definitely going to owe him a six-figure bonus again this year.

He gives me an update on who's pulled their business from us this week. Brady's more concerned than I am. Frankly, I wouldn't give a shit if the whole damn company folded, if I didn't have people that depended on me for their livelihood. I do my best to assure him everything will settle, but it's difficult since I'm not sure I even believe my own words.

New York makes it easy to blend in. So many people, a frantic flow of pedestrians maneuver to their destination, most even avoiding eye contact. Perfect after the chaos I've been putting up with in D.C. Walking everywhere is so much more appealing than the usual darkly tinted glass town car I've grown accustomed to being shuttled in from place to place.

Opening the door to the gym, I'm greeted by a muscle head standing behind the desk. He looks up anxiously as I enter, catches sight of me, and practically snarls. Clearly I'm not who he was expecting.

Walking to the desk, I expect him to look back up, but he pretends I'm not standing right in front of him, even though I'm less than two feet from his face. So much for the customer service in this damn place.

"Think you can direct me to a trainer named Marco? I'm supposed to meet him here."

Muscle head points to the back, but never looks up again. Welcome to New York.

Marco is the cousin of my trainer in D.C. Although I've never met him before, I would've recognized him anywhere. He's the spitting image of his cousin Mario, only some silver has started to gleam through his thick, shoe polish black mane. It's slicked back in that Soprano-ish way that few young guys can pull off without looking like they're wearing a costume. This guy wouldn't look right with anything else. We train for close to three hours, yet a hair isn't out of place when we're done.

"How long you in town for? Mario said maybe I could look into some local fights for you." Marco stops me as I walk out of the locker room, my hair still damp from the long shower.

I laugh to myself, but Marco doesn't get the joke. His cousin Mario's been trying to get me in the ring for some real fights for years. Not a day has gone by in eight years where we didn't end a session with him asking, "Want me to book you a fight? You're ready, you know."

I've been fighting since I was a kid. The trainers tell me I'm good enough to make a go of it in the ring, but I've never really given it any serious consideration. I was always *expected* to do something more appropriate for a living. "After all, you are a Knight," My father would always say.

"I'm not sure how long I'm staying yet." I pause, allowing myself for the first time since I was a kid with dreams of my own to seriously think about getting in the ring for a real fight. Getting in the ring for a pro fight wasn't part of my plan, but that's the beauty of having your *own* plan and not living up to anyone else's expectations. My plans can change…because they're *mine*. "You know what, I'll think about it, Marco." And for the first time, I really might.

6

Marco nods. "Stop at the front desk. Get on my schedule for the rest of the week, either way."

Slinging the strap to my gym bag diagonally over my chest, I wave goodbye to one of the guys I sparred with and head toward the door with a chin lift back to Marco. I expect to find Mr. Friendly from this morning at the reception desk, but instead, the scenery is much better. A beautiful woman sits behind the long counter. She's completely engrossed in what she's doing. Unlike the asshole from this morning who intentionally ignored me, she has no idea I'm even standing in front of her. I can't help but smile as I watch her thick gray pencil move feverishly over the sketch paper, her petite hands half covered in charcoal. A slight smile on her face tells me she's in another place...a good one. One that must be her escape. I can't take my eyes off her as she studies the drawing, her smile growing even bigger when she lifts her head to take in the full sight of her page. She likes what she sees on the paper, almost as much as I like what I see in front of me.

Long blond wavy hair, half of it tied on top of her head haphazardly in some sort of a twist, the other half hangs loosely framing her porcelain skinned face. Big, bright, blue-green eyes, I get the urge to move closer so I can study them close up to debate the actual color. Her smooth skin is devoid of the makeup that woman as beautiful as her seem to think makes them look better, only it usually doesn't. Thick black eyelashes frame her almond shaped eyes. Full pink lips, half the bottom one sucked in, gripped between her teeth as she concentrates, studying her drawing. Beautiful. It almost seems a shame to interrupt her.

"Hi." Eventually beginning to feel guilty for my staring, I finally speak. Her head comes up, eyes traveling slowly up to my face before finally reaching mine. For a few seconds, she still doesn't see me, even though she's looking right at me. Until she comes back from wherever her head has been and our eyes lock, her full lips part, and the jolt from finding me standing there knocks her right off her chair.

Chapter 2

Lily

I knew what being late to work meant. Caden was going to go apeshit, only it had nothing to do with him having to cover for me at the front desk for less than an hour. In his twisted mind, the only reason I could possibly be fifty minutes late to work on a Friday morning was that I was sleeping with someone. It didn't matter who. The waiter from dinner, the guy that politely and innocently opened the door for me at the coffee shop, or perhaps even the teller at the bank where I took too long to make a deposit the other day.

I don't remember the exact moment the jealousy and possessiveness started. Maybe it was always there, only I was too desperate to see it. But by the time I opened my eyes, accusations were part of our daily routine. I guess it doesn't help that I own a gym. A place filled with hulking men ramped up with too much testosterone. The place Caden also happens to spend most days training for his upcoming fight at the MMA Open.

Ralley's Gyms were started by my Dad and his partner, Caden's Uncle, Joe Ralley. The two men were best friends since they were kids. Both dedicated to the sport of fighting, my Dad made his name as a fighter and Joe as a professional trainer. Fifteen years ago my Dad, known to everyone in the fighting world only as "The Saint", retired as Middleweight Champion of the US Boxing Conference. Capitalizing on his fame, and Joe's talent as a trainer, the two best friends decided to open a gym dedicated to Mixed Martial Arts Training. At the time, the sport was just gaining national popularity and there were few gyms devoted to training fighters who wanted to go into MMA professionally. The dynamic duo's gym took off as the sport grew rapidly. One gym turned into two, then four, then eighteen after only three years. Today, the Ralley name has the east coast fighter market locked up, operating sixty-two locations.

Reluctantly, I peer through the glass front door of the gym. I feel a sigh of relief that he's not there. Sitting. Stewing. Waiting for me to walk in for a full onslaught inquisition. But the damn bells tied to the top of the door rattle loudly, even though I try my best to open the door quietly. Shit, I need to get rid of those things.

"Where you been?" Caden's on me before my jacket is even fully off.

"I overslept. Sorry you had to cover for me." Giving him a hesitant, forced smile, I shrug, trying to sound casual and grab the mail on the counter at the front reception desk.

"Then why didn't your phone wake you? I called. You must have been too *busy* to pick up." There's no mistaking the anger in his voice and the bite of sarcasm at my being *busy*.

Digging my phone from my purse, I look at the screen finding eleven missed calls. All from Caden. A quick survey of the times tells me he was growing impatient. Fast. The first few calls were five minutes apart...the last few, less than a minute elapsed before he was hitting redial. "Sorry. I must've forgotten to turn the ringer back on last night. I went to class and then fell asleep."

"You're sorry for a lot this morning, aren't you?"

I lower my voice, I really don't want a scene. Not again. "Please don't do this now, Caden. I went to class and then home. I didn't hear my phone alarm go off for the same reason I didn't hear your calls. My ringer was off. Don't turn it into something more than it is." I pause, deliberating my words for a few seconds. "And you need to stop acting like we're still together, Caden." I don't want to be hurtful, but he needs more than a subtle reminder he has no right to question what I'm doing anymore. I know he's nervous about his big fight coming up, so I've been treading lightly. Obviously lightly isn't the right tactic.

Pete, Caden's regular sparring partner, whistles from a distance. Caden looks torn between interrogating me more and getting back to his training. Lucky for me, a loud, impatient shout from Pete helps him make the decision, which earns me a reprieve. A temporary one, anyway.

Pointing an angry finger at me before leaving the front desk area, Caden warns, "This conversation isn't over." But it's definitely over for me.

Even with my lateness, I'm able to get all my work done by the early afternoon. Caden may not be the right man for me, but over the last nine months, he's done so much to make managing things easier. After my father's heart attack, I was barely able to function, let alone keep up with the business of running sixty-two independently operated gyms. Caden's uncle is a great guy, but managing the business end of things was Dad's responsibility. Joe's idea of keeping the books straight meant throwing receipts in a shoe box. Literally, a shoe box.

Reeling from the death of the only parent I'd ever known, I was lucky to have Caden. He computerized the books, set up a payroll system, and even got the trainer's schedules online for customers to book. All while I was barely functioning. A state of shock had set in after my father's unexpected death rendering me almost useless at work. Truly, I'm not sure what I would have done without him. I only wish things between us would have stayed professional. Getting involved with him romantically just happened. He wasn't shy about wanting to be with me, and I, well, I didn't say no. Devastated from the loss of a man who had been the center of my universe, I was desperate to fill a void. I thought Caden was the answer at the time. Boy was I wrong.

With Caden out for a few hours this afternoon at a meeting with his agent and fight promoter, and the phones oddly silent for a change, I'm able to get almost a solid hour of sketching in before the sound of a man's voice startles me. Completely engrossed in my drawing, the deep, raspy sound takes me by surprise and I jump half out of my seat. Unfortunately, *half* out of your seat doesn't end nearly as well as jumping *fully* out of your seat. Because I'm sitting Indian style, one leg gets stuck in the arm of the chair as my body jerks forward in reaction to the sound which catches me off guard. The momentum of my weight falling one way has the opposite reaction on the chair I'm still half sitting on. It tips backwards, falls to the floor, taking my leg with it. Of course, my entire body is forced to follow my leg. I land flat on my back. Somehow the chair I was entangled in, now on top of me.

"Are you okay? I didn't mean to scare you," says the deep voice that started this mess. Lifting the chair from on top of me, one large hand extends down, offering assistance, which I take, thoroughly embarrassed at my clumsiness.

Back on my feet, I right my clothes, pulling down my top, which seems to have sailed in the opposite direction when I tumbled down in a wholly unladylike fashion. Finally looking up to clearly see the face attached to the deep voice, my gaze is met by a tall, broad, extraordinarily beautiful man. Feeling flustered from the combination of falling off my chair and finding a devastatingly beautiful creature standing so close to me, I'm relieved to see my sketches strewn all over the floor. It allows me a minute to collect my wits. Reaching down, I begin to collect my papers, but beautiful man is a gentleman too. Crouching down to his knees, he helps gather the books and loose drawings that dislodged from my sketchbook.

"I'm sorry, I didn't hear you come in." Of course, now that I want the bells to sound, they're no longer there…mostly because I untied them from the door the minute Caden left. Perhaps they really did serve a purpose other than just alerting Caden to my arrival.

Beautiful man smiles, "I didn't just walk in, I've been here for hours. I was in the back with Marco."

"Oh."

Extending the papers he's collected in my direction, he asks, "You drew these?"

I nod.

"All of them?" Beautiful man motions to the half dozen or so sketches he's collected from the floor.

I nod again.

"Mind if I look?"

I shake my head no. He smirks, likely at my inability to form verbal responses. What the hell, did my little fall turn me into a mute?

As the stranger slowly studies my drawings, I slowly study him. Dirty blond hair, damp from a recent shower, cut short and styled haphazardly in a sexy, *I just got laid* kind of way. My eyes follow the chiseled line of his jaw from one side to the other. Michelangelo couldn't have created a stronger male profile. Unable to stop myself, I chance a glance down lower to what appears to be an equally stunning carved physique beneath a thin white shirt straining slightly to cover his broad chest.

Taking more willpower than I care to admit, I force my eyes back to the man just as he looks back to me. Pale blue eyes peek out from beneath long, thick dark eyelashes, the raw beauty knocks the breath right out of me and I actually gasp a little. No man should be so stunning. He really requires a warning before he enters a room.

A slight uptick on the right side of his perfectly full lips tells me he knows the effect he has on me. I mean how can he not? What woman doesn't this beautiful man affect at first glance?

"You're good." His deep voice is smooth, like running your hand across thick, plush velvet.

Brows furrowed, I haven't a clue what he's talking about. Mr. Beautiful chuckles a bit, realizing I'm lost. "Your drawings, they're really good."

"Thank you."

"Do you show your work?"

"No. It's just a hobby. I take a few art classes."

"Well you're good enough for it to be more than a hobby."

"Oh, thank you." I smile. "I'd love to draw you." The statement blurts from my lips before my brain catches up. I slap my hand across my mouth in a lame, late attempt to try to stop the words, but it's too late, they're already out there.

He smiles, looking amused at my fumbling, and arches one eyebrow intrigued. "I'd love that."

"You'd love what?" Caden's angry voice booms from behind Mr. Beautiful. Taking that bell down really was a mistake. I seem to be oblivious to people coming and going today.

"Ummm."

Mr. Beautiful turns, catching just a glimpse of the anger resonating from Caden. He throws me a lifeline, "I'm visiting for a few weeks. I have some business with Joe Ralley. I need to schedule some more times with Marco while I'm here. Miss..." he turns back in my direction, waiting for me to fill in the blank.

I do. "It's Lily."

"Lily." He nods and the corner of his mouth twitches up just slightly, but I notice it. "Was going to work out a schedule for me." He tilts his head and squints his eyes, a realization of some sort coming to him, he smiles. "You wouldn't happen to be The Saint's daughter, would you?"

Confused at how he would know, I answer, "I am."

Caden takes a moment, looking between the two of us, assessing the situation. "I'll schedule your trainer times. Lily has more important things to take care of." His tone makes it obvious it's not a suggestion, it's been decided already.

"There's nothing more important than helping our customers," I admonish, turning to face Caden. His jaw tenses, eyes darkened with fury squint, and the vein in his neck throbs. He looks ready to explode. We stare at each other for a few seconds before I finally give in, blowing out a breath in frustration. "Fine," I say before turning back to Mr. Beautiful. "Caden will set up your schedule. If you need anything else, just let me know."

"Sounds good." Mr. Beautiful extends his hand in Caden's direction. "Jackson," he offers to Caden, but turns his head to me with a grin.

Caden hesitates, but eventually clasps the man's hand with a curt nod. "Caden Ralley."

I was supposed to be at the restaurant five minutes ago, yet here I am lining my eyes with a thick, smoky gray pencil as if I'm an hour early. I finish my makeup, checking my face in the mirror and liking the results. It's been a while since I've had the urge to girly myself up. I've always liked clothes, the way the right pencil skirt and strappy shoes can lift my mood, making me feel like a beautiful woman instead of the gym rat I've let my appearance turn into over the last few months.

I smile as I look in the mirror, remembering the last business meeting I went to with Joe and my dad. A protein powder rep had invited us out, hoping to convince us to sell his line of products in our gyms. Everything was going well, until the poor salesman paid me an innocent compliment. "You look so different than when we met at the gym," he commented, his tone reflecting *different* was meant in a good way.

"Thank you." I motioned to my fancy shoes with the dangerously thin high heel. "These two don't like it when my stilettos put holes in the floor mats."

"Well you're beautiful either way. But the shoes…," the salesman trailed off into a low catcall whistle, "…the shoes are sexy as hell."

Dad signed on with the competing protein powder company the next morning.

Fashionably late by more than a half hour, I finally make it to Osteria Madena, Joe's favorite Italian restaurant. It's small, everyone squeezed together so tightly the waiters have to be thin just to fit between the tables. I look around the packed room, not finding Joe and the man we're supposed to be meeting at first glance. I check my watch, hoping they didn't leave. I'm late, but nothing Joe isn't used to by now.

"Ahh…the beautiful Bambino. There she is." Fredo, the owner of the restaurant kisses both my cheeks. Dad, Joe and I have been coming here for years, a signed picture of my dad hangs proudly over the bar. He clasps both my hands and pulls back to examine me. "You're too skinny, my bella donna! Tonight…tonight we feed you a big plate of pasta, no? Fredo fatten you up a bit, yes?"

I smile, knowing I'm getting pasta, even if I order chicken. "Is Joe here? I'm supposed to meet him, but I don't see him around."

"Yes, yes. Mr. Joe is at the bar waiting for you. Come." Fredo takes my hand and walks me to the other side of the bar that wasn't visible from the entry where I was standing.

Joe stands when he sees me. "You look lovely." He kisses my cheek then shakes his head. "And you should considering how long you kept us waiting."

"Sorry. I lost track of time," I offer, noticing an empty seat next to Joe. "Did I miss the broker?"

"No, he just stepped away to take a call. Actually, here he is now." Joe motions behind me.

I turn ready to apologize for my lateness, but I'm stopped in my tracks when my eyes fall on Mr. Beautiful from the gym today.

"Jackson Knight, this is my partner, Lily St. Claire," Joe makes the obligatory introduction.

Jackson lifts a brow, a slow smirk tipping one corner of his mouth. "We've met." He shakes my hand, not letting go right away. His eyes make a quick sweep of me from head to toe and I arch an eyebrow when his eyes make their way back to mine, letting him know I've watched him check me out. Instead of being embarrassed at being caught, Jackson's smirk turns to a full, panty-dropping smile. Seriously? Ridiculously handsome *and* cocky.

"Sorry I'm late," I muster when he eventually releases my hand.

"No problem. I'm sure you have a lot of important things to do." Jackson grins, referencing Caden's comment from earlier.

"I didn't realize you two had met already?" Joe interrupts.

"We met at the gym today," I explain to Joe, my gaze never leaving Jackson as I speak. "Jackson failed to mention that he was your business broker, Mr. Knight."

"Did I fail to mention that?" Jackson flirts knowingly.

"I'm pretty sure you did." I quirk an eyebrow and smile.

"Hmmm, maybe I did. I seem to recall we were interrupted."

Fredo reappears out of nowhere, taking my hand. "Come. We feed you now. Si?" He looks back to Jackson as we begin walking. "She's molto bello, yes?"

"Absolutely. Stunningly so," he adds to Fredo's *very beautiful* compliment spoken in Italian.

"But she's too skinny, si? Tonight we plump her up with some homemade carbonara. Yes?" He doesn't wait for a response before showing us to our table. It's the best table in the restaurant, the far left corner, one of the few places where there's room between tables.

Jackson pulls my chair out for me to sit, waiting until I'm seated to take the seat next to me.

"I bring more vino and we make special dishes for our special customers." Fredo disappears.

"I guess we don't need to look at the menu then?" Jackson asks amused.

"You can if you want. But if Fredo doesn't like what you pick, he's only going to change it anyway."

Fifteen minutes later, Fredo brings more food than three people could ever eat. As promised, a heaping serving of fettuccine carbonara is placed in front of me. The three of us talk throughout our meal, the conversation flowing as easily as the wine.

Jackson Knight is the owner of Knight Investments, the firm that put together a group of silent investors interested in buying half of Ralley's Gyms so Joe can retire. Joe took Dad's death almost as hard as I did. It made him think twice about all the hours he works, instead of spending time with his family. I'm glad he is going to retire, but I'd be lying if I said I wasn't terrified at the thought of losing him on a day-to-day basis.

I groan when Fredo has a huge tray of desserts delivered to our table. I'm stuffed, but the chocolate cake here is out of this world. I can't resist at least a taste.

"He seems to be pretty intent on packing you with calories," Jackson says as the table fills with deliciousness.

"Apparently I've lost a few pounds and he's determined to help me find them to fix my body."

Joe is busy talking with Fredo so he doesn't catch Jackson's response. "You look pretty perfect to me." He says directly into my eyes and then they drop, roaming over my body slowly before returning his gaze to mine. "There's nothing you need to fix."

Flustered, I change the subject. "So why didn't you mention you were coming?" I fork a piece of the chocolate cake.

"I thought I'd check out how things ran, without knowing anyone was watching." He pauses, then adds, "For the investors. You find out a lot more about a business when you drop in and get treated like any other client. Since the funding is coming from a group of anonymous investors with limited voting rights, I handle the due diligence and report back." Jackson lifts his fork and motions to the cake in front of me. "You mind?"

"By all means, help yourself. It's less that I'll have to run off tomorrow." He grins and forks a piece of the cake sitting in front of me. I watch a little too intently as he swallows, riveted by the sight of his throat working.

"Some things you get one taste of and want to consume the whole thing." Jackson's voice brings my focus back from his throat.

Trying to ignore how truly sexy his voice is, I respond looking away. "Yes, the chocolate cake here is out of this world."

"That too." Jackson replies, his eyes sparkling mischievously.

The two men argue over paying the bill and then our conversation goes back to business for a few minutes more before we leave.

"So tell me, Lily, what's your biggest concern about the investment group buying out Joe's half of the gym?" Jackson asks pointedly.

I think for a minute. "It's important to me to keep my dad's vision for the gyms. He didn't want them turned into generic exercise gyms just to grow membership. The focus needs to stay on training fighters. I guess I'm concerned the focus of the investors won't be the same. I know we're doing this with silent investors who will have limited voting rights, they're basically becoming stockholders, but it still makes me nervous bringing in any outsiders."

Jackson nods. "That's good to know. I've been training at the Ralley's in D.C. for years and it's one of the things that set the gym apart from other places. It would be shortsighted to turn the gyms into something else. Chains of exercise gyms come and go. The members aren't loyal because there are a dozen places they can get the same service. Ralley's is different, and if it stays different, it can continue growth with the sport. Joe and I spoke a bit about the cash flow shortage Ralley's has been having lately. It isn't uncommon for businesses that grow fast to feel some growing pains. Hopefully having investors with deep pockets will also give you some relief from relying on the banks too much. "

It's a relief to know at least someone involved in the buyout understands what makes Ralley's so special. The worries that keep me up at night. "I'm glad you understand Ralley's. It's more than just a business to me. To us."

Jackson nods. "Do you have management lined up to help out? One of the drawbacks in doing a silent investor deal is your new partner doesn't take on any of the responsibility of the day to day operations."

"I'm still figuring that part out," I say cryptically. Joe and I need to have a long conversation about Caden's involvement once he leaves. I'm not sure he is the right person for the job anymore. He's a bit too hotheaded and his people skills aren't the greatest, to put it mildly.

We talk for a little while more about our long-term vision for Ralley's. I'm impressed at how much Jackson knows and how easily he seems to comprehend my concerns. Eventually we say our goodbyes to Fredo and walk outside into the warm, late summer evening. "How long are you in town, Jackson?" Joe asks as he hails a cab for us. I only live a few blocks away, but I learned long ago that Joe will never let me walk home in the dark alone.

"I'm not sure yet. The bank is coming in to go through the books next week, so a couple of weeks at least."

A cab pulls up at the curb. "I'll be going out of town for a few days while you're here. But I'm sure Lily will take good care of you." The two men shake hands.

Jackson turns to me, a seductive smile warming me inside and out. He leans in to say goodnight as Joe opens the cab door and speaks to the driver. "I look forward to you taking good care of me," he whispers and kisses my cheek. I climb inside the car before he can see the heat spreading across my face.

The next day when I come in, I scour the gym, trying not to make it obvious who I'm looking for. When my gaze finds the man I'm hoping to see again, he's jumping rope at warp speed, but his eyes are locked on me already. Feeling flustered for being caught, I practically run back to the reception area. Throughout the day, I sneak a few glances at Jackson as he works out. A few times he catches me and smiles. Luckily, Caden doesn't notice. The last thing I need is another scene in the gym.

Freshly showered after his workout, I'm grateful Caden is already gone when Mr. Beautiful stops at the front desk on his way out. His hair damp and a towel around his neck, he's certainly a feast for the eyes. Although his body looks sufficiently trained, something about him doesn't seem to fit with the guys that usually train at Ralley's. He's different, and it's not just that he's devoid of tattoos on his arms and scars on his face. Something in the way he speaks and carries himself sets him apart from the normal fighters I see.

"So, I have to admit, I thought you would be different than you are based on our emails over the last few months." I say to Jackson, trying to ignore the effect that seeing his damp, freshly exercised body has on me. We've emailed back and forth a lot over the last few months. I provided reports he requested and answered questions about Ralley's to help him put together the offering to attract investors. But our communications have been strictly professional. He was all business, nothing like the playful demeanor of the man before me.

"What did you think I would be like?" he asks, setting his bag on the floor.

"I don't know. Just different. Older I guess." I smile. "You're much friendlier in person."

"So my emails are old and unfriendly?" he teases.

"I didn't say that. They just come off more formal. That's probably why I thought you were older."

"Well I hope you like the real thing better than what you imagined."

I laugh. "Yes, I do."

"Good. Anything else you've imagined about me that I can work on beating your expectation of?"

I flush. I've imagined more than I care to share, but I don't want to let on that he's been infiltrating my thoughts since I laid eyes on him yesterday. "Are you always such a flirt?" I tilt my head and ask coyly.

"This isn't flirting," he responds with a sexy grin.

"It's not? Then what would you call it?"

His eyes glimmer. "Foreplay."

I roll my eyes and laugh off the comment as playful. Although the heat in his eyes makes me think he really isn't kidding. It makes my stomach flutter and my palms sweaty. Growing up surrounded by alpha males who speak their minds, it generally takes a lot for me to embarrass. Yet something about the way he looks at me when he speaks makes me feel like a teenage girl.

I try to force our conversation back to the gym. I've mixed business with pleasure enough lately, learning my lesson the hard way. "Well, how do you like our gym, Jackson?" I ask, trying hard to keep my eyes trained on his and not ogle the plethora of beauty south of his magnetic blue eyes. He's cocky enough, I don't need to give him anymore ammunition.

"I think I'm going to like it here." His wry grin speaks volumes and it leaves me feeling like his statement has little to do with his actual training.

"People call me Jax, by the way."

"Not Jackson?"

"My friends call me Jax."

"So we're going to be friends then?" I tease.

"I hope so." His smile widens.

"I noticed you didn't tell Caden to call you Jax yesterday."

"Something tells me Caden and I aren't going to be friends." My new friend arches an eyebrow and grins a devilish grin. He slings his bag diagonally across his shoulder. "I have to run for a video conference call. You here tomorrow?"

"I'm here almost every day."

"See you tomorrow then, Lily." Jax smiles and walks out the door.

Chapter 3

Jax

My body aches after a good workout, but it's a feeling I relish. No pain, no gain. The old mantra has a lot of truth to it. High on adrenaline, it's the first time in more than six months that I feel like I'm going the right direction. Hell, it's the first time, in a very long time, I feel like I have *any* direction. And damn if Lily isn't the icing on the cake to a deal I was already thinking was going to work out perfectly for me.

If I had any doubts I was making the right choice buying these gyms, getting a look at her little body and the way her nipples perked up when we touched just sealed the deal. You just never know what might throw a buyer over the edge when they're teetering on a multi-million dollar purchase. I smile to myself wondering how many deals may actually have been sealed by a sexy woman.

Joe was adamant that the only type of investor he was looking for was a silent partner. I'd prefer a hand in managing the business right from the beginning, but the deal was too good for me to pass up, even without the opportunity to operate the company. But I figured once I formed a relationship with my new partner, I could open the door to taking on a less silent role. Now my mind is stuck thinking of a different type of role I'd like to take with Lily.

Women have been on the back burner in my private life lately. Desire sort of goes out the window when your life implodes all around you. The one bright spot I've been looking forward to has been closing the deal on Ralley's Gyms. The fact that my prospective partner is smokin hot is a total damn bonus.

Still unable to shake the energy as night falls, I go for a run. Weaving in and out of pedestrians isn't something I'm a stranger to, being from D.C., but the volume is vastly different in New York. Throngs of people still clutter the streets even though it's after nine. Oddly, I don't find it annoying. Instead I make it a challenge to maneuver through the chaos without breaking a stride.

Back in my ridiculously oversized hotel suite, I shower and slip into bed feeling good – something I haven't felt in a long time. Lily's smile keeps me company as I drift off to sleep, a perfect combination of exhilarated and exhausted.

Opening the door to the gym, I'm greeted with a smile by Lily. Now that's a face I could get used to seeing every day. "Morning," I smile back.

"Good morning, Jax." Jax, not Jackson or Mr. Knight. I told her my friends call me Jax, yet I can't help but think how much I'd like to hear Mr. Knight roll off her tongue. Perhaps in a breathless throaty voice between pants.

Stepping up to the desk she sits behind, I peer over at what she's working on. She has her sketchpad and a narrow charcoal pencil, working on the start of something with fluid curved lines, but I can't tell what the subject is yet.

"So when do you want to do it?"

Lily's face pinks up. I hadn't thought about the multiple ways my question could be taken, but I like the way she's thinking.

She coughs to clear her throat and takes a sip from a bottle of water before speaking. "Do what?"

"Draw me."

"Oh."

"What did you think I was talking about?" I arch an eyebrow suggestively and the pink in her face darkens to a crimson shade of red.

"Oh…I…it's okay, you don't have to. I shouldn't have said anything."

"I don't mind." I won't tell her I've spent half my life posing for pictures. The fewer people that know the details of my life here, the better.

"Well…I…"

The door behind me opens, interrupting us. I know who it is without turning, just from the look on Lily's face.

"Can I help you with something?" Shoulders back, Caden steps between me and where Lily's sitting, looking like he's ten seconds away from exploding. This guy must have radar, he seems to show every time I come within ten feet of Lily.

"Nope. All good." I stand my position, completely aware he is trying to intimidate me and is not so subtly telling me to get lost.

"Lily's busy. She's trying to work here." Caden folds his arms over his chest.

"Caden," Lily warns. "I'm fine here. Why don't you go do whatever it is you came in to do."

"This guy doesn't seem to understand you're trying to work."

"Then why don't you let her work. We were just scheduling something." Jackson suggests sternly, but Caden ignores what both of us are telling him.

"Whatever you need, you can schedule it with me." Caden walks around the counter.

"I need a sparring partner for tomorrow," I lie. Well, I do need a partner, but that's not what I was trying to schedule.

A twisted smile on his face, I know what the asshole's answer is going to be before he opens his mouth. "It would be my pleasure."

Chapter 4

Lily

I met Reed Baxter the first day of middle school in art class. Even at thirteen he knew exactly who he was. The boy already had style back then. He didn't care that he looked different. He wanted to look different, aspired to be truly who he was. I admired him instantly.

At sixteen, when my first boyfriend broke up with me to go out with Candy Lattington because I wouldn't let him get to third base, I cried on Reed's shoulder. He held me and told me Candy was a slut. At nineteen when I drank too much liquor and could barely walk, Reed came and got me at the bar. He held my hair back while I threw up and then brought me home with him and tucked me into his bed. At twenty-four when my father died at only fifty-eight years old after a massive heart attack, he held my hand as we made funeral arrangements and spooned me for two days, holding me until the last sob racked through me. Reed Baxter is the best friend I've ever had.

"Love the blue dress. It brings out the color of your eyes." He's so good for my self esteem.

"Thank you." I reach up and kiss his cheek. "Caden bought it for me." I smirk, knowing what his response will be.

Reed crinkles his nose. "Maybe the dress isn't that nice after all," he teases. These days, I'm starting to wonder if I should've listened to Reed's opinion on Caden a year ago.

Reed surveys the gym, it's filled with its usual assortment of muscular men in various shapes and sizes. "Tell me again why I don't come pick you up from work every day?" He sighs, looking around like a hungry lumberjack at a smorgasbord.

"Because you hate fighting." I smile, pointing out the bigger obstacle, "And Caden."

"Speak of the devil," Reed mumbles. I turn to see Caden approaching.

"Reed." He nods his head curtly in the general direction of Reed. The two men have a severe dislike for each other. But Caden has always known Reed is a deal breaker, so he keeps his distance and minds his manners. Well, sort of.

"Caden." Reed mimics the head nod and curt gesture, but Caden doesn't even notice he's being mocked.

"Call me when you get in tonight," Caden orders dryly.

"It's probably going to be late."

"Doesn't matter." Caden nods to Reed again and attempts to kiss me on the lips before walking out the door. I turn just in time and he gets the corner of my mouth. Luckily Caden misses the salute that Reed offers to his back.

"Didn't you dump him? Why is he kissing you still?" Reed questions with sincerity.

Pensively, I bite my bottom lip, "He's not exactly accepting of our break up."

"What does that mean? He doesn't get a choice to accept it or not. You dump him. He's dumped. It's pretty simple actually."

"It's a long story."

"We have all night. I can't wait to hear this one."

Before he begins the lecture I'm positive is about to come, I grab my purse and take off toward the back of the gym, "Going to run to the ladies room to freshen up. You can stand around and take in the sites."

A few minutes later, I round the corner from the ladies room and find Reed leaning casually against the front counter, ankles crossed, elbows supporting his weight. A crooked smile and sparkly eyes, I'd know that look anywhere. He's crushing on someone. I just hope it isn't one of the muscle head gym rats who'll get physical when he realizes another guy's hitting on him.

Another couple of steps and the object of Reed's attention comes into my line of vision. I can't help but smile, sometimes we really do have similar taste.

"Hey, Jax. I thought I saw you leave earlier," I say, at first not noticing he's no longer dressed in gym clothes. He's wearing dark jeans, a navy shirt that accentuates the light color of his eyes and a darker navy lightweight pea coat. Simple. Understated. Urbane and absolute perfection. No wonder he seems to have caught Reed's attention.

"I forgot something. I just stopped back to see if it was still here."

"Oh. What did you forget? We have a lost and found." I walk behind the reception counter, ready to grab the box we collect all the lost ear buds and lifting gloves in.

Jax looks to Reed, some unspoken man language transpires and Reed holds his hands up. "I play for the other team, dude." Reed shrugs casually, Jax chuckles.

"I was going to see if I could take you up on that offer?"

Brows drawn. "Offer?"

"To draw me."

Reed laughs. No, actually he snorts. "Don't let her take advantage of you. She uses that artist crap to get men to take off their clothes all the time."

Slapping Reed's chest, I know he's teasing, and I know Jax knows he's teasing too, yet I can't stop the blush that creeps up my face showing my embarrassment. "Don't pay attention to Reed, he's still mad because I wouldn't let him ask out the model the night we were sketching male nudes."

Jax smiles, he looks entertained by the banter between Reed and I, so different than the reaction we'd get from Caden. Caden was always jealous of my relationship with Reed, even though he knows nothing can ever happen.

"We're heading to my gallery showing in SoHo. Why don't you come along...I think you'll appreciate some of the paintings of naked women." Reed offers with a wink.

My eyes widen when I realize what he's doing. Feeling panicky, I stumble over my own words. "Actually, it's going to be packed as is. Reed over invited the guest list, as usual."

The disappointment is evident on Jax's face, but he's gracious nonetheless. "That's okay. Another night maybe?"

Shit. Now he thinks I'm trying to blow him off, back peddle away from Reed's invitation because I don't want him going.

"I'm sorry. That didn't come out right. I'd love for you to join us. It's just..." I trail off, biting my bottom lip anxiously as I look for the right words.

"She's going to be buck ass naked," Reed finishes the rest of my sentence. Not exactly how I was going to put it, but it does save me the trouble from having to say the words.

Although confused by Reed's statement, Jax gets there's more to the story and he seems intrigued. "You're getting naked at a gallery?" A hint of a grin on his ridiculously handsome face doesn't make it any easier for me to explain.

"I let Reed paint me," quietly, I explain. "We painted each other." Rethinking my choice of words, I clarify. "Not actually painting each other's bodies, I mean painting on canvas," I stumble nervously over my words. "It was our project for class. He's included it as part of his show."

Jax arches a perfect brow, "So the gallery is displaying a painting of you in the nude?"

"Yep, and her painting got a big fat A." Reed answers before I can open my mouth to respond. "I think she's planning on having me stand in front of it all night."

"And I think you're only having the gallery showing so you had an excuse to invite Frederick," I counter.

"Frederick?" Jax inquires, trying to keep up.

"The male nude, the one I wouldn't let him ask out in class while we sketched."

Laughing, Jax shakes his head, "Sounds like you may have trouble getting him to stand in front of your painting if Frederick is walking around the gallery. But you two have fun. Another time, maybe?"

I nod and watch as Jax happily shakes Reed's hand. Just before he reaches for the door, my mouth utters words before my brain can override the decision. "Why don't you come with us?"

Turning back, he's hesitant to accept my offer. Squinting to assess my sincerity, he asks, "You sure?"

I nod and respond teasingly, "You're bigger than Reed, you can block more of the painting."

He smiles and nods. "You got it."

Chapter 5

Jax

The gallery is packed when we enter, but a short woman dressed in all black with tattoo's covering every inch of her exposed arms finds us immediately.

"Lily! Oh my god, everyone is raving about your painting!" The woman hugs Lily, but I catch Lily's face wilt at her words. Face tense, Lily bites down hard on her lower lip and tries to smile, wanting to share in her friend's excitement, but it's obvious she's nervous.

A man with a heavy French accent grabs Reed's arm, grumbles a few words, and the two disappear as quickly as he came with a promise to return him as soon as he can.

"You okay?" Leaning down, I whisper to Lily.

"Does it show I'm not?"

"Not too much," I smile as I lie.

Lily laughs, "I'm sorry. I just didn't realize how difficult it would be for me when people see it. I see models all the time without clothes and it doesn't bother me a bit. I see art, not a naked woman. Yet when it's me, I'm totally freaked out that people are going to see me naked."

Stopping a waitress as she passes, I grab two crystal flutes and offer one to Lily. She declines. "You sure? Might help you calm your nerves."

"I'm sure." A weak smile teases her lips. "Do I look as nervous as I feel?"

"You look beautiful," I tell her, and not because I want to calm her nerves and make her feel better. She just is. The carefully angled lighting in the gallery picks up the highlights in her wavy long blond hair, setting off a shimmer of gold that reflects off the green in her blue eyes. A few scarcely visible light freckles dot her perfect thin nose, leading down to full pink lips. Her gym attire is gone, traded in for a sexy electric blue dress that hugs her in all the right places. The hint of cleavage showing has me distracted as hell. If the painting is half as good as the real thing, it's going to be a masterpiece.

A few minutes later, Reed returns an empty crystal flute in each hand. "You ready to go see it?"

I watch as she takes a deep breath and nervously fidgets with her hair. But then something changes. A determination passes over her delicate features. If I wasn't watching her so closely I probably wouldn't have even seen it. But I catch it and it makes me smile. She's tougher than she looks on the outside and it makes her even sexier to me, if that's even possible.

Together the three of us walk through the gallery, stopping to view each picture in silence. As we move onto each successive painting, I find my pulse beginning to quicken, wondering if the next painting will be the one.

After a dozen paintings, I'm growing impatient. Anxious, although I have no idea why. I've seen plenty of naked women before, both in person and painted. Hell, I grew up around art, so why is each step making my heart thud louder in my chest with anticipation?

Turning the corner, a crowd mills around a large piece, the murmur of quiet discussions louder than anywhere else. I know before we reach the viewing area, it's going to be her. As we approach, two tall men step to the next painting, leaving a small clearing in the lingering crowd...perfect for my line of vision. Frozen in mid step, my breathing becomes more labored as my eyes take in the most beautiful sight they've ever seen.

Sitting on a sparse bed with nothing but a white sheet that looks as if it was gently dropped from covering her radiant skin, her head slightly bowed, captivating blue eyes look up at the artist from underneath long thick eyelashes. She looks like an angel. I really can't decide if the pose is innocent or alluring, but the sexual tension that radiates from the canvas is palpable. It's the sexiest god damn thing I've ever seen in my life. Sweet, yet incredibly seductive. Sensual. Beautiful. Every curve of her body soft and inviting, yet hard and incredibly erotic at the same time. The pink swells of her perky nipples jut from her lush pale skin, one hand rests casually on her slightly parted thighs, giving the illusion of seeing what lies between her perfectly posed legs, although nothing really shows.

My mouth unable to form words, I don't answer as Lily looks up at me. Forcing my labored breath slower, I swallow hard, reaching for control of my thoughts. A nervous smile on her face, her voice so low I can barely hear it over the sound of my heart thumping against my chest wall, "What do you think?"

Struggling to direct my gaze to the woman that speaks and not the painting I can't seem to take my eyes off, I respond, "I'm thinking I'm going to stand in front of it to block it, facing it."

Lily smiles and elbows me in the ribs. "You're impossible."

"What? I'm a fan of the arts. I need to study the lines. And the curves. Definitely the curves," I respond.

A man's voice from behind me changes the tension I'm feeling from sexual to angry, taking me from the peaceful place the beautiful vision had brought me to fists balling up at my sides in just three words. *I'd fuck her.*

Unfortunately, I'm not the only one who hears it. Lily looks horrified, and the two classless assholes are lucky I make the snap decision to move Lily away from their comment and not knock them both on their asses. As I usher Lily to the next painting, I catch Reed quietly grumbling something to the men through gritted teeth before they both scurry away swiftly with pale faces.

At the next painting I excuse myself for a few minutes. I meet back up with Reed and Lily just as they complete their viewing of the exhibit.

"I have to do the meet and greet thing. I know it will be torture, but would you mind hanging with Lily for a while?" Reed asks jokingly when I return. He turns. "And you...don't let it go to your head, I made you that beautiful. You're really an ugly wench."

Leaning down to kiss her gently on the forehead, he squeezes both shoulders. I hear him speak quietly to her, "Your painting is gorgeous, just like you. Relax and enjoy."

She rolls her eyes playfully.

Extending his hand to me with a wink that Lily doesn't catch, "Take good care of my girl."

I nod and smile. "Of course."

We wander around for another hour, talking nonstop. Eventually the gallery moves from the early phase of serious viewers to the beginnings of an after party, Lily looks around uncomfortably.

"You want to get out of here?" I ask.

"Would you mind? It sort of freaks me out to be in the same room with that painting." She motions in the direction of the corner her portrait hangs in. It's still the busiest area of the room.

As we make our way to the door, I watch as the gallery owner places a cover over Lily's painting, marking it as privately sold. Luckily, Lily doesn't notice.

Chapter 6

Lily

The streets of New York are oddly quiet for midnight on a Friday. Together, Jax and I walk unhurriedly with conversation flowing easily.

"So why do you know so much about art? Who are you really Jackson Knight?" I tease, although I am really curious why every comment he made at the viewing tonight was so spot on. Relating parts of an artist's work back to anyone but the well known masters such as Van Gogh, Chopin, Dali, Munich, usually takes a trained eye. But Jax was able to pull out understated qualities and relate them back to the lesser known artists.

"No one important." I expect Jax's typical witty and cocky response, but instead he smiles halfheartedly and shrugs his shoulders. "My mother just thought I should be well cultured. Art history was my minor in college."

"Well cultured, huh? Are you a prep school brat?" Playfully, I bump my shoulder into his as we wait for the light to change.

Jax volleys the focus back to me. "Tell me about you. Did you ever consider being an artist as a profession or has it always been your dream to own a chain of gyms filled with testosterone flaring men?"

"Nope. When I was little I dreamed about being a ballerina," I respond proudly.

"A ballerina, huh?"

"Yep."

"So what happened?"

"You witnessed how graceful I am first hand the other day when I fell out of my chair. Need I explain more?"

"That wasn't just a one time thing, huh?" Jax chuckles as he speaks.

"Unfortunately not." I smile.

"How old were you when you figured out it wasn't going to happen for you as a ballerina?" Jax asks with a smirk.

"Six."

"And how, exactly, did you figure out that you weren't suited for the role of ballerina?"

"I fell off the stage while trying to pirouette at my first ballet recital."

Jax stops in place, smiling, but looking at me with disbelief. "You fell off the stage?"

"Yep."

"Then what happened?"

"I cried. My father came to the front of the stage and got me. The next year when he went to sign me up, the instructor suggested I might be suited more for karate." I pout my response.

Unable to contain his amusement, Jax breaks into laughter, throwing his head back, enjoying a good laugh at my expense. I feign being annoyed, but he can tell I'm not.

"I'm sorry. I don't mean to laugh. But that's pretty funny."

"You owe me an embarrassing story now," I declare.

"Okay, but I may need some time to come up with one. I'm pretty damn near perfect you know."

"And pretty damn full of yourself too."

"That too." He smiles. "So being a gym mogul was your second choice?"

"Maybe third. I might have wanted to be a butterfly in between a ballerina and a mogul." I admit. "What did you want to be when you were little?"

"A professional boxer."

"Are you training for a fight now?"

"Not really. It's more of a hobby."

"So Knight Investments is your passion?"

"Not really. Fighting was always my passion. But I'm good at what I do with Knight Investments."

"And that's what? You help people sell businesses?"

"Sometimes. I manage other people's money."

"Like a stock broker?"

"Sort of. I help them figure out what to invest in. Sometimes it can be a business, sometimes it can be a fund. Depends on what they're looking for and how much risk they're willing to take."

"Why would people want to take risks with their money?"

"Because usually the more risk you take, the bigger the reward."

"Sounds sort of boring," I tease.

"It is," Jax laughs.

"So why do you do it?"

Jax quiets for a minute as he considers his answer. "I don't even know anymore." There's sadness in his face, although he tries to hide it with a forced smile.

Too soon, we arrive at my building. "This is me." I point to the ten story dated apartment building set between towering modern skyscrapers.

Jax turns toward me, taking a step closer. Slowly, he reaches down and takes one of my hands into his. I don't even notice I'm avoiding eye contact until he calls my name.

"Lily."

My eyes jump to meet his. Being so close to this man makes me nervous for some reason. "I'd love to see you again." He smiles. "And you don't even have to show me yourself naked next time." A dirty grin replaces the smile. "Unless you want to, of course."

I can't help but smile back. Although the thought of having to decline an invitation for a real date with Jax, makes my smile wilt quickly. "I'm sorry. I'd love to, but I can't."

His smile falters too. "You'd love to, but you can't?" Questioning, Jax tries to make sense of my response.

"Mixing business with my personal life hasn't turned out so well for me. I went down that road with my ex boyfriend and I'm still struggling to extract the personal mess from the business." I pause. "I like you, Jax, I really do. But I'm not sure it's a good idea"

"You're not sure if it's a good idea?" Jax asks.

"Yes. That's what I said." Confused, I confirm my words.

Jax smirks. "I can work with that."

"You can work with that?"

"You said *you're not sure* it's a good idea. You don't sound that committed to your new rule." He shrugs and smiles.

I laugh. "Good night, Jax."

Pulling the hand he's been holding to bring me closer, Jax leans in for an unexpected hug. As he pulls away, his mouth close to my ear, he whispers in a deep voice that sends chills racing up my spine, "The painting was beautiful."

Pulling his head back, his mouth curves into a sinful smile, "Going to make for some sweet dreams tonight." Leaving me speechless, he turns and walks away, smiling back at me as he

44

glances over his shoulder while I'm still glued to the spot where he left me.

Chapter 7

Jax

I wasn't kidding when I told Lily last night I was going to have pleasant dreams after seeing her painting. Although half my dreams turned out to be daydreams, rather than sleep dreams, since I tossed and turned trying to fall asleep with visions of her sexy body in my head all night. A sleepless night because I can't get Lily out of my mind is a hell of a lot better than a sleepless night because of the crap that's kept me awake the last six months.

Dragging my tired ass out of bed, my one track mind still stuck on the vision of Lily's painting, I don't even notice the two men with cameras outside of the gym until it's too late.

"Jackson, how do you feel about your father announcing his bid for re-election the same day your estranged brother announces he will be hosting the annual MMA Open in Vegas this year? Is it true, you've broken ties with your family? Are you training here to get in the cage with your brother, Vince Stone?" The two photographers snap pictures and yell questions at me as I push past and make my way into the gym. They attempt to follow me in, but are stopped at the door.

"This is a private business. You're not welcome in here." Lily snaps and shuts the door in their face, pulling the blind down so no one can see in.

"Thank you." So much for anonymity.

"You're no one important, huh?" Lily throws my words from last night back at me, but she's smiling when she says them. Teasing.

"I'm really not. They're interested in my family, not me."

Caden appears from the back of the gym. Does this guy ever go home? "What's going on?" He directs his question at Lily in a tone that makes me tense just hearing it.

"Nothing. You ready to spar?" I respond even though he wasn't speaking to me.

A twisted smile lights up Caden's face, "You bet pretty boy. You can be my warm up."

"Tell Uncle Joe our flight was pushed back to two when he comes in." Caden barks at Lily. Something in the way he speaks to her just pisses me off. And it's more than just the tone, I can't put my finger on it, but it feels like he's bullying her, taking advantage somehow.

"Okay," she responds quietly.

Caden turns and heads back to the gym. Lifting my gym bag strap back over my chest, I begin to follow and then stop, turning back.

"Lily?"

She looks up.

"Is he what made you come up with your new rule?" I nod my head in the direction of Caden Ralley.

She bites her lip, not responding right away. "It's a long story."

I nod and head back to change, looking forward to taking out my frustration on my sparring partner more than I ever thought possible.

Some people need alcohol or drugs to get high. Me, just give me a good day of fighting and everything seems easier. Sparring is supposed to be going through the motions of boxing, practicing your technique and tightening up your strikes, without actually landing any heavy blows. But you wouldn't know that from my spar with Caden this morning. If it wasn't for Joe Ralley breaking us apart a few times, Caden and I would've wound up in a full on brawl.

I definitely surprised him. I usually do when it comes to gym rats that are stupid enough to judge a person's ability to fight by what they look like. What moron decided only fully tatted up, shaved head, scarred face bullies with anger issues could have talent in the ring? A degree from an Ivy League school and they assume you're soft. Days like today, the preconceived notion works for me. Caden wasn't expecting *Pretty Boy* to knock him on his ass. More than once. He definitely didn't see the bloody nose coming either. But this morning, I had a lot to take out in the ring, and Caden was just the right asshole for the job.

The hour long spar and my morning workout still not enough to bring me down, adrenaline pumps wildly through my veins as I begin a ten mile run on the treadmill. It's not unintentional that I pick the machine all the way at the end, the one that gives me a clear line of vision to the reception area. A clear line of vision to Lily. The first ten minutes, I watch as she's engrossed in sketching something. She looks intent and focused, consumed by whatever her imagination sends flowing to the paper as her hand works furiously.

Then Caden approaches, fresh from the shower, a large black duffle bag thrown over his back, he doesn't even consider she's working when he interrupts her. She smiles as he talks, but it's weak and forced, a polite smile at best. A few minutes later, Joe Ralley walks to the front desk and the three of them talk for a while. Joe points to the door and says something and Lily responds, looking around the gym, finding me quickly and points in my direction. The two men look my way as she speaks. I guess the reporters haven't left.

Caden eventually walks around the reception desk, hooking a hand around Lily's neck as she sits. He leans down and pulls her face toward him, venturing in for a kiss on the mouth, but at the last second she turns her head, leaving him with a cheek to kiss. Perfect. Absolutely, fucking perfect. I finish my run and take my time in the showers, hoping the reporters will have given up by the time I venture back outside.

Lily smiles at me, a hesitant smile on her face, as I approach the reception desk.

"Everything okay?" Her face makes it clear that it's not.

"Ummm. The reporters are still out there." Her voice is uncertain.

Curiously, I walk to the door, peering out through the side of the drawn shade. The two reporters from this morning have multiplied. *Ten fold.* At least.

"Shit." Wrenching my fingers through my damp hair, the thought of being chased down the street by a bunch of reporters, yet again, brings back all the stress my spar seemed to work out earlier.

"I know. I'm sorry. They've been doubling by the hour since the two saw you come in this morning."

"I'm going to have to change hotels again. It's getting old. Anytime my family does anything, it starts all over again," I grumble to myself.

"Won't they just follow you from where you're staying to the new one?"

Blowing out a deep breath, Lily's words ring true, even though I wish they were anything but. "Yeah, you're probably right."

Together, we stand quietly for a few minutes, listening to the hoard of reporters making a commotion just a few feet away, on the other side of the door.

Lily breaks our silence, "I have an idea. There's an empty apartment upstairs. Joe's son just moved out last month. He used to be a trainer here, but he decided he wanted to be an actor instead, so he moved to LA. We're going to rent it out eventually, but maybe if you stayed a few days, the reporters might think you left and go away. There's an inside entrance from the gym, through the back, at least you'd be able to come in and out to train and meet with Joe without being bothered."

"How would the Ralley men feel about that?" Not that I give a shit if Caden is unhappy, but I wouldn't want to cause Lily trouble at work.

"Joe's excited you're here. Remember at dinner the other night he told me to take good care of you?" She grins mischievously. "Plus, Joe and Caden just left together for five days, so they wouldn't even know. Joe is looking at buying a small gym down south when he retires and Caden went with him to check it out. Then they're heading to Vegas for some promo work for Caden's next fight."

Not having to be hounded by reporters every time I make a move is tempting. And the thought of being closer to Lily is definitely appealing. "If you don't mind me hanging around a lot more, that would be great, actually."

Chapter 8

Lily

It seemed like a great idea in the moment, but as I walk up the narrow staircase to the apartment above the gym, I'm wondering if maybe it was a mistake to invite Jax to stay at the gym. Caden will likely have a shit fit and being around Jax is a not too subtle reminder of the reasons I broke things off with Caden to begin with.

Jax stirs something inside of me. Something that Caden doesn't anymore. Or maybe he never did. There's definitely something to be said about not getting involved with anyone soon after the loss of a loved one. But, as usual, I didn't listen to anyone. Desperate for something that would ease the pain from the sudden loss of my father, Caden was there to fill a void. I was shattered and he jumped to pick up the pieces. I let him, not looking ahead to the consequences of having to extricate lingering personal conflict from my business when we broke up. I can't just shut the door and walk away from his continued possessive behavior. I've tried politely, but with him working and training at the gym, as well as being Joe's nephew, every time I shut the door, he opens it with the damn key. Then there's my own guilt, allowing him to help me through such a deeply difficult time, only to dump him when I'm able to stand on my own again. I never meant to hurt him. I can't go back, but I can learn from my mistakes.

Slipping the key into the lock, I attempt to turn it, but it sticks. Jiggling it doesn't even make it budge.

"Here, let me," Jax's voice is low, he's standing a step or two below me. But he makes his way up the final steps to just shy of pressing against me as his arms reach around, one hand with the keys, the other a firm grip on the knob, caging me between the door and his warm body. The little hairs on the back of my neck stand up, taking notice of the heavenly body standing so near. *Definitely not a good idea.*

Too quickly, the lock gives and the door opens, forcing me to step inside, although I would have preferred to spend a little more time tightly pressed against the door with Jax so close behind me.

I flip the switch on the lights and the dark room comes into focus. It's simple, but neat and clean. "It's not much, but you won't be bothered coming in and out at least."

Jax looks around and smiles warmly. "It's perfect."

"Do you want me to go get some of your stuff from your hotel?"

Jax looks conflicted, almost as if he wants me to, but doesn't want to ask.

"I don't mind. Really." I encourage.

His gaze slowly searches my face, "Okay, but you have to let me buy you dinner."

"I have to, huh?" I tease.

"Yep, or I won't let you do any more nice things for me."

"And that would be tragic." Placing my hands over my heart, I feign disappointment.

"Wiseass," Jax rebuts, smiling.

"You better be nice, Jackson, or I'll show the reporters the way up."

"Jackson, huh? I thought it was Jax, since we're friends and all."

"Jackson just seems to slip out when I need to put you in your place."

Jax laughs. A deep, real, natural laugh, the kind you can't fake. The sound makes me smile.

"I'll call my driver and have him pick you up and take you to my hotel. He can pick us up some dinner from the restaurant while you're grabbing my things."

"Your driver? I thought you weren't important?"

Jax opens his wallet and slips a sleek black hotel key card out and hands it to me. "I'm not. Doesn't mean I always need to walk." He grins.

I roll my eyes.

The unmarked black town car pulls up to the hotel and the driver turns to hand me a business card. Through a thick Russian accent, he introduces himself as Alex and says, "Mr. Knight requested I pick up dinner while you're inside. Please call when you're ready and I'll be outside waiting."

Stepping out of the car, I look up at the beautiful architectural feat. I've passed the San Marzo hotel before, and thought about drawing it, but never actually gone inside. As I approach the impressive double doors, a uniformed doorman opens the door and tips his hat with a nod. "Good evening."

Inside, the grandeur of the hotel takes my breath away. Jax is lucky I don't have my sketch pad with me, or he'd be eating his dinner for breakfast cold, wearing the same clothes as he has on now.

After a few starry eyed minutes, I force myself to stop ogling the lobby. I enter the elevator and insert the key as Jax instructed, the car begins moving without my even pressing any buttons. A long, but rapid, climb takes me to the top of the building and then the elevator doors open. Although they don't open to a hallway as I would have expected. Instead, they open directly to the penthouse. A beautiful, elegant, completely intimidating suite with a living room that's larger than my entire apartment.

Grateful that I'm alone, it gives me a few minutes to nose around, checking out the place in its entirety. Finding closets large enough to contain my wardrobe makes me wonder, do people live here or come for a few nights? The first bathroom I enter gleams in floor to ceiling white marble. There's a tub large enough to hold six and a separate shower with at least half a dozen shower heads. Two smaller bathrooms are equally as lush, one off the living room and the other off the second bedroom. *Really, who needs three bathrooms when you're alone in a hotel?*

The door to the master bedroom is open, the oversized four poster bed adorned with sumptuous deep burgundy and gold colored fabric. Two chocolates wrapped in gold foil rest lovingly in the middle of the pile of fluffy pillows. The only sign anyone has even visited the insanely luxurious suite is in the closet, where Jax told me I would find his bag and some clothes. Feeling slightly guilty for going through his things, although not enough to stop me, I examine the labels as I fold each garment into his bag. Expensive. Not flashy, but the feel of the fabric and the names of the designers tell me they likely cost a small fortune.

I pack enough clothes for a few days, and grab the toiletries he has in the bathroom, rolling the full suitcase back to the elevator doors. I look around as I wait for the elevator to rise, a small round table with a wooden tray catches my eye. A few folded up papers and some keys sit, likely the contents of Jax's pocket at one time. Curiosity gets the best of me as I wait, and I find myself unfolding a newspaper article before I can think better of my snooping. *Middleweight Champion, Vince "The Invincible" Stone, confirms rumors he is the lovechild of Senator Preston Knight.* The photo shows a handsome man pushing a photographer with one hand, his other arm wrapped protectively around a pretty auburn haired woman as they attempt to walk past throngs of media staked out in front of a gym. The elevator doors open. And then close after a few minutes, my nose still buried in the last of the two page article.

The date of the article catches my eye. He's been carrying it around for a while. Not long after I lost my father, so did Jax. It may not have been a physical loss, as mine was, but if he admired his father a fraction of how much I did mine, it must have been a devastating loss all the same.

Carefully, I fold the newspaper back up into the little square it was when I found it, moving on to examine the business cards held in a beautiful monogrammed silver clip, *JPK*. I run my fingers over the unusual cards, they're not paper, instead some sort of silver metal, paper thin, but strong. Raised engraved lettering displays a simple three line message. *Knight International Investments. Jackson P. Knight. President.* Only one simple phone number on the card, rather than the usual six lines of email, fax, and other means of communication listed. The card matches the man. Intriguing, strong, edgy, yet with a regal air…and pretty damn sexy too.

Jax unloads half a dozen takeout containers from the bag. Unless he's planning on feeding the reporters, there is definitely going to be a ton of leftovers. He fills two plates with a little from each container and sets them down on the small kitchen table. "I had Alex pick up a bottle of red to go with dinner, I hope you like it." He pulls a bottle out of the bag and begins to open drawers in search of a corkscrew.

"Just water for me, thank you."

"Looks like it will be just water for both of us, who doesn't have a corkscrew?"

"Joe's son is more of a beer type guy."

Filling two wine glasses with water, Jax sets them on the table and looks up at me. "What makes a guy a beer type guy?" He asks with a playful, crooked grin. He pulls out a chair and stands behind it, waiting for me to sit, before he takes his own seat across from me.

I think for a minute. It's difficult to put a "type" of guy into words, you just know it when you come across him. "The type that doesn't pull out my chair at the table," I offer with a smirk.

Jax chuckles at my definition and responds, "I didn't realize manners matched with beverage preference."

"I think it might, *Mr. Knight.*"

One eye arches in surprise, questioning, waiting for more.

"The doorman, the driver, the penthouse suite…just feels more like Mr. Knight than Jax."

He nods, but stays silent.

"Why is it I feel like I'm missing a few pieces to the puzzle?" There's a shift in him when I ask the question. He looks at me, searching, deliberating over his response. But too much thinking hinders an unfettered response, so I push a bit.

"Well…" I wait expectedly.

Drawing a deep breath in, Jax begins, "My father is a Senator. You've probably seen his face on TV…in the papers. Preston Knight. He's been in the news lately. A lot. For some pretty crappy stuff he did. His story made headlines six months ago when it came out he had an illegitimate son. My half-brother is Vince Stone, reigning MMA Middleweight Champ. The story broke right after Vince won the title. Took my family by surprise. Things had just started to settle down finally after six months. Then my father decides to announce he is running for re-election the same day it's announced Vince is hosting the MMA Open and the media circus started right back up again. And somehow that makes me newsworthy by association."

I nod, not knowing exactly what to say. "So you thought you'd get some peace here in New York while you checked out the gym and the press found you?"

Jax feigns a conciliatory smile. "I live in D.C., I changed hotels twice there, thought maybe if I came to New York for a while, I could get away from the circus."

"Your plan seems to be working well," I quip, full of teasing sarcasm, before biting into a ravioli from my plate.

Both Jax's eyebrows shoot up, surprised at my comment, but he looks amused too. "Watch it, or I won't let you do me any more favors, you keep being a smartass like that."

"Oh my god." I close my eyes to savor the taste on my tongue, it's just that good. "This is the best thing I've ever eaten, what's in them?"

Jax smiles knowingly. "Brown butter lobster ravioli."

"God, if I was a dog, I'd be wagging my tail. They're heavenly."

He laughs. "It's the only reason I stay at that hotel when I come into town."

Swallowing another forkful of the sinfully delicious pasta I've shoved into my mouth, I tease, "So it's not for the marble floors and three bathrooms?"

Jax arches one eyebrow, "Snooped around while you were there, I see."

I feel the pink color flush on my face. Sheepishly, I respond, "Sorry. I've never seen anything like it, I couldn't help myself."

"Don't worry about it, I'm just teasing."

"Can I ask you something?"

"Anything you want."

"Really?"

"Sure. I didn't say I was going to answer, but you can definitely ask me anything you want," he chuckles.

I ball up my napkin and throw it across the table, hitting him in the nose.

"Very mature." Jax smiles, lifting his tall glass of water, he dips his fingers into it, and flicks them at me. Water drops hit my cheeks, nose, and forehead.

Eyes wide, surprised by his action, I squint, staring at him for a few seconds. He holds my gaze, his face showing he's feeling sure of himself. Never breaking eye contact, I reach across the table and fork his ravioli onto my utensil, quickly shoving the whole thing into my mouth.

Shaking his head, he reaches over to my plate and steals one of my two meatballs, shoving the entire large globe into his mouth.

When he finishes chewing, he reaches over to my plate, cutting the other meatball in half and bringing it to his lips. "So what question did you want to ask me?" He grins, before taking the half meatball into his mouth.

Following his lead, I reach over to Jax's plate, cut his meatball in half and bring it almost all the way to my lips before

60

speaking. "Why do you need such a huge hotel suite, if you're just one person?" I eat the half meatball, waiting for his answer. God, it's delicious too.

Jax reaches over to my side of the table, his fingers wrapping around my water glass, he brings it to his mouth and downs almost half the glass, returning it to my side of the table. He shrugs, "I have absolutely no idea."

His honest answer takes me by surprise. "Seems like a waste," I declare.

He smiles and then concedes, "It is a bit excessive, isn't it?"

"Yes, Mr. Knight. It is." I chide playfully.

Jax tells me a little bit more about his father, but most of it I knew from my snooping of the newspaper article in his suite. Plates bare, we finish dinner eating each other's meal without ever discussing our actions verbally, but the smiles exchanged speak volumes.

After dinner, we clean up together, storing all the leftovers in the refrigerator. "Thank you for dinner."

"Thank you for sharing yours with me," Jax smirks, leaning casually against the counter, arms folded across his chest. We're both quiet for a moment. There's a shift in the air, a tension I breathe in that spreads warmth throughout my body. I feel his eyes on me, watching me intently.

"I should go."

One of Jax's arms reaches out to me and hooks around my neck. "Come here."

Lips parted, I take a deep breath in as he pulls me closer to him. His face six inches from mine, he stops. Looking into his pale blue eyes, I get lost for a minute. The hand not around my neck, reaches up and his thumb rubs the side of my mouth.

"Sauce," he whispers through his grin.

"Ummm...thanks." He releases his grip around my neck, but his hand lazily slides down my spine where the other arm joins, locking around my waist, keeping me close. I know I should step away, but electricity tingles all over my skin. And the way he looks at me, so intense and focused, my eyes lock on to his and everything else blurs in the background.

"You really are beautiful," Jax studies my face as he speaks. His voice is low and raspy, there's a rawness that does something to me. The combination of the seductive sound and the close proximity turns my breath ragged.

My heart pounding in my chest, I stare up at him, forgetting everything else for a moment in time. His grip around my waist tightens. Slowly he pulls me to him, closing the small distance between us, until our bodies are finally flush. His eyes never leave mine, forcing my head to tilt up to keep our gaze as our bodies draw closer. Feeling the warmth of his hard chest pressed against my soft, my eyes drift closed. It feels so good, so right, so natural.

Taking a deep breath, I open my eyes. Jax's gaze, roaming my face, meets mine again. And holds. Our lips are so close, if either of us were to move the slightest bit, we'd connect. Wetting his lips, Jax's eyes drop to my mouth and my heart rate careens out of control with nerves and excitement all rolled into a big ball of anticipation. Slowly, they lift back to find mine, only now they're hooded, changing from sweet and adoring to desire and need. Full of want and raw passion. The look sends my libido into overdrive.

"Your body feels so right connected to mine," Jax whispers, his words coming out labored, like it's difficult for him to speak too.

Swallowing hard, I avert my eyes, knowing he's watching me, waiting for me to give him something. Anything. But even though I feel his words ringing true, his body feels so right connected to mine, something inside of me won't let me give in to what I'm feeling. What I know we both feel. "I should go," I say again avoiding his eyes.

We're both quiet for a minute, my mind racing as fast as my heart. "Lily?" One hand locking me in place lifts to my chin, gently forcing my gaze to meet his. I watch as he studies my face, slowly taking in each and every inch. Finally, as our eyes meet again, he whispers hoarsely, "Don't leave yet."

Unable to say no to his eyes, knowing they could easily change my mind, I look away, speaking with a low voice, "I have to. I, I…need to go." Taking two steps back from his hold, Jax releases me without struggle.

As much as I want to stay, I haven't even fixed the mess I've gotten myself into with Caden yet. I know it's a bad idea to get involved with anyone connected to my business again. Especially someone so important to Joe right now.

Scurrying to collect my bag, I make my way to the door and smile back halfheartedly as I reach for the handle. "Good night, Jax."

Still leaning against the counter, I see a look of confusion as I hurry out the door, practically sprinting down the steps.

Chapter 9

Lily

My phone rings for the fifth time as I walk into my apartment, only this time I don't hit REJECT. Feeling guilty, even though I haven't done anything wrong, I answer. "Hello."

"Finally." Caden's voice is laced with impatience and anger. "I've been trying to reach you for an hour."

"I was in the shower," I lie because it's just easier to.

"For an hour?"

"I dried my hair afterwards." My words met with silence, I decide to attempt to change the direction I know the conversation is about to go. "How is your trip?"

"Do you even really care, Lily?" he replies curtly.

"Please, Caden. I do care. You've been very good to me. I know that. It's just, I need some space. I told you that. If it's going to work out with us being friends and working together, we need more space between us."

"You didn't need space when I was there for you every night while you were crying after you lost your Dad." Guilt pours over me. Not just for spending time with Jax, but for leaning on Caden so hard and then pulling away as soon as I was strong enough to stand on my own.

"I'm sorry, Caden."

"There's someone else, isn't there?"

Taking a deep breath, I force myself to remember how good he was to me when I needed him most. Holding me while I cried. Wiping my tears. Stepping in for me at the gym when I couldn't function. He gave me what I needed and it's wrong of me to completely push him out. "There isn't anyone else." It's not a lie, nothing happened between me and Jax, yet it feels like a lie to tell him there's no one else.

We talk for another ten minutes. I do my best to keep the conversation light, focusing on small talk…the weather, plans for the next day. Eventually he lets me hang up, promising to call first thing in the morning. The concept of giving me space either not registering with him or he chooses to ignore it.

Falling into my bed, my brain mentally exhausted, I fall asleep thinking about only one man…Jackson Knight.

Even though I ran out the door last night, literally running from Jax's arms, I'm up extra early, anxious to get back to the gym just to see him again. I stop by the grocery store and pick up a few things, knowing his fridge is filled with only dinner leftovers and wine with no corkscrew.

Reporters are still camped out in front of the gym when I arrive an hour before opening time. Ignoring their questions, I slip inside quickly, lock the door and pull the shade down once again. I flip on a few lights and make my way to the door in the back that leads up to the apartment.

At the top of the dark stairs, I knock on the door gently, it dawning on me for the first time that I have no idea if he even gets up this early. Feeling disappointed when Jax doesn't answer, I turn around, beginning to make my way back down the stairs, when I hear the lock open.

"Lily?" Jax's voice is throaty, full of morning grog.

I turn, a few steps from the top of the stairs, bags raised in hands to explain along with my words. "I figured you'd need some food in there. The reporters are still outside."

Jax makes his way down to me, taking the bags from my hands, "Thank you, but you didn't have to do that."

"I'm sorry I woke you."

"I'm not." He grins. "Will you come in?"

I hesitate, feeling conflicted. Jax assesses me before speaking, "Come in, Lily. I promise to keep three feet back at all times," he says only half teasing.

Feeling ridiculous for not going inside when I feel perfectly safe around him, I concede. Jax carries the bags into the dark apartment, flicking on a light as he passes. Catching a glimpse of what he's wearing, or not wearing, I feel my face flush, yet I don't turn away.

He's shirtless. I take in what I'd imagined he'd looked like, only the real thing is even better. He's thick, well defined…muscles sculpted over flawless smooth skin. Although that isn't what leaves me speechless, it's the bottom half that has my mouth hanging. He's wearing only skin hugging, solid black boxer briefs. Ones that leave little to the imagination, although my imagination immediately starts running wild.

Jax turns back after setting the grocery bags on the counter and catches me staring. Looking down as if just realizing himself what he's wearing, he smirks and says, "Sorry. I was sleeping. I'll go throw on some pants." Though his grin tells me he's not really sorry at all.

A minute later, Jax emerges from the small bedroom in the back, wearing the grey sweatpants I packed yesterday, still no shirt. Taking the entirety of him in, the way the sweats hang low on his hips, the deep sculpted v that leads down to a place I already know is well stocked, I think to myself that the underwear might have been easier to handle.

Feeling flustered, I busy myself with unpacking the groceries as soon as I force my eyes off of the feast they've encountered. It's not an easy task.

"The reporters are still outside?" Jax asks, sounding somewhat deflated.

"Yes." I unpack a bag. "I'm sorry I woke you. I didn't even think maybe you weren't a morning person."

"I actually am a morning person." Jax joins me in unpacking the bags. "I'm usually out for a run by six and in the office by seven." Catching my eyes, he smiles and continues, "Just had some trouble falling asleep last night."

"Probably the strange place."

Jax shakes his head, slowly. "That's not what it was." There's no need for him to spell it out, we both know what kept the sandman away last night. For both of us.

"Dark chocolate syrup?" he questions with one eyebrow arched.

"You don't like dark chocolate?"

"I love it. You?"

"It's my weakness."

We unpack the rest of the groceries - eggs, cheese, bread, milk, peanuts, turkey, protein shake mix. Jax reaches into the bag for the last item and smiles as he lifts out the corkscrew.

"Now you'll have to come back tonight to have that glass of wine," he says with a boyish grin and sparkle in his eyes that I can't help but smile back at.

We put away the few things I've purchased in the bare kitchen cabinets and I tell him I better get downstairs to work.

Heading to the door, I ask, "You training today?"

"Ten with Marco."

"I'll see you later then."

Jax nods.

I open the door and Jax's voice stops me. "Lily?"

I turn back.

"About last night...," he says, his voice drifting off.

"It's fine. Nothing happened."

"No. But I wanted something to," he admits with a coy smile.

"Jax, I..."

He interrupts, "You don't have to explain. I just wanted to apologize. Let me make it up to you with dinner?"

Fighting a smile, I warn, "Jax."

"Lily," he counters just as sternly as my warning, maybe more so. "Come on, friends can have dinner, right?"

"I suppose, but..."

"Let's start over." Jax walks to me, extending his hand. "Hi, I'm Jax Knight."

I can't help but smile, even though he's doing his best attempt at serious. "Lily St. Claire." I meet his extended hand with my own.

His eyes squint ever so slightly as they gleam. "Listen, *friend.*" He draws out the word friend. "I'm new in town, and I'm sort of holed up in this place. Would you like to have a purely platonic dinner?"

Narrowing my eyes to gauge his sincerity, I say, my tone making it clear I'm not convinced, "Purely platonic, huh?"

"Absolutely." He nods his head.

"Okay."

"Okay?" His questioning tone reveals I was easier to convince than he thought.

"I guess we're having turkey sandwiches?" I tease.

"Nope."

"Eggs?"

"Nope."

"You don't have much else."

"I'll take care of everything."

Walking through the doorway, a smile already on my face, Jax stops me again. "Lily St. Claire."

"Yes." I have no idea why, but the sound of my name rolling off his tongue does something to me. My smile broadens.

"Your name is beautiful. It fits you."

Shaking my head with a laugh, I walk out, not turning back when I say, "See you later, *friend.*"

The morning goes by so smoothly, I actually find myself whistling as I unpack the supplies that were just delivered. Unsure if it's the lack of Caden or the frequent smiles I get from Jax when our glances catch, but I feel more relaxed than I have in months. The day only gets better when Reed walks in unexpectedly. He kisses my forehead and wraps a crimson red scarf around my neck.

"Don't you look gorgeous today," he says with an accent of some sort, although I have no idea what it's supposed to be. Bad Australian, perhaps?

"Thought you liked me with my hair back and no makeup?" I grin at my best friend, throwing his own words back in his face.

"I only say that when we're late and I want you to hurry up and get ready." He smirks, reaching forward and turning my sketch book to see what I'm working on.

Not looking up, Reed traces the pencil outline of my drawing with his finger, the ridges of the carved faceless torso, beginning to take form. "Is Mr. Panty Dropper here today?"

Pretending I have no idea who he's talking about, I furrow my brow. Mentioning I look nice followed by asking if Jax is around...am I really that obvious? I hadn't given it any thought this morning, but I did try on a few outfits and blow out my hair instead of my usual ponytail and whatever's clean wardrobe decision. I look over at Jax and Reed traces my line of sight. Feeling four eyes staring at him, he looks up and smiles at us, lifting his chin at Reed in a guy hello.

We both stare for a little too long, neither of us wanting to pull our eyes away from the sweaty man on the other side of the room. His white shirt clings to his pectoral muscles with every upward thrust on the chin up bar, a glimpse of tan skin revealing itself on each draw down. Both of us sigh at the same time.

Forcing my attention away from the vision of perfection, I bring my focus back to Reed. "So what brings you down here? You slumming?" Though you'd never know it by his attitude, Reed is probably the wealthiest person I've ever met. Well, maybe not, after seeing the hotel suite that Jax was checked into. His father is the CEO for one of the largest utility companies in the United States. And also an opinionated, card carrying, staunch conservative. Money driven and resistant to change, he's the antithesis of everything Reed is.

"Ummm...we're supposed to go to lunch, remember? And what's with all the people camped out outside?"

"Long story."

"Give me the short version."

"They're trying to get to Jax."

71

"Why?" Reed leans his elbows on the front desk, propping his head up on his hands, readying himself for some juicy gossip. The man is a fiend when it comes to gossip. He doesn't even need to know the person to be interested in someone else's dirty laundry.

"Father's a senator. Cheated. Found out he has a brother. Brother is the current Middleweight MMA Champion. Father is running for re-election anyway. They followed him here from D.C."

"Get. Out." Reed says each word staccato, total drama queen rearing its prissy head.

Looking back to Jax, Reed sighs again loudly. "Rich boy. Daddy issues? Are you sure he's not gay. He'd be perfect for me."

"He's *definitely* not gay." My tone gives away more than I intended.

Reed's eyes go wide as saucers and his mouth hangs open a minute before he speaks. "You didn't?" He accuses with a smile so wide it leaves no room for doubt that he'd be thrilled if I did.

"No. I didn't."

"But you wanted to."

"I didn't say that either."

"So what are you saying?"

"I'm not saying anything! You're putting words in my mouth."

Looking over at Jax again, Reed smiles and waves enthusiastically. "That man is sin on a stick." He sighs dramatically.

Glancing in Jax's direction, he smiles at us again. It's painfully obvious that we're talking about him, but Reed's right, and it's hard to tear my eyes away even when I should. It's my turn to sigh loudly. "I can't argue with you there."

"He seems like a nice guy too."

"He is."

Reed folds his arms over his chest as he speaks to me in a patronizing tone, "So he's gorgeous, nice, I'm guessing rich and smart too with daddy being a Senator, I can see why you'd keep away." He wrinkles his nose like he just smelled something foul, "Total loser. You're much better off with Caden." He lifts his hand melodramatically and begins ticking off comparable traits with his fingers. "Let's see, Caden's not gorgeous, not nice, not rich, and not too smart. Of course you'd pick Caden, and pass on Jax."

"It's complicated and you know it."

"Doesn't have to be."

Frustrated, I know there is no winning this conversation, so I change the subject, "I'm sorry...I completely forgot about lunch. I can't leave, there's no one here to cover for me. Joe's still traveling."

Reed shrugs, he's the most flexible person I know. "So we'll order in." It really is pretty amazing how malleable he is considering he's the product of two of the most inflexible people in the word. He pulls his cell from his pocket and orders sushi, without needing to ask what I want.

I pull the scarf he draped around my neck and examine it closer. Chanel. I squint, knowing how the generous man works. "The scarf is beautiful." I pause, fingering it between my hands. "Tell me about the guy you met."

"What guy?" Reed responds in a guilty voice that confirms my suspicion.

"Barneys and Bergdorf when you meet a new guy. Swap meets and second hand shops when you break up."

"I do n...," Reed trails off, his brain going through a mental rolodex of the timing of his last few shopping trips. He goes to finish his sentence twice, each time thinking better of it. Eventually he gives in, rolling his eyes, but his eyes light up as he speaks. "He's my TA."

Reed's working toward his degree in Art History. We decided two years ago we would go back to school together part time to finish the degrees we had started. I'm a business major with a minor in Art. He's an Art major with a minor in business. We always find a way to take a class together each semester. "Isn't that against the rules?"

"I hope so. That'll make it hotter." Grinning at the thought of forbidden lust, Reed turns as the bells sound on the door. Fleeting are the thoughts of his TA, as he's quickly distracted by a handsome delivery boy who walks in. He's waif thin and looks like he just woke up from a three day binge, although he is cute if you look past the protruding cheekbones.

"Delivery for Mr. Knight?"

Not taking his eyes off the poor delivery boy, Reed waves in my direction. "Go get whatshisname."

"Whatshisname?" So fickle. It didn't take long for him to forget he was drooling over Jax not five minutes ago and about to spill the details of his crush on his TA.

Chin ups done, Jax is hitting the speedball as I make my way to the back of the gym. His arms bulge with each punch and it pains me to have to interrupt him and spoil the view. "You have a delivery here."

"Thanks." He grabs a towel and wipes his head and tucks it into the waist of his shorts, making them hang even lower. A scant amount of bare skin shows as he reaches up and runs his fingers through his messy, yet sexy, hair. My eyes linger for a second too long, Jax catches it and grins.

Reed is busy chatting up the waif boy, so Jax and I hang back a few steps and wait. He leans in close to me and whispers so only I can hear him, "You smell incredible."

I smile, leaning back a little so my head is closer to his, but I keep my face forward as I respond, "You just think that because you probably smell from being all sweaty."

Jax turns, shifting his body to face me, "I bet you smell good even when you're sweaty."

Combatting the looming feeling of fluster creeping up, I attempt to lighten the feeling being so close to this man brings, "Think we should interrupt the lovebirds so you can get your delivery?"

Reed finally acknowledges we're waiting and arches his eyebrows at me as Jax steps forward to sign for the delivery.

"I'll get the rest of the bags," the delivery boy says in the direction of Jax, but never takes his eyes off of Reed.

"I'll help you." Reed follows the barely legal looking boy-man out the door.

Jax sets the bags down on the reception desk, his attention caught by my sketch pad. Picking it up, he studies the faceless form taking shape in my drawing. "Anyone I know?" He asks knowingly, his eyes gleaming with delight.

"No," I lie, but the pink on my cheeks gives me away easily.

Luckily Reed comes back, forcing Jax's focus back to the task at hand. Jax takes the bag handoff from Reed.

"Can I get a rain check for lunch?" Sheepishly, Reed asks with a dirty grin just below the surface.

I roll my eyes, but he knows I'm not upset. He kisses me on the cheek and talks over my head to Jax. "You like Dragon rolls?

"Sure."

"Great. Lunch will be here in twenty minutes." He tosses a fifty down on the reception counter. "Enjoy you two." Kissing me on the forehead and practically running to the door, Reed leaves me no chance to argue.

Twenty minutes later, a freshly showered Jax comes back down just as I'm setting out our lunch. As usual, Reed ordered enough food for a family of five, even though it was to only be the two of us.

"I can't leave the front desk, hope you don't mind." I motion to the chair I've pulled up next to me behind the counter.

"Works for me." Jax smiles as he walks behind the tall front counter, he brushes against my back ever so slightly, his hand lingering just a second too long on my lower back as he squeezes past me. My entire body becomes acutely aware of the close proximity, with tension gripping at my knees. He waits for me to sit, pushing in my chair before taking his own seat.

I start to open the takeout containers when my phone begins to buzz. Joe Ralley flashes on the screen for us both to read. "Sorry, it's Joe…I should answer."

"Hello."

Jax takes over setting up the sushi, opening the dips and putting the ginger and wasabi on one plate between us to share.

"Yes, everything's good. Quiet." Joe asks me about Jax. "Yes, Mr. Knight seems happy with everything at the gym." Jax looks up, wiggles his eyebrows playfully, a smirk on his face. Joe and I talk for a few minutes more and then he hands the phone to Caden before I can conjure up a way to politely ask him not to. Joe knows we broke up, but I haven't let on Caden's behavior is borderline stalkerish. I was hoping to unravel my personal life from our business without dragging Joe into it and muddying the water more than it already is.

"Hey." My voice goes lower, less enthusiastic. "How is the trip?"

"Fine," he responds. The creek of a door closing echoes in the background and then he immediately moves the conversation to the topic of getting back together, asking if we could go away next weekend and try to work things out. "I was thinking, with Joe's retirement coming soon, I should probably take on a bigger role with Ralley's too."

He refuses to accept what I keep telling him. If I had known Caden was going to get on the phone, I would've let the call go to voicemail. He's been more persistent than usual, the entire conversation is obviously going to come to a head, but I'd rather have this conversation later, rather than now. And without Jax sitting next to me. "I don't think so, Caden. I'm sorry."

"You don't want to go away or don't want me to help you run Ralley's?"

I pause. Hating to hurt him, but he needs to hear the truth. "Both."

Jax looks at me, catching my eye, and I do my best to smile, but it comes out timid and forced. His eyes scour my face and then he pauses for a second and smiles. It's a boyish smile and I can tell he's up to something. Reaching over with his chopsticks to the Alaska roll positioned in front of me, Jax plucks a roll from my plate and deposits the entire piece in his mouth in one bite.

My eyes widen and I lose focus on the conversation I'm supposed to be having with Caden. I pick up my chopsticks, Jax watching and grinning as he chews, reach over to his plate snatching a piece of his Dragon roll, and deposit it into my mouth through smiling lips. It's a mouthful, leaving me unable to respond to the question Caden shoots at me from the phone.

"Sorry...someone came in," I finally say as I swallow the last bit in my mouth. Jax grins at my lie.

"No. I'm busy Caden. I'm not ignoring you."

Jax arches his eyebrows, enjoying what he can hear from my half of the conversation and attempts to take another piece of my lunch from my plate. Only this time I smack him in the knuckles with my chopstick and the piece he has gripped between his sticks falls back to my plate. I point my finger at him and give him my best mock glare warning him to behave himself.

"Can we talk about it when you get back?" I ask and pause listening to him again tell me my decisions are wrong. Of course, he throws in how he was there for me when I needed him.

Not about to let me off the phone, even though I've told him I'm busy, Caden continues pushing. "You're not even listening to me," he accuses with a hardened tone.

"I'm listening to you. And I'm responding. You just don't like what I have to say." I pause, sighing with frustration. "I have to go, Caden."

"You okay?" Jax asks with concern evident in his voice after I hang up, his playful face gone.

"I'm fine. Sorry about that."

"You want to talk about it?" His voice is low and cautious, but he looks directly into my eyes, showing his offer is sincere.

"No. But thank you."

Feeling the need to lighten the mood, I reach over to his plate and grab another piece of sushi, smiling as I bring it to my lips.

"So what did you have delivered in all those bags?" I say before popping another bite of sushi into my mouth.

"Just some stuff for dinner with my friend." Jax shoots me a wry smile.

"Do you realize that we will have shared all three meals together by the end of the day?"

"I'm a lucky guy," Jax replies. "And when you say shared, it's a pretty literal use of the word." He pinches another piece of sushi from my plate and brings it half way to his mouth. "You want to try a piece of my Alaska roll?" Grinning, he holds up the piece.

"Sure."

Jax brings the sushi to my lips and I open, he gently slips the roll into my mouth. His eyes focused completely on my lips, I feel the heat of his gaze and it warms me inside.

We finish our lunch taking turns eating off each other's plate and occasionally feeding each other. The conversation flows easily, we compare art and business classes I'm taking to the ones he took in college. He tells me how he visited the Louvre in Paris and I tell him about the dozens of museums in the city he hasn't been to yet. Both of us seemingly content with sitting around talking. Until my phone buzzes again and we both glance down at the same time to see the name flashing. Caden. Again.

"He's persistent, I'll give him that." I try my best at sounding casual, but fail.

"Guess I don't blame him." Jax pauses, catching my eyes in his beautiful blue gaze. "I'm not a man who's easily deterred when there's something I want either."

His words scare the hell out of me, but make me feel oddly hopeful at the same time.

Chapter 10

Jax

Growing up with a house full of staff doesn't lend itself to learning to cook many things. But I can make a few good meals, mostly because my grandmother taught me to make them when my parents would dump me in Cape Cod every summer.

Lily knocks right at seven. She looks beautiful in faded old jeans, a simple white tank top and colorful flip flops. Her thick hair is braided to one side and her face is almost free of makeup, except for some sort of dark liner that makes her blue-green eyes look more jade than blue tonight.

Lily's different than the women I usually date, she doesn't look like a designer picked out her clothes and a makeup artist airbrushed her face picture perfect. She's truly a natural beauty, the kind that doesn't have to work at it. It's effortless and simple, and the sexiest damn thing I've ever seen.

Growing up surrounded by men, being the daughter of The Saint, I would guess she'd been propped up on a pedestal. But she doesn't act like a trophy. Instead she has a quiet, feminine confidence. No flaunting required for my thoughts to race from awe to indecent.

"Are you okay?" she asks, tilting her head to assess me as I stare, lost in her beauty.

"I'm great." I smile, wrapping a hand around her waist and leaning down to kiss her on the cheek. Catching her scent, my head lingers a bit longer than it should to kiss a friend hello. "You smell good," I whisper with my mouth close to her ear. A little tremble runs through her, I feel it, but she tries to hide it.

"Thank you," she answers breathlessly, but with a flicker of uncertainty in her face. It makes me relieved to know I'm not the only one affected by being so near.

Reigning in a breath, I try to collect my thoughts. "I made stuffed artichokes and steaks."

"Mmm…" Lily closes her eyes, "It smells delicious in here."

It sure does, but it has nothing to do with the food in the oven.

"You want a glass of wine? I have a corkscrew now." Lily follows me into the kitchen and opens the oven door to peak in.

"No, thanks."

"Do you not like red? I had white delivered just in case." I show her the bottle that I have chilling in the fridge.

"No, I like red, I'm just a lightweight. Two glasses and I'll be sleeping on your couch."

"I'll give you the bed."

She shakes her head, amused. "Always the gentleman, you'll give me your bed and sleep on that little couch." She points to the living room couch that could possibly hold half my body.

"Who said anything about my sleeping on the couch?" I dig the corkscrew into the bottle and arch an eyebrow suggestively.

Her face flushes a bit, so she tries to change the subject. "So you cook?" She leans against the counter as I take our dinner out of the oven.

"It's one of my many talents."

"*Many* talents?" She rolls her eyes playfully, but asks anyway, "I'll bite, although something tells me I'm going to regret asking, but what are your other *many* talents?"

"Oh, the list is pretty long." I grin. "I can walk on my hands."

Lily smiles. "That *is* a talent. What else you got?"

"I can say the alphabet backwards, as fast as most people say it forward."

"Why would you want to do that?"

I shrug, "Why not?"

She giggles.

"You want to hear it, don't you?"

Smiling, she admits, "I actually do, although I have no idea why."

"zyxwvutsrqponmlkjihgfedcba" I run through the stream of letters rapidly.

Lily laughs, "Oddly, that really is pretty impressive."

"What talents do you have?"

"Did you run out of talents already?"

"Definitely not. I have plenty more where those come from. But I don't want to intimidate you with all my talent, so I need to slow it down a bit," I tease.

Lily contemplates for a moment. "I can touch my nose with my tongue."

My eyebrows arch and other parts of my body perk up at her talent confession. Folding my arms across my chest, I lean against the kitchen counter and nod my head, silently giving her the floor to demonstrate. And she does. Her tiny, perfectly pink tongue darts out of her mouth and curls high, touching the tip of her nose. My pants get a bit snugger.

"Nice." I blow out a ragged breath, filling a glass of wine and handing her one. I take a long gulp, hoping the chilled fluid will cool the heat I feel steaming from my body.

"I can tell when people lie by their body language," I offer, trying to impress her with a never ending list of talents.

"I'd like to see *that one* demonstrated."

"You got it. Tell me three things about yourself and I'll tell you which is a lie."

Lily ponders for a moment, nibbling unconsciously on her bottom lip as she considers what she is about to share. I get the urge to pull her plumb bottom lip from beneath her teeth and sooth it with my tongue. Fuck, this being friends thing is not going to be easy.

Shifting her shoulders back a bit, she stands taller and brings her eyes to mine, locking our gaze and standing steady as she speaks. "My favorite color is green. I've dipped my toes in Bethesda Fountain in Central Park. The smell of mustard makes me gag." She smiles confidently, sure she's going to prove my talent a lie.

"That's a shame, I hear the water's pretty nice in Bethesda Fountain."

Her eyes go wide. "How did you know?"

"Body language."

"But I didn't move. I made sure of it."

"Ahh…so you were trying to prove me wrong."

"Of course. Let's try it again. That was totally beginner's luck."

I smirk, already having figured out her tell, it should be a piece of cake. "Go for it," I say confidently, tilting my glass to her before downing more.

Lily concentrates for a moment, avoiding eye contact, but I don't take my eyes from her. I like watching her think, catching the slightest uptick from the corner of her mouth as she comes up with something she thinks will fool me.

"My Dad's nickname for me was Lily Vanilly. I've kissed a girl. I had a pet turtle named Speedy." Confident that she's got me, I play with her a little. But there's no mistaking the dilation in her pupil when she lies, even though she tries her hardest to still herself completely as she lists her three facts.

Rubbing my chin as though I'm pondering, I pretend I'm having a hard time deciding the fake fact. "You know, I've kissed a girl, maybe you should really try it sometime, it works for me."

Lily slaps me playfully. "How do you do that?"

"Talent. I told you."

"Let me try. Tell me three facts."

"Okay." I think for a second, locking our eyes, I speak directly to hers, never even blinking to disrupt our gaze. "Boats make me seasick. I've been to forty-nine states. I have a crush on a friend of mine."

Her face pinks a bit and her eyes squint as she tries to read me. "Boats don't make you seasick," she says without too much confidence.

"Yep. They do. But I've only been to forty-eight states."

The buzzer sounds on the stove, interrupting our game playing. Lily helps me bring everything to the table and together we sit.

"Which two?"

Confused, I furrow my brow.

"States. Which two haven't been graced with your presence?" she chides sarcastically at one of my facts.

I'm just about to respond, when Lily's phone starts to buzz. We both look down, finding the name Caden flashing on the screen. Her face changes, a sadness taking over her carefree happiness. Before either of us can comment, my phone joins in on the buzzing. 'Dad' appears on the screen. Ignoring the vibration on the table I smile, reaching over to pluck a leaf from her stuffed artichoke, and bringing it to my mouth to scrape the edible meat between my teeth.

Lily looks torn. Glancing at the buzzing phones lying at our sides on the table and back to me twice, eventually she smiles as she makes her decision without words. Reaching over to my plate, she plucks a leaf from my artichoke and brings it to her mouth smiling. Both of us pretend not to notice the phones jumping around the table.

My father and Caden call twice more each during dinner. We never discuss the calls, but we smile, ignore the sound, and keep on eating.

We clean up together in the little kitchen. I intentionally brush past her lightly as I reach over her head to put dishes on the top shelf. When she's in the fridge putting the leftovers away, I snake my arm through hers to put a jar on the door. I could have waited my turn, but I love the way her body reacts at the slightest contact we make. It can't help it, even though I see her trying to hide it, control it. Mine reacts too…a twitch, a swell, a thickening, an ache, a damn fire in my pants. Yeah, without a doubt, my body likes brushing against hers too.

"You feeling daring enough to do something with me?" I rub my chin, an idea popping into my head.

A blush creeps up Lily's cheeks. "I, I…" Lily's voice trails off, making me realize what she must think I'm asking.

A slow smile curls up on my lips. "You have a dirty mind. I was going to ask you if you were up for attempting an escape and ditching the photographers."

Her sweet, pink cheeks darkening with embarrassment, she attempts to recover, "I wasn't thinking anything dirty." We both know she's lying.

She's leaning against the kitchen counter, I close the distance between us, standing in her personal space, but our bodies aren't touching. "Yes. You were." I lean in a hair more. "Haven't we already established I can pick off lies easily?"

She swallows, wanting to deny, but instead attempts to change the subject. "What is it you wanted to do?"

Closing the small gap left between us, my body now lightly brushed up against hers, it forces me to look down to her. I say nothing, until she looks up at me. "Well I'm not sure now. What did you have in mind? I think I might like what you want to do better." I tease, although we're so near, she can probably feel the hard on through my pants and guess what I'd really like to do with her.

A look of disbelief mixed with embarrassment passes across Lily's face, "You're unbelievable."

I smile, taking her words as a compliment. "Thank you."

"I didn't mean it as a compliment."

Ignoring her retort, I continue with a one-track mind. "Tell me what you thought I meant."

"You know what I thought you meant."

"Yes. But I want to hear you say it."

"Why?" Lily's eyes bulge at my admission, clearly she can't believe the words I'm sharing.

"Because I want to hear you talk dirty to me."

Placing her hands on my chest, she shoves a bit, but not enough to really want me to move. "Use your imagination."

Gripping the counter she's leaning against on either side, I cage her in. She looks to the right and left, seeing the position I've moved into and there's no mistaking her breath hitches. She likes it and so do I.

"Oh, I've been using my imagination a lot lately." I smirk, then pause. "Tell me, or I'm not letting you go."

"I'm not telling you anything, you crazy man."

"Then we're going to be here for a while." I settle in place, my eyes telling her I'm serious about keeping her right where she is. It's a no lose situation for me. If she doesn't tell me, I keep her incredible body pressed up against mine. If she does tell me what she was thinking, I get to hear her admit she had dirty thoughts about me. I'm not sure which option appeals to me more right about now.

"You're going to keep me pinned against the counter?"

"I kinda like it here."

"I thought we were having a platonic dinner?"

"We were. Until you started to think dirty thoughts about me."

"You're impossible!" Lily shrieks, but there's still a smile on her face, even though she tries to disguise it.

I lean down slightly, forcing her back to arch a bit. "On second thought, don't tell me." I pause, my eyes dropping to look at her plump full mouth. Her lips part slightly as she watches me. Returning my eyes to hers, I continue, "I'd rather stay right here."

She sucks in a breath and I lean down closer. Only this time she doesn't arch anymore, so we're face to face. "You like me here. This close to you. Pinning you so you can't move. Don't you?"

She gasps, but averts her eyes.

"Lily." I say her name sternly. Her eyes jump back to mine. "Answer me."

She looks conflicted, but whispers her truth anyway, "Yes."

"You have till three, but I'm kissing you, crossing the line from business to pleasure or not, unless you stop me."

Her eyes widen, but she doesn't say anything. We're still pressed tightly against each other, there's no way she can miss the erection testing the limits of the seams of my jeans.

"3," I begin my countdown.

Her eyes widen more.

"2."

Her mouth opens but no words tumble out.

"1." The second the number leaves my mouth, I kiss her. Her lips may have begun to open to protest, but I don't give her a chance to get the word out.

At first it's gentle, our lips softly touching and tongues beginning to explore each other. Until I feel her push her breasts against my chest, a silent affirmation that she wants the kiss as much as I do. Then I can't get enough fast enough. The hand that was gently weaving through her thick blond hair, clenches a fistful and I tug, forcing her head back more so I can deepen the kiss. Lily moans in response to the harshness of my action and it makes me god damn wild. Pilfering her mouth, pushing harder against her, I reach down and grab one leg firmly, lifting it and guiding it to wrap around my waist. Her other leg follows without my direction.

Her thighs spread wide, legs wrapped around my waist, the heat between us blends to the point of combustion. There's fire pulsating through my veins, and my mind and body join together with only one purpose. This kiss. It consumes me as quickly as it started. Her smell, her moan, the feel of her luscious body pressed hard against mine. I have no idea how long it lasts, but however long it is, it's definitely too damn short. Breathless, we both come up for air. But I'm not ready to let go just yet. I take her bottom lip, the one that has been taunting me since I met her, between my teeth and nibble on it. When my nip turns harsher, she makes a sound that is a cross between a gasp and a moan, and it takes every ounce of my self-control to not carry her into my bedroom while keeping our mouths locked so she can't object to my ramming myself into her.

As difficult as it is, I force my self-control back. Eventually I release her mouth and we stay quiet, both of us panting uncontrollably, our foreheads pressed against each other, eyes closed, until our breathing returns to normal.

Lily's the first one to speak, although her voice is more of a whisper. "You didn't count from one to zero."

"I'm a go on one guy, Angel." I brush a lock of hair that has fallen free from her braid back behind her ear.

She smiles, but I see her senses are starting to flood back. Whatever is holding her back, regains its grip on her mind. "We can't, Jax," she whispers, her voice sounding as disappointed to say the words as it does for me to hear them spoken.

We're both silent for a minute, both of us staring into each other's eyes. As if on cue, the sound of one of our phones buzzing on the nearby table catches both our attention.

"Yours or mine?" I ask without moving. She looks around me to check. Her phone is jumping around the table, the vibration making a tapping sound against the wood.

"Mine." Her face saddens. Before her phone can even stop buzzing, a second buzz begins, signaling my phone now has a caller too. Looking over at the table and then back to me, the corner of her lips turning upward, a hint of amusement showing, she says, "And yours."

Breaking the tension the kiss left in its wake, we both laugh, neither of us even attempting to answer the calls. I step back a little, not wanting to force her into something, even though her body seems to be doing the talking. Strands falling loosely from her braid, her cheeks flushed and lips swollen from my kiss, she looks beautiful. Not ready for her to leave, fearing she will run out on me again like she did last night if I don't give her some space, I decide my original plan still might be fun.

"You think you can outrun a few photographers?"

She smiles, perking up at the thought of an adventure. "Absolutely."

The evening crowd has dwindled, only a handful of diehard paparazzi still wait, hanging around the darkened gym. Both donning sweatshirts pulled up covering half our faces, I tell Lily to go right and I go left when we open the door and make a run for it. Lily locks the door before she leaves, allowing the photographers to begin snapping pictures and shouting out questions to her. I make a mad dash left, half of the photographers following me.

Ten minutes later we meet at our planned location, both of us able to lose the photographers on the chase.

"Nice work," I say, impressed at her ability to lose people during a chase.

"Not the first time I've had to run to get away from someone." Lily smiles mischievously, there's a whole story there I want to hear about. But for now, we need to keep moving, put more distance between the mice and the cheese.

We walk a block, both of us spotting one of the photographers that was giving chase on the other side of the street, before he spots us. I grab Lily's hand, changing direction and increasing our pace to a jog. "Come on."

Chapter 11

Lily

We weave in and out of streets for almost half an hour, until Jax is comfortable no one is following us anymore. Our fingers still woven and hands tightly entwined, I'm not even paying attention to where we are heading. Content in easy conversation that comes effortlessly, and the feeling of Jax's big hand meshed with mine, I stop as we arrive at where Jax must have been heading all along. Bethesda Fountain.

"Now you won't have that one to use as a lie anymore," Jax says with a grin, pulling me toward the fountain.

"I think you really are crazy." I tease, laughing that he brought me to the fountain just so I could dip my feet in. "Have *you* dipped your feet in?"

Slowly, Jax shakes his head back and forth, no.

"Well take your shoes off, Mister. I'm not getting cholera alone."

Without argument, he does. I reach over and pensively feel the water…it's freezing and the cool air of the late summer evening doesn't make me want to jump in so quickly. "It's cold," I whine, sounding like a little girl, my nose crinkling.

Jax reaches down and feels the water. A wicked smile crosses his lips...just before he splashes me with a wall of water from the fountain, drenching me completely from head to toe.

"You. Did. Not. Just do that," I growl, shocked by his actions.

Jax stands, folding his arms over his chest, an undeterred smile still spread wide across his perfect face. "I did."

Trying my best to gather as much water as possible, I splash as much as I can back in his direction. Jax jumps back and not one drop hits him. He arches one eyebrow.

"I'm soaked!" I shriek, to which Jax's dirty grin and another playful arch tell me where his gutter brain took my comment without the necessity of words.

I try again, in vain, to splash him, but it's no use. I don't have the element of surprise like he did and he sees it coming every time.

"Jackson Knight!" I scold, water still dripping from my nose.

"Lily St. Claire," he mocks me in response.

"You wait. I'll get even when you least expect it." It's a promise, not a threat. He doesn't know it, but I can be a grudge holder, playing at getting even is a sport to me.

"Can't wait." He has the audacity to smile, like it's something he actually is looking forward to. "Now, go on, dip your toes in."

"Dip my toes in? Half my body is soaked, I hardly think it's necessary for my toe to go in at this point."

"Oh it's necessary, alright." Jax heads toward me, a look of determination on his face. I run the other way. It takes less than one full lap around the fountain until he catches up with me. Lifting under my knees, he cradles me as he walks toward the cold, flowing water. My playful cries completely ignored as he steps over the concrete circular bench surrounding the fountain and walks straight in with me in his arms.

"No!" I squeal, realizing he's heading straight for the center of the fountain, where the waterfall is still running. I try my best to get out of his grip, kicking and screaming, flailing my legs around, but it's no use. He only smiles with delight at my attempts as he steps under the ice-cold cascading water. We're both drenched from head to toe by the time he climbs out of the fountain, me still in his arms.

I should be angry, but the whole scene is comical. It's late, yet there are still a few people milling around and they've all stopped to watch the scene we've created. Some aren't sure whether I'm really angry or we're playing. Either way, with the size of Jax, and the muscles rippling through his wet shirt, not too many people would intervene anyway.

Both still laughing, Jax eventually places me back on my feet, sliding me down his wet, hard body. I'm not sure if it's intentional or not, but the man has a way of heating me up, even when I'm soaked, wet and freezing. A chill passes over me as my chest glides over his.

"Cold?" Jax asks.

"What would give you that idea?" I reply sarcastically as I ring a puddle of water out from my hair.

Jax looks to my nipples and back to me and smiles. No response necessary. "Here, put this on." He hands me his sweatshirt. It's as equally drenched as everything I'm wearing.

"Umm…I don't think that's necessary. I have my own dripping sweatshirt."

"Your dripping sweatshirt is white and you're cold. Put it on."

I look down to find my nipples protruding and my three layers of white clothes almost transparent. Jax is helping me put on his sweatshirt before I even agree.

The dripping has stopped by the time we arrive back at my apartment, but that's the extent we have dried off.

"Do you want to come up and dry off? The paparazzi will probably have a field day if you go walking up looking like that."

"Finally, something good coming from the photographers that hound me. I get an invite up," Jax says with a devilish grin on his face.

After seeing his hotel suite, I'm pretty sure my place is going to look like a closet to him. It's unlike me to be self-conscious about things, yet I can't help but be a bit nervous as I invite him in.

"This is me. It's not exactly a suite at the San Marcos, but make yourself at home."

Jax looks around, taking in my shabby chic style. My old butcher block kitchen table surrounded by four different, ornately decorated, lush fabric chairs. Nothing matches, but it all works together. At least I think so.

"I feel like I just walked into one of those high end stores that are trying to look funky and chic. Except they come off as copied and imitating the real thing. I just never knew what they were trying to copy, until now. This place is great."

I smile, keeping the fact that I designed and made half of the pieces to myself.

"Come on…I'll give you something to change into."

Jax follows me into my tiny bedroom. The closet is organized, but filled to the brim. I pull out a pair of men's sweatpants and a t-shirt and hand it to him.

He takes it, but looks up at me hesitantly. "Are these…"

"Reed's," I fill in the blank. "He won't mind. We keep clothes at each other's apartments. Sometimes we do movie marathons and lay in bed for two days in a row."

Jax nods, looking relieved. "Have you two been close since you were little?" He begins to peel off his pants.

"Umm…there's a bathroom right over there." I point down the hall.

"Sorry. Figured we were past the shy stage. You already saw me in my boxers." He grins and wiggles his eyebrows. "And I saw you naked."

"Yes, but your boxers are soaked too…aren't you going to take them off?"

Jax stops undressing and looks at me appalled. "It's not cool to go commando in another guy's pants."

I giggle, "I'm pretty sure if Reed found out you were commando in his pants, he'd never wash them again."

"On second thought, maybe I'll keep my wet clothes on," Jax teases.

"Just change in here. Take everything off and I'll dry it for you."

"If you wanted me out of my clothes, you could have just asked," he flirts his response.

"You're unbelievable." I grab my clothes, toss a pillow at his face, and head to the bathroom. I hear Jax's low chuckle all the way down the hall.

Chapter 12

Jax

ily wipes her face clean of the makeup that was smudged and dries her hair with a towel. Emerging from the bathroom wearing a pair of sweatpants rolled down at the waist and a pink tank top, I catch a sliver of her slim waist as she ties her damp hair back into a ponytail. She's the girl next door. The one that makes a boy have sweet dreams for years without even trying. Wet, sweet dreams.

"What?" She tilts her head and looks herself up and down. My stare making her think something is out of place.

"Nothing." I grin. Jesus Christ this woman gives me a hard on wearing sweats.

"You're staring at me like I have my underwear on the outside," she teases.

Underwear. Lily's underwear. Get control of yourself man, or she's going to kick you out wearing some other guy's clothes. "I like you with no makeup." *And your nipples are erect in that damn little tank top. Don't stare, eyes high, stay on the face. Face only.* I try to talk my eyes into working with me. It doesn't work, like a magnet to its pull, they drop.

She squints, not sure if I'm teasing her or not and shakes her head with a smile. "I'll throw your clothes in to dry. You want something to drink?" She asks over her shoulder as she tucks my clothes into the dryer.

"Sure. Whatever you're having."

Grabbing two bottles of water, she hands me one, her face faltering a bit as she speaks, "I don't have much else in the house. Hope this is okay?"

"It's great." I try to assure her. I really could care less, but something seems to have shifted, her mood blue and distant.

We settle in on the couch together. I'm glad it's small, even though she sits at the other end, it's still nice and close. "Here, give me your feet." Reaching down, I pull her legs up and settle them on my lap. "They're freezing," I say as I take one into my hands. Her tiny pink painted toes are like little icicles.

"That's because someone soaked me in a cold fountain," she teases, the smile coming back to her face.

"That's terrible." I smirk as I begin rubbing her feet.

"Wow. That feels good."

"I'm good with my hands," I quickly counter, wishing I was showing her what I could do with them *other* places on her body.

"Mmmm." She closes her eyes and let's out a small moan of appreciation as I work the arch of her foot with my thumbs. I rub up and down methodically, enjoying watching her face go slack as she relaxes into my touch. Perhaps I enjoy it a little too much, forcing me to shift slightly to disguise the bulge growing in my pants before she sees it.

After another ten minutes, Lily opens her eyes, now hooded from the massage. "Seriously, that was incredible. I don't even like people touching my feet."

"I'm not just any people," I offer, trying to mask just how much I was enjoying touching any part of her. At this point, I'll take what I can get. Sadly, I'll settle for a foot.

Lily rolls her eyes and attempts to pull her feet away, but I grab them, stopping her from recoiling.

"What are you doing?" She asks as I hold firm on her feet

"Keeping you comfortable."

Lily squints, eyeing me suspiciously. "With my feet on your lap?"

"It's a small couch. You shouldn't have to be squished just because I'm here." I offer as an explanation, although her face tells me she's not buying it. Yet she doesn't attempt to pull her feet away again.

"So, tell me, Jackson Knight. Do you have a girlfriend back home?"

I shake my head no, grinning almost questioningly at her. "The position is open if you know someone."

"Hmmm..." she replies, teasingly, "...maybe I do. Tell me what you're looking for."

Clasping my hands behind my neck, I pretend to deliberate over my answer. But I know exactly what I'm looking for. "She has to be smart," I begin. "And love art."

"Art, huh?" Lily questions suspiciously.

"Yep. You know, with my being an art history minor and all."

"Uh huh." She plays along with a smile.

"And I tend to like blondes, my preference with long wavy hair. Maybe the kind that picks up flecks of light, reminding you of spun gold."

"That's pretty specific."

"Hey. I know what I like." I shrug.

"Of course you do," she patronizes me.

"And blue eyes. I'm definitely a sucker for blue eyes. There's actually a certain blue that has a hint of green in it, almost like they can change based on mood." I pause. "They're pretty rare. But that's the color I like best."

"Anything else?" She dares to ask.

"Curves. I like a woman with curves. Not too skinny. Maybe about five foot three." I rub my chin as if I'm pondering the description of the perfect woman. Although all I have to do is look in front of me if I forget anything.

"Not five foot six? You sure?" Lily teases.

"Positive. I'm pretty specific about the height."

"I'll try to remember that. Anything else?"

"Hmmm…" I pretend to give it due consideration before dishing out my final requirement. "She has to like foot massages."

"Foot massages?"

"Yeah. I like to start at the foot."

Lily swallows, trying to pretend I'm not getting to her, but I can tell that I am. "Start?"

I nod slowly. "I like to take my time. Get the tension out of her feet before I make my way up the leg. The calf. The inside of the thigh. The…"

Lily jumps from the couch abruptly. "I should check on your clothes. They were pretty soaked. One cycle might not be enough." I smile watching her walk away, and not just because of the view. Seeing her flustered as I spoke, told her what I liked, gives me hope I might have a chance.

A little while later, we're back on the couch and I know my clothes have to be close to dry. We're comfortable with each other, so I try to broach what her deal with Caden is.

"So Caden seems protective of you."

Lily forces a smile, although the mention of Caden definitely changes the mood. "That he is," her tone tells me it's not something she's too happy about.

Quiet for a moment, I try to think of a tactful way to ask the question, but sometimes direct is just the fastest way to where you want to go and causes the least amount of resistance. "Are you together?" Looking her in the eye, I ask pointedly.

"No. Not anymore."

"But you were?"

"Yes, we were." She pauses then adds, "It's complicated."

"So you're not sleeping together?"

"No!" She answers, shocked that I would ask such a question. But there's no way in hell I would share a woman like Lily.

"So it's not complicated then."

"You don't..." The dryer buzzer interrupts our conversation and Lily's too eager to make an escape. A minute later she brings back my clothes.

"They're dry," she says, and I think I hear a bit of disappointment in her voice. I change in the bathroom, putting on my warm pants but realize she's given me one of her shirts instead of mine.

"I don't think this is going to fit me?" I emerge from the bathroom shirtless, holding her shirt up.

Lily turns around. Not answering with words, I watch as her eyes drop from my face to my body. Swallowing hard, slowly her eyes trace the length of me, stopping at the top of my unbuttoned jeans. Her lips part and with a salacious gaze, I hear a small gasp that makes me lose the little resolve to be a gentleman I have left. "Oh fuck this," I growl, taking the two strides to reach her quickly, finding all the emotions in her eyes that I feel deep inside of me. Lust. Need. Desire. Hunger so deep, it consumes me.

Walking us two steps until her back is to the wall, I reach down and lift her up easily. Pinning her body between mine and the wall, I wrap her legs around my waist and bury my face into her neck, breathing deeply to take in her scent.

Heat pulsating wildly through my veins, I pull my head back, dig my hips deeply into her parted legs so she can feel how hard she's affecting me and claim her mouth in a kiss.

A low moan escapes her mouth as we come up for air, both panting, our chests rising and falling in rhythm pressed firmly up against each other. "God I love that sound," I growl, sealing my mouth back over hers before we've even both caught our breath.

She tastes fucking incredible. How can someone taste so damn good? Sweet and addicting, like a drug you know you shouldn't take the first time, because there's no going back to how you were before you had it. You need it. Want it. Crave it.

Dropping my mouth to her neck, I lick and suck, making my way to her ear where I bite down on her tender lobe. I listen to her breathing change, learning what she likes as my tongue explores every inch of what I can reach. But it's not enough. I need more. "Jesus, what I'm gonna do to you," I groan.

Slipping one hand behind her head and the other lifting her weight at the curve of her ass, I unpin her from against the wall and carry her over to the couch. Gently, I lay her down, her back to the soft leather, and lean over her. Her wide blue-green eyes look up at me with hooded need, but there's something else there. Something that stops me no matter how bad I want to keep going.

"You okay, Angel?" I ask, my voice hoarse, straining to control myself.

She hesitates, "I...I shouldn't."

The simple two words are the equivalent of someone pouring a bucket of cold water over my head. *Shit.* I stand, raking my hands through my hair, taking my frustration out as I tug mindlessly at my own locks. Why the hell did I need to ruin the moment by stopping to talk, we were doing just fine without conversation.

"I'm sorry," Lily says in a timid voice, sitting up and pulling her knees to her chest.

"Don't be. It's my fault. I should go." Turning my back on her, I grab Reed's shirt, rather than wait for her to get mine from the dryer and take off toward the door. It's barely over my head when I reach for my shoes and walk out without looking back.

I replay the last twenty minutes over and over in my head as I make my way down the four flights to the lobby. *I shouldn't,* she said, not I don't want to. Turning around, I take the stairs back up two at a time.

Chapter 13

Lily

What the hell is wrong with me? I can't remember ever wanting something so badly, yet I chase him out the door. And for what? Because of a bad experience getting involved, or rather getting uninvolved, with Caden? Because I feel badly for breaking it off with a man I'm not in love with? A man I've never wanted like I do Jax. For almost a year I've walked around numb, filled with an emptiness I never thought would be filled. Then a man comes along that makes me feel more alive than I ever have, and what do I do? Push him away like an idiot.

I pick up my phone to call Reed, as I always do whenever I have a problem. But half way through dialing I realize I know what he's going to say. Screw this. I'll figure the rest out tomorrow. Flinging open the door to my apartment, I don't bother to put on shoes as I make my way to the stairwell, hoping I'm not too late. Just as I reach my hand forward to open the heavy door leading to the stairs, it flies open and I'm met by the most beautiful blue eyes staring down at me.

"Where are you going?" he asks, his chest heaving up and down like he just sprinted up the four long flights of stairs.

"To get you," I whisper.

Taking a step closer to me, Jax cups my chin, sliding his thumb across my bottom lip longingly, before tilting my head up so my eyes can meet his gaze. "You said you shouldn't. You didn't say you didn't want to." He searches my eyes, waiting for something, although I'm not sure what else he needs. I've come after him.

"Say it," Jax demands, lowering his face so we're eye to eye. "Tell me you want me as much as I want you. I don't give a shit what you should or shouldn't do. I just need to hear you say it. Tell me you want me."

"I do." I breathe out, feeling relief just saying the words.

"Say it then," Jax commands more firmly as he takes a step closer. We're practically touching, but it isn't enough. I want him against me, his hard body crushing against mine again.

"I want you," I squeak out, little more than a whisper.

"Again. Louder," Jax wraps one arm around my waist, pulling me close to him. The other hand grips the back of my head, threading his fingers through my hair, he tugs my head back. It doesn't hurt, but I feel the strength in his hands and it gets my attention, forcing me to look up...maybe even leaving a little more wetness between my legs. Staring back at him, he waits patiently. He wants me to say it to his eyes.

"I want you," I say louder, with more force, more meaning.

A wicked smile crosses his face that speaks volumes. He lifts me, our mouths colliding with need so consuming I don't even realize he's carried us back into my apartment until the door slams closed with my back up against it.

One of his large hands grips both my wrists and pulls them high above my head. It makes me feel small and vulnerable, but instead of scaring me, it turns me on. I want him to take me. I don't even care if it's right here against the wall, my whole body yearns with desire.

Leaning down, I think he's going to kiss me, but instead he buries his head in my neck, the feeling of his warm breath near my ear, ratcheting up my need to an excruciating level. My hands held tightly over my head, I have no way to grab him, bring his mouth to me where I need him, so I do the only thing I can do to force more contact. Arching my back, I push my body deeply into his until we're pressed tightly against each other. But it's not enough, I still need more.

"Please," I say, almost pleading. I need to feel him back against me, know that he's really here again. "Kiss me." I groan as he nibbles his way down my neck to the tender skin at the crook of my shoulder.

Pulling his head back, his voice no more than a rough whisper, a delightful twitch of his sinful mouth, he says, "Oh, I'm going to kiss you, Angel. Every part of you. From the tips of your toes to the top of your head. I'm going to bury my mouth so deep inside of you that you're going to beg for me to *stop* kissing you." Distantly I register Jax lifting me and my being carried; but I'm too busy concentrating on the way he sucks my tongue into his mouth as he kisses me with more passion than I've ever been kissed.

He lays me down on the bed and stands, looking down at me with hunger in his eyes that brings goosebumps to my skin, even though he hasn't even touched me yet.

I reach up, offering my hand, wanting him near me, but he grins and shakes his head no. His gaze almost predatory, he leans down, his face aligned with my breasts, and pushes down the fabric to my thin tank top, revealing a very protruding, and wanting, nipple.

"It was killing me knowing you had no bra on under here," he hisses, then drops his head without warning, sucking deeply on one nipple while staring up at me…watching my reaction. His tongue swirls around my pebbled bundle of nerves before biting down and I gasp at the unexpected pain. Although it's the kind of pain that feels good, and he quickly lavishes sweet kisses making it all better anyway.

Discarding my tank top for better access, he shifts his attention to the other breast. His tongue again swirling around in gentle circles, awakening every nerve ending, setting my body on high alert, before biting down with just enough force to make me gasp.

My nails dig into his shoulders and I try to pull him up, but he doesn't budge. Not upwards anyway. With a nearly maddening slow pace, he kisses and nibbles his way down from my breasts, inch by inch, leaving no skin untouched as he makes his way down to the edge of the bed.

Dropping to his knees, he watches me, his captivating blue eyes searing into me as he pulls me down the bed until my ass hovers near the edge. He slips off my pants in one fluid motion, leaving me lying bare in only my skimpy black lace panties.

He strokes his fingers languidly along the edge of the lace, before his hand slips underneath, his thumb grazing lightly over my clit, but it's enough to have me panting at his simple touch and my body throbbing for him. The tension inside of me builds even more as he slips one finger inside of me, finding me already slick from my own juices. "You're so wet for me," he murmurs approvingly.

Adding a second finger, he pushes in and out in a slow, steady, unhurried rhythm. Keenly focused on my eyes, he watches how my body reacts to his every touch. Seeing him fixated on learning my body's reactions only serves to heighten the intensity of what I'm feeling. I never knew how incredibly sexy it could be for a man to be so focused on bringing a woman pleasure. Bringing *me* pleasure.

He speeds up the pace and I feel my body climbing higher and higher with each blissful pump. But I want him with me. Want him inside of me when I come, need him to fall with me when I spiral down from the mountain he's brought me to the top of.

"Please, Jax," I breathe, reaching down, trying to grasp his shoulders and bring him up to me.

"Shh…later, I promise." A dirty grin crosses his face, "I'm just getting started." He adds his thumb to my clit, rubbing gentle circles around as he continues to push two fingers into me. Fast and firmly, his fingers glide in and out, in and out. I'm so close…dangling over the tunnel that leads straight to euphoria.

"I need to watch you come. Your sweet little pussy is tightening around me. Let it happen, Angel. I can't wait to spread you out and lick every drop from you." His words enough to send me spiraling over the edge, my body begins to convulse, clamping down around his fingers as I climax. Between the innate instinct to close my eyes and let it wash over me and the intimacy of the moment, I struggle to hold his gaze. But I do, because it's the only thing I can give him in the moment, and his eyes flare with satisfaction as he watches me, brings me to this place.

Barely recovered, I'm in a fog as he slips off my now soaked panties. Jax lifts one leg high, starting at my ankle and kisses his way gently up to my thigh. Slowly, he lifts and worships my other leg, only this time, when he reaches the top, he arranges both legs over his shoulders.

The first lick from his hot tongue elicits an unexpected shudder that runs through my body. I moan, a feeling of ecstasy taking over me, between the strength of my orgasm just a few minutes ago and the feeling of his tongue lapping hungrily, almost needily, at my juices, my emotions consume me.

My body arches off the bed, greedily craving more. And he gives it to me selflessly, his tongue tunneling deep inside me, licking and sucking, drinking in all my body gives as if he needed it to survive.

My breath quickening, one throaty moan leading directly into the next, my body begins to tremble against his mouth. Clutching and tugging at his hair as my orgasm washes over me like a tidal wave, it pulls me under in its fury until I have to struggle to breathe.

In a euphoric haze, I sense the activity around me, but my brain doesn't register what's happening until I hear the crinkle of a wrapper and feel the brush of Jax's thick erection waiting patiently near my opening.

Hovering over me, Jax hesitates, one arm supporting his weight, the other hand brushes my hair from my face with a tender touch. "You okay, Angel?" he asks, true concern in his voice even though I should be the one asking if he's okay after the marathon treatment he's just delivered.

I nod, a goofy grin on my face, which apparently he finds amusing. Taking his time, he gently kisses around every inch of my lips, his tongue dipping in to mingle with mine leisurely. His smile is still firmly in place as he pulls his head back to look into my eyes. I lift my pelvis slightly under his weight, silently urging him to take me. He knows what I want and I watch as his eyes change from playful to hungry, filled with raw desire. "You want my cock inside of you?" he groans.

I nod again. My thirst for this man is barely quenched even after what he's already done to me. Keeping his eyes locked with mine, with a strong thrust of his hips, he finally sinks into me. Slowly. He's long. And thick. I've never seen him naked before this so I don't know what to expect. But whatever I expected, the reality blows the fantasy away. Painstakingly slow, he rocks into me a little at a time, stretching me unhurriedly, like he knows he

112

needs to take his time, until the base of him is finally flush against me.

It feels heavenly. More than just him inside of me, I feel filled by him, possessed completely and totally connected. Like we've just shut ourselves off from the world and only the two of us exist. Together, as one.

He takes his time, giving me a chance to adjust to his wide girth, before he begins moving. Our fingers linked together tightly, he sets our rhythm. At first it's slow and sweet. I wrap my legs tightly around him, allowing him to sink even deeper than he already is. I moan his name and Jax responds with a sound that can only be described as a growl. And then slow and steady goes out the window. Jax slams into me hard and fast, relentlessly pounding over and over until my furious grip on his back goes limp and both of us climax with a ferocious groan that he silences with a kiss.

I don't remember falling asleep, but I wake completely tangled with Jax, our arms and legs wrapped around each other in a vice like grip. My head on his chest, I tilt my eyes up, expecting to find him still asleep, but he's already awake.

"Morning," he says in a low, gravelly morning voice that is sexy as all hell.

"Morning." I smile at him and snuggle a bit closer. It feels so good. So right. I spent months with Caden and never wanted to spend the entire day in bed. Snuggling was just never my thing...until now.

"How long have you been up for?" I ask.

Jax strokes my hair back, his touch soothing more than my morning bed head. "I don't know. An hour maybe."

"Do you have to be somewhere?" I ask, quietly hoping he doesn't.

"Nope. You?"

"It's my day off from the gym. The uptown manager is covering for me today." I pause. "Although I do need to do a little sketching at some point. I'm a bit behind because of all the extra hours I've been putting in at the gym with Joe away."

Flipping me over onto my back in one swift move I didn't see coming, Jax pulls the sheet covering my body down, sucking one nipple into his mouth. "You can sketch me."

"I can, can I?" I tease, pretending he's arrogant and I don't really want to sketch him. Even though I've wanted nothing more than to capture his jaw line on paper since the first time I laid eyes on him.

"Yep." He smiles, moving his attention to my other nipple and biting down until I yelp. "Naked."

"What if I don't want to draw you naked?"

"Then you can do other things to me naked." He wiggles his eyebrows playfully.

"Hmm. Tough choice. I really do like to draw, what other things did you have in mind? I need a little more specifics before I can decide," I tease.

"Let's see...my cock has so many ideas...." He slides two fingers inside of me.

I gasp. "I can sketch later."

"Good choice, Angel."

If morning sex was always like we just had, I'd be anxious to get to bed every night, just to wake up. Sitting in my kitchen wearing nothing but tight black boxer briefs, Jax keeps me company as I finish up making us pancakes.

"Can I ask you something?"

"Sixteen," Jax answers without hearing my question.

"Sixteen what?" I'm almost afraid to ask.

"That's the answer to your question."

"But I didn't ask a question yet."

"Oh. I just assumed you were going to ask me how many times I thought I could service you in one day," Jax grins as he speaks.

"Wiseass…wait, what? Sixteen?"

"You think I'm exaggerating?"

"I do."

He reaches over to my plate and tears a piece of my pancake, bringing it to his lips, but falling short of stuffing it into his mouth. "Only one way to find out?"

"Let me guess. We give it a try?" I roll my eyes playfully.

"You got it." He rewards me with a full dimpled smile.

My cell phone rings on the nearby counter. It's the third time in an hour. I'm almost positive that it's Caden, but I reach to grab it and check anyway. I hit REJECT and slide it back onto the counter.

Almost immediately, Jax's phone starts ringing. "Guess we're pretty popular." He reaches down to his phone, finds his father's name on the caller ID and hits REJECT with a clench of his jaw.

"So what's the question?" He tries to resume our playful banter, even though I see the name on the screen has shifted his mood.

"How come you don't fight professionally? Marco says you're good enough."

Jax arches an eyebrow, a satisfied boyish grin tilts upward at the corner of his mouth as he speaks, "Asked about me, did you?" He forks another bite of pancake from my plate.

Of course I did, but I hadn't meant to let him know that. This man has seen every part of my body. Hell, he's licked, sucked and nipped at most of it...you'd think I'd be past the point of shyness, yet I feel my face flush at being caught simply digging a little bit...asking about him.

Attempting to avoid the question, I reach across to his plate, fork a pancake, and swirl it around in the syrup leisurely. Flush rises up my face. His eyes never leaving mine, he watches me intently. Bringing the fork to my mouth, I attempt to deflect, "Are you avoiding my question, Jackson Knight?"

"Maybe." His face turns serious. "I guess I just wish I had a better reason to tell you." He pauses, reflecting on something before continuing, "I wish I had a better reason for myself."

"I'm sure whatever you decided, you had good reason at the time. Sometimes things we choose to do make perfect sense at one time...but later, in hindsight, we can't imagine what we must have been thinking."

Jax searches my eyes, "I guess you're right."

"I usually am," I tease, an attempt to lighten the mood.

"Well, I could have used you ten years ago, when I decided to follow my father's choice of careers for me, instead of my own."

"Is that why you didn't fight? You didn't want to disappoint your father?"

Jax's face tenses, "Not my finest hour."

"Actually, I think it's honorable that you followed his guidance."

"At the time I thought he was an honorable person."

I've always known how lucky I was to have the father I did. It saddens me to think Jax's father let him down when he looked up to him so much. I try to offer comfort, "Parents are human too. Sometimes they make bad decisions."

Standing, Jax looks anxious to change the subject, but not before delivering his final thought, "And sometimes they're just bad people."

Together, we clean up breakfast in relative quiet. Although the quiet isn't the same comfortable one as it was earlier. It feels like he built a wall and I'm on the other side of it. The recent conversation is still obviously weighing on him.

"I'm going to take a quick shower."

Jax nods.

The warmth of the pulsating shower helps to soothe my aching muscles. It's been a while since I've used some of them. Closing my eyes, I smile as the memories of last night play over in my head. Sex with Caden, even in the beginning when things were good, was never like it was with Jax last night. It was just sex. An activity. A mutual release, which I enjoyed at the time, but we never had a connection to elevate things from sex to making love. Last night felt more like making love than I'd ever experienced in my life. I didn't just give over my body to Jax…it was more. I let him in, gave him a piece of me. Maybe even a piece I'll never get back.

When I'm sufficiently pruney, I wrap a towel around my body and open the bathroom door which leads to my bedroom and find Jax lying in my bed. The sheet covering to his waist, the sight of his shirtless torso enough to bring my body that just relaxed in the long, hot shower back to life.

"Hey," Jax says softly.

"Hey." I smile and make my way over to the dresser to grab some clothes.

"Come here," His voice is low, but his tone makes the simple two words more of a demand than a question, it stirs something inside of me.

Still wrapped in my towel, I sit on the edge of the bed next to him.

"I'm sorry."

"For what? You didn't do anything."

Jax strokes the wet strands of hair away from my face. "I shut you out when you were only trying to get to know me better."

I smile, appreciating the thought he's given to our conversation and his ability to recognize what he'd done. A sign of maturity, something I'm not used to with the men I've dated over the years.

"Thank you." I smile.

Jax nods. Folding his hands behind his head, he leans back leisurely on the headboard. "I had an epiphany while you were in the shower."

"An epiphany, huh?" I arch an eyebrow. My shower seems to have washed away something for both of us.

"Yep. I'm turning over a new leaf. From now on, I'm not hiding what I want. No more worrying about my family, the media, the reflection my actions might take on the precious Knight legacy. Let them snap pictures. I know who I am."

"That sounds perfect," I say, because it really does...and he makes it sound so easy.

Jax leans forward and pulls me back onto the bed, then lifts me onto his lap. "What are you doing?" I giggle.

"I'm starting on my first order of business," he says, fingering the top of my towel until he loosens the tight wrap and the towel falls around me.

Already squirming while sitting on his lap completely naked, Jax runs both hands down the sides of my arms. Goosebumps flare on my skin. "And your first order of business is..."

"Watching you ride me." His arms tighten around my waist. He visually assaults my still damp body now bared completely before him as the midmorning sun shines through the nearby window.

Jax's epiphany may just leave me walking a little funny tomorrow. But I'll worry about that then.

Chapter 14

Jax

Peace. That's what I feel as I wake in the late afternoon. I can't remember the last time I took a midday nap. But it feels damn incredible. Although it likely has something to do with the beautiful angel who's wrapped around me, her head snuggled close, cheek pressed warmly right above my heart. I listen to the quiet sounds of her breathing. Watch her slow even breaths, the way her mouth twitches up slightly every once in a while, like whatever she's dreaming is making her happy. I can't help but smile each time it happens. Somehow seeing her happiness becomes enough to bring my own.

From the nightstand, her phone buzzes yet again. The sound makes her rustle in her sleep. A few minutes later it happens again, this time she lifts her head. I reach for her phone and look at it. Fucking Caden. Whatever peace I was enjoying is quickly replaced by a host of other emotions. Anger, jealousy, somehow even a little hurt, even though she's done nothing herself to make me feel this way.

"Mine or yours?" she whispers, her voice filled with sleep.

"Yours." Unintentionally, the word comes out a bit clipped.

She reaches up, assuming I'm going to hand it to her, but I don't. Instead I push REJECT and toss it back on the nightstand.

Looking up at me, her brows drawn together in confusion at first then a look of understanding replaces it quickly. "Caden?" she asks softly.

I've never been the jealous type. But even hearing her say his name evokes a feeling of turmoil inside of me. I have to force myself to not wonder if he's been in this bed, lying how I'm lying at this very moment. "What's the deal with that guy?"

Lily's eyes dart up to mine. She looks into my eyes, maybe searching for how she should answer, but I only stare, patiently waiting for her response.

She closes her eyes briefly and then opens them. She had said it was a long story. I'm not sure I want to hear the whole thing, but I need to know something. Seeing another man's name repeatedly flash on her phone as I lie in bed falling for her a little more each minute isn't going to fly for long.

"We were together for a while," she says, trailing off.

My jaw clenches. I already knew it was more than a one night stand…she just isn't that type of girl and there's some sort of loyalty there. Which I'd normally respect, but having my eyes opened recently makes me leery of misplaced loyalty to a man who doesn't deserve it.

"When my Dad died I was a disaster. Caden had moved to the city a few months before to train with someone Joe thought might be a good fit. We also hired him part time to help out around the gym. We were friendly, but didn't really know each other well. But when my Dad died, he was there for me. He helped me through it." My grip around her tightens automatically, without giving it any thought whatsoever. I'm not sure if it's

122

because she said she went through a tough time or I'm feeling jealous just hearing the asshole's name spill from her lips. Both, likely.

"He wasn't always a jerk." Her eyes look away from mine as she thinks for a moment, then she shrugs and smiles almost regretfully. "Maybe he was, I just wasn't in a place to see it right away." She pauses and then looks up at me. "He's possessive of me. Doesn't quite take the hint, even though I keep politely reminding him we're over. He also has this way of making me feel guilty…reminding me how he helped me get through a hard time." She trails off for a moment, thinking. "Sometimes I think I let him bully me into things."

A burn in my stomach ignites and grows to my face. "What kind of things?" I ask because I need to know, but I'm not sure I want to hear her answer.

She shakes her head, her face paling at the thought. "Oh god. No, it's not what you think." Relief floods me. "I don't even know if he does it on purpose. But he reminds me of everything he's done for me and it makes me feel bad."

"It's on purpose. Trust me." Sounds all too familiar. Fucking manipulator. Why is it the one being manipulated never sees it until it's too late? "When did it end?"

She bites her lower lip, nervously. Shit. You've got to be kidding me. My stomach turns as she looks away with shame on her face.

"Lily?" Anxiousness with a bit of anger laces my voice. She looks up at me. "You're still sleeping with him?"

"No!" Lily glares at me. "I wouldn't be here with you if I was still sleeping with him!" She's angry I thought so little of her. I don't blame her. But what the fuck? She couldn't answer when it ended. Pulling away from me, she tries to move to the other side of the bed, but I pull her back.

"I'm sorry. It's just…you didn't answer me when I asked you how long ago it ended." I don't like talking to her back. Instead of pulling her to where she was lying, I gently guide her onto her back, so I can see her eyes when we talk. Her face is still angry. "I'm sorry." I speak slowly, directly into her eyes, my voice filled with sincerity. Her face softens a bit. "It's just…I like you. A lot. The thought of you with another man…" My jaw clenches and voice trails off.

Sensing I'm being genuine, she reaches up and touches my face. "It's okay. I guess I could have explained better." She pauses. "I broke up with him two months ago, but I felt bad and sort of agreed maybe I'd reconsider in the future." Trying to hide my reaction isn't easy, but I do a halfway decent job as I wait for her to continue. "I knew it was over, and I wasn't really going to reconsider, but he was just so persistent. He's Joe's nephew, works at my business, and I see him almost every day at the gym. I realize now it was the cowardly way to handle things, but he relented a bit when I said that. I figured he'd move on, realize I wasn't really reconsidering anything after a while." She pauses. "Like I said, he helped me when I was in a bad place." She frowns. "Now he has a big fight coming up soon. I think he's nervous about it, even though he walks around like a pompous ass full of confidence. I told him a few weeks ago I would be there for him. But as a friend, that I didn't want more."

"Guess he doesn't take a hint too well."

Lily attempts a smile, but it falls short of real. The kind that seems to be on her face a lot when we are together. Except when the asshole interrupts us. "No, he doesn't. We haven't been together…together…," her voice dips in that way to explain the word together means fucking, it's cute that she won't say it, "…in months, but even the other day when he said goodbye, he tried to kiss me as more than a friend."

As if on cue, her phone buzzes again. It's on vibrate, but it bounces around against the wood on the table like a tiny drumroll anxiously leading up to the flashing name. "Think he needs it reinforced that it's over," I say, picking up the phone. I'm about to answer, when Lily shrieks at me.

"Don't!" I stop, my finger freezing, hovering over the buttons. "I'll talk to him again."

"It sounds like you've tried. Maybe my telling him you've moved on, will help him do the same."

"He's got some anger issues and *that* would definitely not sit well."

"I don't really give a shit about any issues he has. His calls and behavior are borderline stalker. He's not hearing what you're saying."

"That's my fault."

"Did you tell him you didn't want to see him anymore and you stopped sleeping with him?"

"Yes."

"Then he's hearing you. He just isn't accepting what you're telling him. I think he needs someone else to explain it to him." The phone is still buzzing in my hand.

"I'll talk to him again when he gets back."

"How about we talk to him together?" I suggest as an alternative.

"That would undoubtedly turn into a physical fight. I'd rather it not turn out that way. I'll talk to him."

"I'm not worried about it turning physical." I might actually enjoy it. Didn't like the asshole the minute I met him, even before I knew he was playing games with Lily.

"I didn't say you were." She takes the phone from my hand and hits the REJECT button. "But I would prefer Caden and I not end that way. Our families have been close for too long. Joe *is* my family." She looks at me and smiles sweetly. "And I don't want you and I to begin that way either."

Begrudgingly, I agree. Although something tells me there's no avoiding a confrontation with the asshole somewhere down the road.

Chapter 15

Lily

Last night, not five minutes after Jax and I talked about my need to have another chat with Caden, my phone started jumping and buzzing all over again. I turned it off. A satisfied grin on his face, Jax joined me, taking it one step further and unplugging my house phone after powering his cell off. Not that anyone ever calls my house phone...I'm not even sure why I still have the thing, but Caden would undoubtedly move on to try a different means after a few hours of going to voicemail on my cell.

We've been together for almost two days, half of the time we spent exploring each other's bodies. Every time we started, the same passion consumed us, stopping only when exhaustion hit, both of us fully sated as we fell into blissful sleep. Although last night after we ordered in Chinese food, we laid entwined with each other for hours watching old movies and eating each other's meals. Oddly, it felt so normal. So comfortable. So inexplicably right.

Finally turning the TV off some time after 2AM, we talked until the sun came up. The more I get to know Jackson Knight, the more I discover I like. He's smart, thoughtful and well mannered. Well, well mannered on the outside, as in opening a door for me or pulling out my chair. It's certainly a whole different ballgame when the door shuts to the bedroom with this man. *Please* turns into *Keep your hand where I put it* and *Thank you* turns into *On your knees now, Angel.* I've always heard the saying men like a lady in the living room and a whore in the bedroom, guess it's not that far off for women either. There's nothing sexier than a man with manners when he's dressed, but a bit caveman-ish when he's in the bedroom. Unfortunately, all I've ever had to compare it to were pure cavemen. The kind that don't treat a woman like a lady. Ever.

Two days of short naps and long stretches of time in the bedroom when it's not even nighttime have my internal clock off kilter. I have no idea what time it is when I wake. I try to untangle myself from Jax's stealth grip as he sleeps, but he's got one arm wrapped tightly around my waist and starts to wake as I gently peel back his fingers. Deciding it's next to impossible to disengage without waking him, I attempt to stretch while in his arms, aiming to reach my phone on the nearby end table. It takes a couple of attempts, and the use of the tips of my fingers, but I'm able to spin the phone toward me a little at a time, until it's finally fully within my reach.

Powering my iPhone back on, I'm not surprised the clock shows it's almost twelve, but I am surprised at the quantity of messages and texts. Knowing Caden would be upset he was unable to reach me, I'd expected a half dozen angry messages. But it's beyond that...my voicemail is completely full and there are sixty-two new texts. More than fifty from Caden, a half dozen from Reed.

I start with Reed's...scrolling to the bottom to read the oldest of the bunch first.

Nice bath in the fountain. NY Post - page 6. Glad ape boy is away or he'd go apeshit for sure.

2 hrs later

Message from Ape on my vm. Not sure how he even got my #. Sounds angry. Did he catch the pic?

10 minutes later.

Ape flying home today. Apeshit for sure.

5 hours later.

Ape called me five times today. He's lost it. He saw the pic.

10 minutes later

Where are you? Why aren't you answering? Call me.

1 hour ago

Just saw your bath on TV. Uh oh.

Shit. Shit. Shit.

I hit Reed's number and try to whisper, but I'm panicked.

"Seriously? I've been trying to reach you for almost two days. I'm on my way to you now. You wait till I get three blocks away and call me? You better be calling to tell me you're dead." Reed rattles off before I've even had the chance to say hello.

"I'm sorry. I turned my phone off. I was with Jax."

"So you haven't spoken to Caden?"

"No."

"Have you seen the picture?"

"I'm not even certain what you're talking about, what picture?"

"You. And Jax. In a fountain. Is that Bethesda, by the way? That thing is filthy. You probably have Legionnaires' disease."

"A picture of us in the fountain?" I turn to Jax, his eyes are open now, my conversation has definitely caught his attention. He squints, silently asking me what I'm talking about.

"You look like Natalie Portman in that bad swan movie."

"*Black* Swan. And it's a Natalie Portman in a Dior perfume commercial where they're in the fountain, not from the movie." I have no idea why I feel the need to correct him.

"Whatever. Mr. Dior will be knocking on your door any minute. You two look *hot* together. It's a still, but I mentally got the visual of you slip sliding all the way down his muscular body. Lucky girl."

"Reed." I sit up. "Who took the photo?"

"How would I know? A paparazzi I guess."

"What are we doing in the fountain?"

"Jax has you lifted up into the air and water is pouring over your head from the top of the fountain. You're looking down and he's looking up. Your faces are maybe a few inches from each other's...but you're both smiling and laughing."

"Shit."

"It could be worse."

"How exactly could that be?"

"You could look bad. You look beautiful. It's a great shot."

"Wonderful."

"Someone is grumpy. Your knight in shining armor keeping you up all night? Did you see what I did there? The pun was intended."

"Reed!" I scold. He's gotten so far off track of where I need this conversation to be.

"Oh my god, he so did! I'm two blocks away. Tell me details until I get there."

"Reed!"

"What? Jesus you're cranky."

"What did Caden say?"

"Oh. That." He sounds deflated. "He's sort of freaking out. He saw the picture on the news."

"Do you know when he's coming back?"

"Tonight."

I close my eyes. Caden is going to be a disaster. He gets jealous when a guy I don't know looks at me the wrong way. I don't even want to think about what he will be like seeing my picture in the paper in another man's arms.

"Okay. I have to go. Have to be at work at two."

"I'm going to be there in five minutes."

"You can't."

"Why not?" Reed sounds blatantly insulted.

"Because." I pause. "I need to talk to Jax."

"We can go see him together. You can fill me in on the way."

"Jax is here. I'll call you later, okay?"

Reed screeches so loudly, I pull the phone away from my ear. Jax smirks and shakes his head...right before he takes my phone out of my hand. I listen to one side of the conversation.

"Reed?" Jax pauses and listens before responding, "Do you know when he lands?"

"Yeah. I don't trust him either. I'm not letting her out of my sight."

"Okay. Later."

He pushes a button and hands me back my phone. "Looks like we get to have that conversation with Caden sooner, rather than later."

"Jax. You don't know him. He's not always logical."

Jax shrugs. "That's why I'm not letting you out of my sight till we have a chat with him."

"Maybe he doesn't know it was you in the picture." I'm grasping at straws.

"So? I'll tell him."

My eyes bulge. "Why would you do that?"

Jax stands, slipping on his sweat pants calmly as he speaks. "Because I'm not going to run away from it. This isn't a one night thing for me, Lily."

"He's going to freak, Jax."

Jax leans down, his face in mine, "Don't worry about it." It's more of a stern warning than a suggestion. Then he kisses me chastely on the lips. "I'll put the coffee on. Freak out for five minutes if you want. Then meet me in the shower."

Jax heads for the kitchen and I do exactly what he said. Sit, freaking out for five minutes until he returns with a steaming mug of coffee for each of us. "You done now?"

I sip my coffee. It's exactly how I take it. Briefly, it makes me feel better. "Done what?"

"Freaking out."

"Not really?" I respond with a question, not a statement.

He takes another big gulp of his coffee and sets the mug down on the end table. "Take another sip," he instructs, before swiping my mug from my hands and setting it besides his. Then he scoops me up into his arms, the sheet covering me falls to reveal my naked body.

"What are you doing?" I ask, not really caring what he's about to do now that I'm in the warmth of his arms.

"Taking a shower."

The press outside the gym quadrupled overnight, Jax wraps his arm around me and does his best to shelter me from the clicking cameras. I have no idea what time Caden will show up at the gym, but I'm glad he's not there when we enter.

I go behind the front desk and get myself settled in. Jax stands watching me fidget nervously. "You going to be okay?"

"Yes," I lie, trying my best to avert my eyes by grabbing a pile of waiting mail. But Jax just waits. Calmly. Patiently. Standing there looking completely undaunted by the fact that all hell is soon going to break loose, he waits till my eyes reach his and I still as he speaks.

"It's going to be fine. He won't get the chance to raise his voice, no less lay a finger on you. I promise. Trust me." He pauses, his eyes probing mine. "Let me take care of it. Okay?"

Incredibly, I believe him. Somehow, I just know everything will turn out okay, so long as he's near me. I smile. It's weak, but genuine, and it earns me a dimpled grin back from Jax. Jesus, even worried and exhausted from two days of life altering sexcapades with this man doesn't quell my desire when he turns on the charm.

"Go!" I point in the direction of the gym, giving him an order. "You're incredibly distracting. Don't you have someone to beat up or some tycooning to do?"

Jax's eyebrows raise in surprise, but he chuckles and walks off shaking his head in amusement.

The afternoon flies by, without both Joe and I here for a day and a half, it takes me hours to get caught up with mail, telephone calls and getting next week's schedules put together. Every once in a while I'd look up, my eyes scanning the room to find Jax. Each and every time, he was already looking back at me by the time my eyes found his. I think Jax may have been on a higher level of alert than I even was. I'd noticed he'd positioned himself for his afternoon workout and sparring so that he can keep an eye on me. It was sweet, so very different from the way Caden kept his eye on me. Caden's never felt protective or warm, instead it was possessive, territorial. And not the sexy kind of possessive I see a sliver of in Jax. His possessiveness is about me. Caden's is about him.

By 8PM, an hour before closing, my nerves have gotten the best of me and I almost jump out of my skin every time the door opens. The rattle of the bells somehow training me like Pavlov to hold my breath as I wait for the person to walk through. I try to sketch, but creativity doesn't mix well with restlessness and anxiety.

Jax comes to the front desk. He's set up a makeshift office in the corner of the small kitchen and I've caught him on more than one occasion raking his fingers through his hair looking stressed himself.

"You okay? You look stressed." It's my turn to check on him.

"Yeah. Just some work fires I needed to put out."

"Mmmm…" I tease, "I like firemen."

Jax leans his elbows on the counter, lowering his frame down so our faces are level. "Better than tycoons?" he questions with a flirty challenge in his voice.

I'm just about to respond when the bells interrupt, bringing me back to the impending doom I'm facing. Jax seems completely unaffected and doesn't budge at the sound of the door opening. I let out a sigh of relief when I see it's only a late night regular. He waves and goes right to the gym.

"You really are afraid of him, aren't you?" Jax wonders aloud.

"I honestly don't really think he would ever hurt me. Not physically anyway. But there's a side of him that scares me a bit. I didn't see it at first…that's a whole other conversation. Someday, maybe. But there's something that lurks just beneath the surface that I'm afraid to see escape."

Jax brushes his knuckles softly along the side of my cheek. My eyes close at the contact. God I even love the simplest of touches. Each one just says so much with him.

"I'm not sure I could handle listening to too much about you and Caden when you were together. Even though I'm glad he was there for you when you needed someone, I wish it would have been me." Gently, he pushes the hair that has fallen on my face back behind my ear. "I want to be there to catch you if you fall from now on, Angel."

Yet another check mark gets ticked off the chart listing the elements of the perfect man. Perceptive. Doesn't just listen to my words, but listens to what I'm not saying. I've only known one other man like that and he had my heart and soul. My dad. My heart swells at both the memory of the man I loved and finding a piece of him in Jax.

When I don't respond right away, Jax gently lifts my chin, bringing my eyes back to meet his. Mine are filled with unshed tears. "Okay?" he says the word in a soft, soothing voice. I nod, swallowing hard, fighting back the thought of my dad being gone. Gently, Jax leans in and kisses my forehead.

"I'm going to lock the door and run up to get my stuff. Don't think it's a good idea to put Joe in a position to keep his nephew away from burning it all." He forces a smile. "Don't open the door unless it's a customer you know. Okay?"

"Okay."

"You close up at 9, right?"

"Yes."

Jax checks his watch. "It's almost 8:45. I'll grab my bag and be back down in a few."

Chapter 16

Jax

Anger boils in the pit of my stomach as I pack up my bag. What kind of a man makes a woman afraid of him? Lily may have said she wasn't physically afraid of him…but her body language over the last few hours tells me something different. She jumps every time the door opens, the anticipation of Caden's reaction, and his ensuing wrath, leaves her nerves frayed. He may not have touched her, but emotional manipulation…instilling the fear of what *could* happen, is just as bad. Reminds me of someone I know. Scare tactics and threats to get what he wants. Some men just aren't men.

I slip the last of my belongings into the duffle bag and sling it over my shoulder. The moment I open the door, I hear it. His voice. I can't make out the words at first, but I can tell from the tone that whatever he's yelling is vile. Pure venom drips from every angry syllable. I dart down the stairs two at a time, the blood coursing through my veins as fast as the pace of my rapid steps.

I see red when I catch sight of him. Caden has Lily pinned up against the wall, his forearm pressed against her neck, forcing her chin up. His face is in hers, wild and angry, his nostrils flare and spit heaves from his mouth as he screams right in her face.

"You're a fucking whore! I should have known you'd open your legs for anyone that came along when I turned my back."

Too busy threatening a woman a quarter of his size to hear my approach, he doesn't expect it when I grab him from behind. Wrapping one arm tightly around his neck, I use my other arm to pull back more, applying even more pressure.

"How do you like it?" I hiss between gritted teeth. "Does it feel good?" I yank even harder, falling short of crushing his windpipe, but definitely constricting his air passage.

"Does it make your feel powerful to hurt a woman?" I turn to Lily. She's slid down the wall, her hands clenching at her throat, tears streaming down her face. "You okay?"

She nods.

"You sure? Let me hear your voice, Lily."

"I'm okay," she whispers, coughing between words.

"You want to hurt someone, come at me. Keep the fuck away from Lily. Keep. The. Fuck. Away. Do you hear me?"

I gotta hand it to the stupid bastard, he's stubborn. I'm about thirty seconds away from choking him out, and just the tiniest bit more pressure and he'd be drinking through a straw for the rest of his life, yet he just glares, trying his best to make eye contact with me. This guy's not backing down. Not even close.

"Don't," Lily says as she attempts to stand. "It's not worth it, Jax." She walks around the counter and pulls something from a drawer. It's a taser of some sort. She walks closer to us, standing at our side. Caden's eyes track her every move, fixated on nothing else. He's so wired, I'm not so sure a taser would even bring him down.

"Go behind me Lily," I instruct. But before she can move, the bells chime as the front door opens and in walks Joe Ralley.

"God damn it! I warned you, Caden." Joe walks toward us, not looking shocked at the scene going on in front of his eyes. Obviously he knows how unstable his nephew is.

He looks to the front door, sees the dangling handle, the result of Caden busting open the lock, and shakes his head. "Now what am I supposed to do here boys?" Calmly, Joe asks, as he walks around the counter, reaches down and comes up with a wooden bat. What the hell else do they have behind there?

"Loosen your grip for me, Jackson," Joe asks. Eyeing him, I don't respond right away. "I didn't say you had to let go. Just give him enough room to breathe so we can all have a little conversation, okay?"

I look around, considering my options. "Okay. But Lily leaves before I let go of him. I want her safe. I don't trust this asshole one bit."

Joe assesses me, realizes quickly it's not a suggestion or a chip I'm willing to bargain, and nods. "Lily, I think that's a good idea. Why don't you go home? Might help defuse the situation we got going on with these two boys." He nods his head in our direction.

Lily looks to me and shakes her head no.

"Go home, Lily. I'll be fine. I'll come to your place as soon as we're done here." Wrong thing to say. My words, or perhaps it's the visual picture of me going to Lily's that does it, but Caden's already steamy temper flares, and he almost gets out of my choke hold. I'm back to barely letting him breathe just to keep him from escaping. "Go, Lily!" I bark.

Thankfully, and surprisingly, she listens. Handing Joe Ralley the taser, she walks to the door and looks back.

"I'll cover tomorrow. Stay home. Get some rest. Come in on Saturday, if you feel up to it." He looks to Caden and then back to Lily. "They say blood is thicker than water, but that's bullshit. Me and The Saint, me and you – we're family. You take care of yourself, and I'm sorry this happened, Lily."

She nods and I watch the tears flow as she reluctantly walks out the door.

Joe closes the door, and turns back to where I'm still restraining Caden in a choke hold from behind. He says nothing for a long moment, assessing how to handle the situation. I've been working with Joe for months now. He seems like a levelheaded guy and it's clear he adores Lily. Smart, fair…I'd even consider him a friend. But I'm not taking any chances. This situation can turn on me in the blink of an eye.

Finally, Joe speaks. "I only know what my nephew has told me, but I saw the picture on the news too. Lily stepping out on Caden with you, son?"

"Lily and Caden broke up two months ago. Lily's not stepping out on anyone. Caden here just doesn't seem to know how to take a hint." Caden attempts to struggle at my words, but I'm ready and a little pressure reminds him who's really in control. He stills, but his nostrils flare and dark eyes go black and stormy. The truth is hard to hear sometimes, especially when you don't like what's being said.

Joe takes a deep breath in and closes his eyes, shaking his head. He's surprised to hear what I have to say, but I can tell he believes me. This definitely isn't the first time he's seen the crazy in his nephew.

"Caden, this score you've come to settle, isn't yours to settle, son. Seems like Lily's made a choice and Jax hasn't shown you any disrespect. This vendetta you're chasing… *Doesn't exist.*" Joe emphasizes the last two words, something in the way he says them, like a parent stressing a point to a small child, tells me he's experienced at handling Caden's one track mind. A mind stuck on a track that leads to nowhere, yet he's physically unable to change course.

"Now." Joe continues. "What we're going to do here is...Jax is going to let go of you. And you're going to stand there and not move a muscle as he collects his things and walks out that door." He tilts his head back, motioning to the door behind him. "You boys want to continue this, we'll set it up. *In the ring*. The way we fight around here. Clean. You got that?"

Caden doesn't move or respond, not that I'm leaving him much room to wiggle in my hold.

"Caden!" Joe warns. "I want to hear you understand what I'm saying. Jax let's go, there will be no fighting in here tonight. You clear with that? Because I'm starting to lose patience. Getting off a plane and chasing your ass here isn't exactly what my nearly sixty year old ass should be doing. So no more shit tonight, tell me you understand what I'm saying. Or, so help me God, I'm dialing 911 and they're taking you out in cuffs for assaulting Lily."

Caden's jaw clenches but he blinks his eyes in agreement.

"Jackson?" Joe questions. "We good?"

I'll probably regret it, but I nod in agreement anyway. Joe nods back. Cautiously, I loosen my hold, but only enough to test the waters...see if Caden tries to turn on me. He doesn't move, so I take the next step, removing my arm wrapped around his neck altogether. He still doesn't move. Grabbing my bag, I head to the door and begin to open it, but I stop and look back, both Caden and Joe in my sight. Caden hasn't moved a muscle, almost makes me think he knows he won't be able to control himself if he does. "I'll take you up on that offer to settle it in the ring, Joe." Joe nods and I turn my attention to Caden. A heinous smile curls up on his lips. If I didn't want to kick his ass so badly for putting his hands on Lily, I might be a bit more concerned how psychotic he really looks. Like a psychopath ready to tear off limbs and gnaw on them for lunch.

Lily must have been standing at the door waiting. She flings it open before I even finish knocking, throwing her arms around my neck in the hallway. Her quiet cries cause me physical pain.

"Shhhh…everything's fine." I pick her up and carry her inside.

"I'm sorry," she whispers between deep breaths as she tries to reign in her tears.

I pull my neck back to look at her. "You think this is your fault?"

"Yes. I knew how Caden would react if I got involved with someone too soon, but I did it anyway."

"Lily…," I pause, putting a finger under her chin, bringing her eyes back to mine. "This isn't your fault. Not one bit. Caden doesn't own you. I know you two have history, but that's what it is. History. He has no right to raise his hand to you, even if you were still together. There is no justification for what he did."

Sniffling, she averts her eyes for a moment. It breaks my heart to see her so upset. Internally, my brain is battling against my emotions, I'm so filled with anger, yet I want to make Lily feel calm. Safe.

"Are you hurt at all?" she asks.

"No."

She tries to force a smile but fails. "He's not going to let it go this easily."

Seeing the warped smile on his face before I walked out of the gym, I couldn't agree more, but I need to calm her, not make her more upset. So I try to make her feel better. "We reached an understanding," I reply cryptically.

Lily furrows her brow, her sweet face a mixture of fear and confusion. "What…"

I lean down and kiss her lips gently, silencing her before she can finish her sentence. "Tomorrow. We'll talk about it more tomorrow. He's consumed enough of our day." I begin walking toward the bedroom with her still cradled in my arms. She rests her head against my chest. "You need to get some rest."

I don't see the full extent of the bruising on her neck until she's lying on the bed. It takes every ounce of self-control to not leave and hunt that motherfucker down and beat him until his entire body is covered with matching bruise marks. But right now, Lily needs me. My retaliation will have to wait. Instead, I grab an ice pack, slip into bed next to her, and lift her on top of me, placing her on my chest. I wrap my arms around her tightly, protectively, making sure she knows nothing is going to happen to her. My own adrenaline still pumping ferociously through my veins, sleep evades me. But I tenderly stroke Lily's hair until I hear her ragged breathing turn peaceful, knowing she's fallen asleep. And even then I keep holding her, stroking her hair, willing her to feel safe in my arms as she sleeps so she can rest.

Chapter 17

Lily

The warmth of the late summer sun peers in through the blinds, the brightness blinding me as my eyes flutter open, then squint, catching a ray of the early morning sunlight.

"Morning, Angel." Jax's throaty voice makes me smile.

"Good morning."

I wake in the same position I fell asleep in, on top of Jax, which is unusual as I usually toss and turn.

"How you feeling?"

"Okay. You?"

"I'm fine. Is your neck sore?"

Without thinking, I reach up and touch it. It's sore to the touch. "It's a little tender I guess." Jax's grip tightens around me.

Gently, he lifts me and rests me on my back. Propped up on one elbow, he leans over me. "It's going to be that way for a while, you're pretty bruised."

"I am?" Guess I hadn't looked in the mirror last night. Mirror. That reminds me, I must be a complete mess. Makeup streaks likely trailed down my face from all my crying.

Jax leans down and kisses my neck, ever so gently. "That hurt?" he questions with his lips still at my neck. I feel the warmth of his breath and it sends a shiver down my spine.

"No," I whisper, hoping he'll continue.

He kisses me again, a tiny bit to the left. "How about that?"

"Nope." A smile cracks through my voice.

He moves a little more to the left, dropping two more tender kisses. "And that?"

"No."

Jax continues kissing along the area that Caden injured with his menacing forearm, not neglecting any of my bruised skin. As he trails soft kisses in a line, I feel his erection growing against my leg. Never a morning person before, a little attention from this man and years of dedication to not smile before 9AM goes out the window.

Pulling his head back to check on me, Jax looks me in the eyes. "You sure you're okay?" He's serious.

"I would be…" I pause, a serious face firmly set before I grin mischievously, "…if you would keep doing what you were doing."

Jax's eyebrows lift with surprise, his mesmerizing sky blue eyes heating dark with desire. He drops his head back to my neck and kisses again, this time adding a flicker of his tongue. "You mean this?"

I nod, even though he doesn't raise his head to see my response.

A few more kisses and he makes his way to my ear. He nibbles on my tiny lobe, tugging at it with his teeth for a second before releasing it. "How about this. Is this good?" he whispers in my ear. The sound of his strained voice is completely erotic and it makes my body perk up with desire.

I nod again. This time, it's because I'm unable to form words. His kisses growing more intense and his hot breath in my ear, I feel heat swelling between my legs.

His hand drops down and he pushes the covers away so he can see my body. With need in his eyes, he teases his fingers around my breasts, circling around my taut nipples, but falling short of grazing them. Leaning into my ear, he whispers in a strained voice, "The first night I met you, I stroked my cock picturing it was you as I rubbed up and down."

Oh god. My body already aroused, it begins to thrum. I groan as he circles closer to my engorged nipple. "I thought about how it would feel to be inside you. Your legs spread wide as I filled you." His hand trails lower down my body, stopping as he reaches just beneath my bellybutton. "Spread your legs, Lily."

Parting my legs, I hope my obeying will get him to give me something. Anything. I need more than just his sweet kisses on my neck and a teasing bite on my ear. Need. Not want.

"More. I want you wide open for me."

Complying, I spread my legs across the width of the bed, feet dangling off the edge of my queen size mattress.

Satisfied with my response to his demand, he trails his hand lower, stopping to rub my clit before he pushes two fingers into me. His fingers instantly slick, he easily burrows deep inside of me, finding a rhythm as he slips in and out. I moan into his touch.

"God, you're beautiful. I love being inside of you. Watching you wiggle as I pump my fingers into that perfect little pussy of yours. There are so many things I want to do to you right now." Increasing the speed of his fingers, my body begins its pursuit of its release, teetering on the edge. I grind up, forcing his fingers even deeper.

I'm so close, just needing a little more to send me over the edge. It doesn't even have to be more penetration. His dirty words are enough to bring me what I need. "Tell me," I beg shamelessly, "what else do you want to do to me."

"I want to taste you. Curl my tongue deep inside of you and feel you come around my mouth as I drink every bit of what you give me. I want to plunge my cock into you and fuck you long and hard. And then, I want to fill your pussy. Make you feel every bit of my hot come as it pours into you."

I moan loudly as his strokes quicken, his thumb reaching up to find my clit as his fingers pump furiously into me. His words consuming my head, his body controlling mine, I give myself over to my orgasm, feeling completely and utterly possessed by this man.

Spent, but feeling the need to reciprocate…wanting to bring pleasure to Jax as he had just done for me, I reach for him, feeling him still hard pushed up against me.

He grabs my hand before I can touch him. "Not yet." Pulling it up, he tenderly kisses my hand. Catching my eyes in his sea of blue, he acknowledges, "It's not that I don't want your hand on me. But we need to talk first."

Chapter 18

Jax

I didn't intentionally start the morning off the way it turned out, but I may as well use it to my advantage. I know Lily isn't going to be happy when I tell her that my fight with Caden from last night wasn't finished, it was merely postponed. We both plan on getting our vengeance out in the ring. A sated Lily would put up less of an argument.

"We need to talk about last night."

Lily's happy, freshly finger fucked face falters, yet another reason for needing to beat the shit out of that asshole. Taking away the afterglow of her orgasm, this had better be the last time Caden Ralley makes his way into the bedroom when I'm with her.

"What about last night?" Lily sits up, her relaxed demeanor instantly growing tense.

"We worked some things out I should tell you about."

"Worked things out? How?" Brows drawn, her face is an open book for me to read. Confusion mixed with a whole lot of concern.

"Caden and I are going to settle our differences in the ring." It sounded much better in my head than spoken aloud.

Lily's eyes go wide as saucers. "What? I hope you're joking."

I hit her with a serious stare, but say nothing.

"You're not joking."

"No. And I'm looking forward to it too. He deserves to get his ass kicked for putting his hands on you."

"That's insane!" she screeches.

"Look at you, Angel. Your neck is purple. God knows what he would have done to you had I not been there."

"Violence isn't the answer to violence." For the daughter of a champion fighter and co-owner of a chain of gyms, I'd think she would be better versed that although it may not be the answer, it goes a hell of a long way in settling a war.

"Maybe not. But it's what is going to happen." I shrug. "It was either that, or go at it last night without a referee and people to stop us from killing each other."

"I don't want to be the cause of you getting hurt."

"And what makes you think *I'm* the one that will get hurt?" I bite back, offended that she doesn't think I can take the asshole. He picks on women for a reason. Can't take a fair fight with a man.

"I didn't mean it like that. He's just, he's just...not right. The last few months, I've seen a side of him that scares me. I don't want you to get in the ring with him. I'd never forgive myself if anything ever happened to you."

"I'll be fine. I've watched the guy fight. I'm going to enjoy kicking his ass. And he deserves every minute of it."

"But..."

"I'm not changing my mind, Lily," I warn, my tone a bit more dismissive than she's ever heard from me.

Looking into my eyes, she sees I'm serious.

"You're doing exactly what Caden did to me. Not listening to what I'm saying."

"Don't compare me to him." My response is clipped.

"But you're not listening to me."

"I'm listening to you. I just don't agree with you. I'll listen to any reasoning you have. Tell me, why shouldn't I get in the ring with Caden? You've grown up around fighting. Obviously you aren't adverse to a good, clean, fair fight."

"Because I don't want to be the cause of the fight."

"He's the cause, Lily. I'm not a nonsensical caveman. We wouldn't even be having this conversation if he didn't put his hands on you. Would I like looking at him, knowing he's your past? No. But I wouldn't start a fight."

"And I don't want you to get hurt," she adds.

"I won't."

"You really are impossible sometimes!" She wraps the sheet around her body and closes herself into the bathroom without a word.

I have no idea what the hell she did in there for an hour. I'd heard the shower go on a few minutes after she went in, but when she finally comes out, her spirit seems lifted. A little bit anyway.

She rests her arms on the kitchen counter, opposite me, as I finish off the breakfast I'm making for us. "It smells good. But what is it?" She says then reaches over and tries to put her finger into the pan. I whack her with the spatula and arch my eyebrow playfully when she looks up at me.

"It's Nutella French toast." I flip the two golden slices of bread stuck together with a heaping pile of hazelnut chocolate like a pro, catching it in the center of the pan.

Lily shakes her head, trying to hold back a smile. "Showoff."

"Always," I retort, plating the sandwich and sliding it over to her on the other side of the counter.

"What do you have planned for the day?" I ask, preparing my own plate. She hops off the stool she's leaning on and walks to the table. I must have been looking down when she came in, because I definitely wouldn't have missed her ass cheeks peeking out from behind the short nightshirt she has on. My pulse quickens and I harden just watching the curve of her ass as she steps.

"Nice shirt," I compliment her wardrobe choice as viewed from behind.

"Thanks. I thought you'd like it."

"I do. And thank you for being so considerate. Consider it one of my personal favorites whenever I'm here."

Lily giggles and the sound does something to me. Wakes something in me I didn't realize was sleeping. She reaches over to my plate and breaks off a piece of my toast creation. Warm, dark chocolate oozes from between the slices. "I don't have any plans. I'm usually at work," she tells me and I see her face fall a little. Until she gets a taste of the Nutella toast. Her eyes light up like I've just given her a new Mercedes. "Oh my god. This is soooo good." Chocolate smudges at the corner of her lip. I reach forward and wipe it off, bringing my finger to my mouth.

"You're right. It is good." I suck the chocolate from my finger.

In what has become our usual eating pattern we both demolish everything on the plate. The plate in front of the other, that is. "Do you want to get out? Do something? It looks nice out today."

Lily shakes her head no. She blushes a little so I know what she's thinking.

"Did you have something else in mind, Lily?"

She nods her head yes, but still doesn't say anything. Rising from her seat, she takes both of our plates and drops them into the sink before returning. But instead of going back to her own chair, she lifts her leg up and over me, straddling my thighs, landing in the perfect place on my lap. The thin fabric of her panties does little to hide the heat radiating between her legs.

I run my hands up and down the outside of her thighs. The feel of her smooth, creamy skin only adds fuel to the growing inferno in my pants. I'm rock hard. Lifting her at the waist, I adjust her position only slightly, but it allows the wide crown of my cock to push up directly against her clit. Her eyes dilate and become hooded.

"So what did you have in mind to do today?"

She bites her lower lip. Dirty talk doesn't come easy to her, but she definitely loves to hear it from my mouth. This time I want to hear it from hers. I run my hands up her back, stopping when I reach her long wavy hair and wrap it around my hands loosely. I tug lightly, but enough so she feels it. "Tell me, Lily. Tell me what you want," I urge.

"You."

"And how do you want me?"

"I...I..."she hesitates briefly. Then she reaches down somewhere deep and surprises me, "I want to ride your cock."

That a girl. The only thing better than hearing those words from her lips is her actually doing it. In one swift motion, I lift her and pull my sweat pants down enough to accommodate her request, freeing my rock hard erection. I sit her back down, my cock pushing up against her, but I don't put myself inside of her. I want her to do it. However she wants it.

She looks down and licks her lips. I nearly explode just watching her mouth. I love that she salivates at the sight of me. It makes me want to beat my chest and yell from a fucking rooftop somewhere.

"Go ahead. I'm all yours," I offer as I stroke my cock. It's already hard as stone, so it's hardly necessary. But something tells me she might like to see me touch myself as much as I'd like to see her. She looks down and gasps. Without hesitation, she wraps her hand around mine and together we stroke up and down a few times. Then she lifts up, allowing enough room to position my broad head at her opening. She circles her hips around a few times, coating my head in her slickness. It feels incredible, all I want to do is ram inside of her. But it's her turn now and I'm not going to rush it. We'd had *the talk* the other night and I knew she was on the pill. Recent checkups and mutual trust cleared the path for future barrier free encounters, but I'd left it up to her to decide if she was ready. It's a gift that she's decided to give. And it means more than just the physical pleasure it brings. There's a trust and it means a lot that she's giving it to me now.

A tremble rocks through her body as she holds herself high above me. Ready to take me, she looks down at me with lust filled eyes. Ever so slightly she allows herself to drop, sheathing just the crown of my aching cock. She waits for a long moment. I have no idea if she senses my impatience or her own is just too much to bear. But instead of doing what I think is going to come next, inching me in a bit at a time, teasingly slow, she puts her hands on my shoulders and slams down on me, taking me in fully in one long stroke. It's fucking incredible and exactly what I needed. To fill her, be inside her, skin against skin.

I try hard to steady myself, allow Lily to set our pace – give her the control this time. But her rough plunge down unleashed something primal inside of me. Without the barrier between us anymore, I feel exactly how hot and tight she is, the sensation overwhelms me. I'm desperate to come inside her, claim her as mine.

I give in to the relentless urge in my core to dominate her, she can have control next time. Grabbing her firmly at the waist, I take over. Lifting her, raising her up all the way, till the tip of my cock is just barely inside her. Then I slam her back down hard. It only takes a few strong thrusts, I watch as her face changes. Her lips part, breathing hitches faster and her jaw goes slack. And I'm right there with her. Together we come hard and fast. The feeling of me spilling inside of her is unlike anything I've ever felt.

We both catch our breath and a goofy, yet incredible smile forms on Lily's face. It makes me forget anything and everything else in the world exists. With all the excesses I've grown up with around me, I realize, I've got all I want right here.

Later in the afternoon, we lay spent on the couch after two more turns exploring. The latter two slower and more passionate, but no less mind-blowing. I flick on the TV and a commercial comes on advertising the MMA Open in three weeks. A picture of my new found brother flashes on the screen. It's a tradition that the current champion hosts the tournament. My finger rolls over the channel button, quickly responding to my innate reaction to avoid anything to do with my father and his spawn.

"I guess I'm going to meet your brother soon." Lily says quietly.

I don't really want to talk about my brother at all, or any member of my family as a matter of fact, but I don't want to hurt her feelings by shutting her out completely. Especially after I upset her this morning. "You have entries in the Open?"

"Yes. We're also sponsors." She pauses. "Can I ask you something?"

I nod.

"Did your brother know about you?"

"As far as I know, he was as surprised as I was."

"Have you ever met him?"

"Once."

"How did that go?"

"Not too good, considering I was hitting on his girlfriend."

"You hit on your brother's girlfriend?" Lily's voice raises and eyes flash wide.

"I didn't know she was my brother's girlfriend. Hell, I didn't even know he was my brother at the time." I chuckle thinking back to our first meeting. I was at an MMA fight and ran into a reporter who had just done a story on my family. A very pretty, sweet reporter. I leave that part out and continue, "I had no idea at the time she was writing an investigative piece on my father and his illegitimate child. Her paper broke the story a week after we met." Lily's brow furrows...it's a hard story to follow. Goes to show the old saying is true, *what a tangled web we weave...*

"So how did you happen to come across your brother's girlfriend if you didn't even know he existed at the time? That's a pretty big coincidence."

"His girlfriend is the reporter. She was writing an expose on my family and my father's secrets."

"His girlfriend is the one that broke the story on your dad?"

"No. She actually buried the story."

"I'm confused."

"I was too for a long time. After everything came out, I had a friend do some digging for me. Turns out, Olivia, his girlfriend, and Vince had history together. She uncovered that Vince was my father's child, but lied to the newspaper she was working for about it. I think she lost her job over it. Vince found out and got her job back by giving her paper an exclusive on the story."

"He sounds like a stand up guy." Lily's not half wrong. I just never let myself give him any credit. I'd basically blamed him for being born. Being the spawn of Satan doesn't automatically make you Satan. At least I hope not. I kiss her lips softly for reminding me I've let my judgment be clouded about a lot lately.

She smiles. "What was that for?"

"Just for being you." Another soft kiss and then, "Tell me about your family."

Sadness colors her otherwise happy face. I regret asking as soon as I see the change.

"I don't have any family anymore. Joe's the closest thing I've got to family."

"I'm sorry." I want to ask questions, find out more about what makes her so sad. But the overwhelming urge to see her spirit rise greatly outweighs my selfish curiosity.

Unshed tears fill her normally sparkling eyes and it feels like someone reached into my chest and squeezed my beating heart. Each pump causing more pain. Lily looks lost for a moment, her memory taking her somewhere else, a place that obviously causes her grief. She begins to speak, but I stop her. "You don't have to. If talking about it is half as painful for you as it is to see the sadness it causes mar your beautiful face, then don't."

She blinks back tears from her big almond shaped eyes. "My mom died when I was three years old. Car accident." She pauses. A small, but real, smile forms on her lips. Her eyes filled with remiss, she reflects back. "After she died, I had bad dreams for a long time, so my Dad would lie with me every night until I fell asleep. When I woke up in the morning, he was always gone, but he left an old pocket watch in his place in my bed.

He left it on purpose, knowing I'd feel better just having something of his near me. The sound of that old watch grew to soothe me in the months after I realized Mom wasn't coming back home to say goodnight to me. Then when I was five, my dad would walk me to school every day. We'd hold hands and swing our joined arms as we walked. One day in kindergarten, some boys made fun of me, calling me a baby, because I still held my dad's hand.

So the next day when we walked to school, Dad went to take my hand and I shoved them into my pockets telling him I was cold. I hated not holding his hand, but I thought I fooled him. Then the next day, it happened again. Dad went to take my hand and I thought my slick move had worked the day before, so I shoved my hands into my pockets again. Only that day, I found Dad's old pocket watch in my pocket.

We smiled at each other but didn't say a word. He slipped it into my pocket every day for the next few years, neither one of us ever talking about it. Somehow it made me feel better having a piece of him always next to me."

I rub her shoulders as she speaks and hold her tight when she's done. "He sounds like an incredible man. I wish I would have met him."

"He was amazing. He was my ground when I felt like the world was spinning out of control. Strong, tough, yet loving and protective." She's silent for a few minutes, memories filling her head. "All those years of just the two of us, we were a team." She pauses. "I gave him a hard time as a teen. But he hung on and waited for me to get through what I needed to go through. He had the patience of a saint." She smiles, thinking back. "The guys used to tease him that he got his name for putting up with me."

I listen quietly, running my hand through her hair as she talks about her father. I love how she lights up when she thinks of her dad, but afterwards the sorrow that ensues is deeper than the glow of the memory.

"Dad never remarried after Mom. He didn't even really date much. He used to say, when you've had the love of your life, anything else just pales by comparison. He threw himself into his career and taking care of me. That's why the gyms are so important. Why Joe and I agreed only a silent investor would work. It means the world to me to keep his vision intact and not turn it into a franchise. Plus, it makes me feel like a piece of him is still with me everyday. He worked so hard to build it to what it is today. He wanted something substantial to leave behind someday. Wanted to make sure I was taken care of when he retired." She pauses. "He didn't realize that someday would be so soon. None of us did."

I pull her close to me, wrapping my arms around her tightly, wishing I could take away the pain I see buried deep. But for now, until she's ready to give it to me to hold, I'll just hold her tight.

Chapter 19

Lily

I'm up early, nervous about going back to work today. Even though what happened the other night was only between Jax, Caden, Joe and I, I'm sure the gym will be buzzing. You'd never guess it, but fighters can gossip better than the ladies that lunch. Sure, they prefer to call it "shooting the shit" but they could have saved Paul Revere a long ride back in the day.

Jax insists on coming with me. I know it's like bringing gasoline to a party filled with sparks, but I have to admit, after the other night, I feel better knowing he'll be near.

After ten minutes of blotting on makeup, I step back from the mirror, afraid to see what my neck looks like. It's no use. The early pink and pale purple bruising has turned a vibrant shade of black and blue. Nothing short of a turtle neck would cover it up. Too bad it's going to be seventy degrees today.

Jax is sitting on the edge of the bed talking on his cell as I emerge from the bathroom, he catches sight of me from the corner of his eye as I walk out the door. His eyes drop to my neck and I watch as his jaw flexes. "I'll meet you there at ten," he says into his phone, before pressing a button and standing.

Dressed in a suit, sleek and confident, he looks every bit the tycoon I've emailed over the last few months and far from the fighter I've gotten to know intimately over the last few weeks.

"Hot date?" I tease.

"Yep. Meeting her at ten." Jax tightens his tie, grabs his jacket, and walks toward me.

Irritation written clear on my face, I squint, my hands on my hips, assessing him. He had better be kidding.

A wry grin crosses his cleanly shaven face. Honestly, he looks so delicious I'm not sure if I prefer sweaty fighter man or sexy business tycoon. "Problem?" He leans down, kissing me chastely on the lips.

"You're dressing up for a date?" I ask, the word *date* said with disdain, annoyance obvious in my voice. I can't help but feel a little territorial when it comes to him.

"Yep. With a banker. 10AM." He grins knowingly, quite enjoying that he's ruffled my feathers.

"Very nice. I'm sure you'd enjoy it if I told you I had a hot d...."

"Don't finish that sentence," Jax growls, pulling me flush against his body in a not too gentle manner.

Inwardly my ego preens, but outwardly I goad him even more. "So you don't want to hear about my dates."

"I won't hear about them, because you won't be having anymore." His voice is low and gruff. I look up into his eyes, expecting to find playful, but he's dead serious. Oddly, his possessiveness totally turns me on, whereas Caden's was a total turnoff.

Jax holds open the front door to Ralley's Gym, and I hold my breath as I walk through. Joe Ralley is at the front desk and my eyes immediately begin scanning the gym before I even acknowledge his existence.

"He's not here."

I turn to face Joe and he repeats himself. "Caden. He's not here. Told him I had a business meeting and didn't want any trouble. He's at the 52nd street location, working the front desk. Brought the front desk person from there over here so you can help out with the banker if we need. They're doing a financing audit. She'll probably need reports. You know me and that stupid computer don't get along."

I exhale noticeably loud, feeling relieved. "Thank you." I walk around and stand on my tiptoes, kissing Joe on the cheek. I'm truly going to miss this man when he retires, for more reasons than just help in running the business.

Joe nods and leans down to me. "You're my girl. I'm sorry things with Caden went as far as they did. Should have seen that coming. The kid's wound too tight." He turns his attention to Jax. "Jackson, why don't you and I go over a few terms of the financing my lawyer asked me to clarify." Joe steps from behind the desk and motions in the direction of his office.

Jax nods. "Give me one minute and I'll join you."

Waiting until Joe is out of earshot, Jax takes my hand as I settle in at the front desk. "You okay?"

"Yes."

"I'll just be in the back office."

"I know."

He gives me a sweet kiss on the lips and takes a few steps away before turning back. "Gertrude," he says over his shoulder with a smirk on his face.

"Gertrude?"

"My 10AM date." He winks.

At precisely ten, Gertrude Waters, managing auditor at City Bank, arrives to meet with Mr. Ralley and Mr. Knight. Happily, I walk the silver haired woman back to the meeting.

The auditor stays for hours and pores over reports. It's nerve-wracking, I really want everything to work out for Joe. Our business is great, membership is at an all time high, though she did seem a little concerned over our tightening cash flow. But Jax was able to alleviate her concern. She left with a pile of data, seemingly pleased with her initial review. Granted the constant smile may have more to do with Jax's presence, and the way he leans over her shoulder to help her figure out things on the reports she's reading, than the actual numbers on the page. He's clueless the effect he has on her, but I saw her blush a few times as he joked with her. If she wasn't almost sixty, I might even be a little jealous at their playful banter.

By late afternoon, with the auditor gone and my bookkeeping work all caught up, I find myself finally relaxed enough to sketch. Taking out my pad, I glance over in the gym where Jax is sparring with Marco. Low hanging exercise shorts, a sweat soaked simple white t-shirt clinging to his chiseled chest, he looks so different than the businessman in the three thousand dollar suit, but every bit as delicious. I smile thinking how lucky I am to have Jackson, the Ivy League refined tycoon pull out my chair and open my door. And Jax, the gritty, dirty talking fighter that commands my body. God, I had no idea such a man existed, he shatters stereotypes. It's as if someone told me to fantasize about sexy men, and then they rolled them all into one perfect prototype. I sigh watching him. I never even knew I was capable of swooning, but that's what the man does to me.

Sensing my staring, I'm caught ogling him when he turns. He arches an eyebrow suggestively and I wave him off as if he's wrong for thinking I was checking him out. But we both know the truth.

My last project of the semester nearly done, I begin packing up my supplies as Joe comes to the front desk seeing Jax approach.

"Caden's set up a time and ref, late next week," Joe says pensively.

"Excellent. Can't wait," Jax responds.

Joe shakes his head and looks at me, attempting to provide an explanation, "Boys will be boys. Lucky for us, it doesn't change." He slaps a hand on Jax's back. "Otherwise, we wouldn't be brokering a deal that will take me long into retirement, would we?"

"No, we certainly wouldn't want anyone to stop fighting before the paperwork was signed." Jax extends his hand to Joe and the two share a smile.

"Lily. Caden's my nephew and I love him. But Jax is a good man, and I know you never showed Caden any disrespect. And I'll make sure he does the same for you. Now you two get on out of here, I'll see you in the morning. I'll make sure he isn't back here until the fight."

Jax insisted we stay at his hotel suite tonight so we could go out to dinner. After almost two weeks hiding out to avoid the media, it feels odd to get ready to go out in public on a date just the two of us. The paparazzi hasn't completely disappeared yet, they still follow us and yell rude questions, but it seems to bother Jax less.

I stand silently at the doorway to the bedroom, leaning my head lazily against the wall, watching Jax's reflection in the mirror in the walk-in closet as he gets ready. He slips on a pair of grey slacks that hang perfectly from his slim waist. Covering up his finely chiseled chest with a crisp white shirt, a small smile forms at the corner of his mouth as he fastens the buttons at his wrists. I wonder what he's thinking that puts the smile on his face. Too curious to keep quiet, I walk to the closet and take over buttoning the front of his dress shirt.

"What were you just thinking about?" I look up at him through my long thick mascara coated lashes as I button.

"I'm not sure you want to know."

I stop buttoning. "Well that might be true. But now I have to know."

Jax motions to the chest high dresser island in the middle of the closet. "I was thinking I want to bend you over that, and watch your face in that mirror while I take you from behind." He lifts his chin, gesturing to the mirror.

His eyes stay fastened on me. I work to keep my face unreadable, but I resume buttoning. Taking my time, I don't respond until I reach the top button. "Maybe I should keep these on, looks like they keep us lined up much better." I pull back a bit and look down, enough so he can catch a glimpse of the five inch heels he hadn't noticed I'd walked in wearing. They're silver with thin straps that wrap up my ankles.

A dirty grin washes over his face. "Those are definitely staying on."

I kiss him chastely on the lips and turn around leaving him watching the sway of my ass as I walk away.

The waiter seats us at a table for two in the corner next to the floor to ceiling windows that face outside to the streets of Manhattan. A beautiful view of the Brooklyn Bridge lights up the clear night sky off in the distance.

"You know we're not getting dessert," Jax says.

"Why not?"

"There's a mirror calling my name upstairs as soon as you're done eating." His voice is low, deep and seductive. I feel the swell in between my legs and cross them to stop it from throbbing. Jax arches an eyebrow with a wicked grin...he knows exactly what I'm doing.

"What can I get for you to drink this evening?" The waiter hands us both the wine selection menu.

Jax looks it over quickly, double checking with me before he orders. "Red?"

"That sounds great."

He hands the menu back to the waiter and orders. The waiter nods and disappears. "So you've mentioned two glasses of wine makes you sleepy. What does one do?" Jax sips his water eyeing me.

"Nothing much," I say, lifting the menu and pretending to read it as I continue. "Except it makes me lose my inhibitions."

I glance up, finding a wicked smile spreading across Jax's handsome face. His eyes sparkle as he leans in to speak. "We could have that glass of wine and skip dinner."

"But I was so looking forward to eating yours," I tease playfully, selecting my words purposefully.

"Oh. I'll give you something to eat."

My face pinks when the waiter clears his throat, no doubt he'd heard Jax's last comment.

"Are you ready to hear the specials?"

"Are we?" Jax arches an eyebrow, his eyes gleaming with delight. He's not the slight bit embarrassed, but knows I am and is enjoying himself.

"Yes. Please." I give him the evil eye and force my full attention to the waiter. The entire time the waiter talks about the specials I feel Jax's eyes burning into me.

"I'll give you a moment to let you decide." Graciously, the waiter excuses himself.

"Why did you do that?" I scold, my voice low.

"Do what?" He leans back in his seat, crossing his arms over his thick chest.

"You know exactly what I'm talking about."

"Do I?"

"You enjoy watching me flustered, don't you?"

Jax arches both eyebrows. Bad choice of words.

"You know what I mean."

Leaning in, his voice gritty and sexy, he looks me straight in the eyes when he speaks. "I love watching you. Period. But what I like best is watching you pretend you're unaffected. It's like an unspoken challenge." He pauses and leans in even closer. "I love the pink that creeps up your cheeks when I say something dirty. The way your pussy throbs when I mention what I'm going to do to you later, and you wiggle in your seat trying to control it. So yeah, I guess I do like watching you flustered. You sit and give your attention to the waiter, trying to pretend you're listening to whatever he's saying instead of thinking of me feeding you my cock later, but we both know you didn't hear one word he said. Hell I didn't hear one word watching you, just knowing what you were thinking about."

This time, I see the waiter before he's close enough to hear us. He smiles as he reaches our table. "So what can I get for you this evening? Did I interest you in one of our specials?"

I look at the waiter, then Jax, who arches an eyebrow with a knowing smirk on his face, then back to the waiter. "The specials all sounded delicious. I just can't decide for myself. I'm going to defer to my date to pick one for me." I return my eyes to Jax with a cheeky grin. He throws his head back with a chuckle and looks at the poor confused waiter.

"We'll take whatever two are your favorites. Surprise us."

The fact that we are sitting in a five star restaurant in a luxury New York City hotel doesn't deter Jax from eating half his meal off my plate. "So have you thought about what you'll do when Joe retires?" Reaching over to my plate, he finishes off my risotto.

"I have, although the thought of him not being around every day seriously freaks me out. I run the business side of things, but there's so much I still don't know about the operations. A few weeks ago I ordered hand wraps for all the locations, they were on sale for a quarter of what we normally pay. It wasn't the Fairtex brand we usually buy, but I figured a hand wrap is a hand wrap." I shrug. "Joe got the delivery when it came in. Told me they were too long and too thick, they wouldn't fit under the gloves. We sent them all back before we opened the cases. I had no idea."

"So you'll hire someone."

"That's easier said than done. You know how many regional managers my dad went through before finding someone he could trust? It seriously took him two years to find Clive, the southern manager. It's hard finding someone with a good business acumen and a love of the sport." I sigh. "I had thought Caden might be a good candidate, but I need to seriously start looking."

Jax jaw clenches at the mention of Caden. "Maybe you would have been better off finding a partner to help you manage things, rather than a silent investor after all?"

"I guess we were just worried I'd get stuck with a partner that wanted to turn Ralley's into a chain with a fancy juice bar and group classes." I smile thinking of a conversation Dad and Joe had when they were approached by a group that wanted to franchise the gym. "Dad said the day he had to put hangers in the lockers, he was out."

Jax furrows his brow. "Hangers?"

"He didn't want the gym turning into a place a suit and tie stopped at on his way home from work."

"A suit and tie?" He arches an eyebrow. "You mean like me?"

"You're not the normal suit and tie."

"I'm not huh?"

"Nope. It wasn't as much the clothes Joe and Dad were talking about as where the heart of the member lies. They wanted to keep the gym to members whose hearts were in the sport, not a hobby."

"So you think my heart is in the right place?" Jax asks, his eyes questioning more than how dedicated he is to the sport.

Holding his gaze, I tilt my head and search his face. "I do. I think your heart is right where it belongs."

A man interrupts. "Jackson, I thought that was you." He slaps his hand on Jax's back. He's tall, probably early sixties, but handsome and very distinguished looking. Jax stands, shaking the man's hand.

"Senator Gorman. It's been a long time."

"It certainly has. You haven't come to the last few Senate family functions. You should come. Your father could certainly use some help with the younger voters."

Jax's jaw clenches and I watch as something comes over him. "Yes, I'm sure he could." He turns his attention to me, doling out his impeccable manners. "This is Lily St. Claire."

The Senator nods. "Nice to meet you Miss. St. Claire."

"You too."

He studies me for a moment. "Any relation to Phillip St. Claire, the state Senator from New Jersey?"

"I don't think so."

Remembering the young woman standing next to him, the Senator clears his throat, making the obligatory introduction, albeit uncomfortably. "And this is Eve Matthews. She's my youth marketing advisor. Keeps me in touch with the young constituents," he says with a nod to the voluptuous twenty-something year old woman standing next to him.

There's little change in Jax's face, but I catch the tightening of his jaw and the glazed over look in his eyes. He nods in response, saying nothing to the woman. Making his point painfully obvious, Jax's eyes fall to the Senator's wedding ring and then his stare returns to the Senator. No words are spoken, yet so much is said.

Sensing it's time to go, the Senator fumbles a bit. "Well you two enjoy your evening." His hand drops to the woman's lower back, a little too low and familiar in his touch for an exchange between just business associates. Jax's eyes catch it to. Turning back, he says, "I hope to see you following your father's footsteps, Jackson. You'd make a fine Senator someday. You're so much like your father was at your age."

Seething, Jax replies, "I'm nothing like my father." Dismissing the Senator as he sits down, he doesn't offer so much as a look back.

We're both quiet for a long moment. The waiter interrupts the thick tension that hangs in the air when he comes to check on us. "Can I interest you in the dessert menu?"

Jax looks to me, his face still riddled with tension, I debate my answer for a moment and then respond. I feel the heat rise in my face before I even finish the sentence. "No thank you. We've already made plans for dessert in our room."

Jax's eyebrows pop up with surprise. The corner of his mouth twitches up. "Just the check, please." Speaking directly to me instead of the waiter, he adds. "And if you can get us out of here in one minute or less, I'll double your tip."

We're weaving our way out of the restaurant with purpose sixty seconds later.

Chapter 20

Jax

Thoughts of all the things I want to do to her beat out any of the frustration I felt listening to Senator Gorman speak.

The elevator fills as an older couple holds the door open for some friends. Lily brushes up against me as she takes a step back. Her sweet fresh smell consumes me with her nearness.

"You smell incredible," I mumble quietly in her ear so only she can hear. My fingertips grip her hipbone on both sides and I pull her back, closing the small gap between us. Her breath hitches when I discreetly push my firm erection against her ass. She elbows me as the doors close in the near capacity elevator car. It only encourages me more.

After four achingly long stops on different floors, it's only us and another couple. I catch our reflection in the shining silver doors and slide my hand hidden against the wall from her hip down to her thigh. "Look forward," I whisper.

Her eyes lock with mine in the reflection. The doors open and the last two people step out. When our reflection comes back into focus as the doors slide closed, I reach up and roughly cup her breast. Her eyes go wide, but she gives in to it quickly when I pinch her protruding nipple. I watch intently as her head lolls back, lips part and her breathing turns harsh when I bring the other hand up to grope her other breast. My head spins watching her – I want to be inside her, make her scream my name over and over so it consumes her and she can think of nothing else but how I make her feel.

Reaching the penthouse, the elevator door opens. Briefly I contemplate staying where we are. My need is so raw and I can't wait too much longer to feel skin against skin. But out of the corner of my eye, a camera reminds me we're not really alone.

"Mirror. Now," I growl and begin to guide her quickly through the suite. Stopping us in the doorway to the closet, I let her gaze settle on the dressing island in the middle and the oversized mirror hanging in front of it.

"You're going to lean over, grip the other side with your hands." She gasps, picturing it before us. "Spread your legs open wide. Position your sweet ass high for me." My grip on her hip tightens, maybe a bit more that it should, but it's either that or it'll be over too fast. "I want you to see everything you do to me in the mirror while I watch you take each inch of me deep inside of you. Don't close your eyes. Watch. Every minute of what I'm going to do to you, Angel."

She murmurs something I can't understand, I'm not even sure if they're words or just a string of sounds blending together with a moan and a sigh that I feel pulsing through my body. I swallow, my mouth salivating at the thought of fucking her for hours. Taking a deep breath, I resist the unbearable urge to just strip her down and drive my throbbing cock inside of her as hard and fast as I can. Instead, I turn her and take her mouth in a kiss. It's passionate and raw, I use all my willpower to keep it from becoming too forceful. The need inside of me is so strong, I'm afraid to allow it to consume me too much. Afraid I'll scare her. The way I feel about this woman, so intense and powerful, it scares the hell out of me.

Lily makes it even more difficult to contain my self-control when she presses her breasts into me firmly, lifts one leg high, and wraps it around my waist. The pointy heel from her sexy shoes dig into my skin. I grab her ass and lift, her other leg wraps tightly around me. I feel how wet she is between her legs even though we're both still fully dressed. It makes my body tremble as I cling to my last bit of resolve to maintain some semblance of control. But then her hand wrapped around my neck moves to my hair and she tugs. Hard. Her newfound boldness is my undoing.

I carry her to the dresser and lower her to the ground, turning her before her feet barely reach the surface. Not willing to waste another second to be inside her, I lift her skirt and tear her panties from her body with one swift tug. She gasps but I don't give her time to catch her breath before my own pants are down and my hand on her back eases her forward.

"Grab." I bend her over the dresser and instruct her to take hold of the other side. She's definitely going to need to hold on. Looking down at the creamy skin of her smooth, tight ass, a feral sound I don't even recognize escapes me. I position the thick, wide head of my cock at her glistening opening and growl one more command. "Watch," I instruct and our eyes meet in the reflection of the mirror. Her blue eyes darkened and hooded, I find my own desire staring back at me.

Thrusting my hips forward I fill her in one long stroke, our eyes never breaking contact. I settle for a moment, circling my hips to ease her body's acceptance of me. The pressure builds from deep within, the minute I begin to move again, a fast and furious rhythm takes over me. Eyes glued to the mirror watching her, I pump in and out, my pace building faster, each gyration of my hips bringing me closer and closer. Her eyes glaze over and I know she's feeling it too. Feeling each and every incredible sensation as her muscles convulse and she clenches down around me and I swell at feeling her greedy pussy milk me.

Swift thrusts turn into rugged pounding and I struggle just to keep my own unrelenting pace. Lily's eyes start to roll into the back of her head as her own orgasm takes over her. But I call her name, her eyes jarring back to awareness momentarily, then glazing over as she calls my name back. Over and over again, my eyes glued to her lips moaning my name, the sound consuming me as I find my own release. The heat from my own orgasm spilling into her causes my body to spasm with delight until I'm finally empty.

Leaning over her, our bodies both covered in a sheen of sweat, I bury my face in her neck as I catch my breath. Eventually my panting slows and I can finally find my voice. "That was seriously fucking incredible."

I can't see her face, but I watch as a goofy grin slowly spreads across her face. "Remind me to find someone to piss you off more often."

Lying in bed, both sated from a physically and emotionally intense night of passion, I watch her face as she deliberates for a few minutes before she speaks. "How long are you staying in New York?" She trails her fingers lightly back and forth across my chest, her head snuggled into the crook of my shoulder as I gently stroke her hair in the dark.

"I was only planning on staying until the deal with Ralley's is finished." It would be the perfect moment to tell her the group of investors I'm bringing to the table is a group of one. Me. But I want to wait till the deal is done, not influence any of her and Joe's decisions because of our relationship. Plus, the bank hasn't signed off on the financing yet and things could still fall through. Lily may not be happy when she eventually finds out I've hidden that I'm the investor, but I think she'll understand my reasoning. I don't want what we have to sway her in negotiations – keeping silent protects her more than me.

"How long is that?" she asks hesitantly.

"Not too much longer. There's this woman that gives me everything I need over at Ralley's. Got the financing fast tracked by having it all put together so nicely," I tease. "Should be done within a few days."

"Oh," she says sounding deflated.

I turn us, gently maneuvering her onto her back, so I can see her face. The room is dark but there's enough moonlight peaking in from the open window to see her eyes. I wipe a stray lock of hair from her face. "But I didn't plan on meeting you."

She nods, but says nothing.

I lean in, kissing her on the neck. "Guess my plans have changed." I leave a trail of wetness as I lick my way up to her ear where I whisper, "You've changed my plans, Lily St. Claire."

Chapter 21

Lily

There's almost always a lull in the middle of a powerful storm. The eye that catches people unprepared because they've let their guard down. I should feel calm, happy even. Lord knows I've had twenty-four hours of bliss. I smile as I walk from the subway, cutting across the parking lot on the way to Advanced Linear Drawing class, thinking of Jax last night. Seeing his face in my mind warms me all over. Yet something sits in the pit of my stomach, warning me that I shouldn't give in to the lull, even though allowing myself to wouldn't take much.

Cars fill almost every spot in the lot, yet there are few people milling around. Early morning college classes tend to be for commuters rather than the younger crew that lives on campus. The kind that come and go with purpose, rather than hanging out with their friends beforehand. I look around, no one seems to be near, yet I have the odd sensation of being watched. Just as I'm about to enter the building, I catch sight of a black town car slowly rolling by. The windows are tinted dark, so I can't see inside, but I have the distinct feeling whoever is inside is looking back at me. It drives off without incident a moment later.

Headphones on, Dave Matthew's soulful voice fills my ears as I allow myself to get lost sketching. The model isn't nude today, but he's shirtless. Thin, more boyish than man. More Reed's type than mine. Adding charcoal, I shade the fine line of his pectoral muscles, the definition coming more from being thin and lacking body fat than the development of actual muscle. Unlike Jax.

My mind drifts as I sketch, to the swell of his chest. The deep defined crevice of each bulging muscle. I exhale audibly as my mind pictures the deep indents of his narrow waist, the deep v that I watched deepen in the mirror last night with each powerful thrust forward.

Pulling me back to reality, my teacher points to the drawing in front of me. "Less bulk, more bone," she comments. I nod noticing for the first time what the drawing on the pad in front of me looks like. I've been drawing more from my own memory and fantasy of a man I can't stop thinking about, and less from the model in front of me.

The parking lot is bustling when I leave. Again I look around, finding no one in particular focusing on me. Yet I get that feeling again. I'm sure it's my paranoia kicking in, but Caden having backed off so easily leaves me feeling unsettled. The fight between Jax and Caden is in seven days, I hadn't really expected Caden to keep away until then.

The packed late morning subway car actually brings me comfort. Oddly, being crammed in like sardines makes me breathe easily. I ride the dozen or so stops to Ralley's Gym and notice a few photographers outside. Jax must be at the gym already. The paparazzi have dwindled over the last few days and only a few diehards follow him back and forth to his hotel now.

I take a deep breath before pulling the door open, even though Joe told me Caden wouldn't be there till the fight next week. Jax is sparring at the back, but he catches my eye the minute I walk through the door.

"Everything okay?" Joe comes out from the back office.

"Yes."

His eyes drop to my neck. The black and blue has faded to a lovely shade of yellow and purple. His jaw tightens. "Caden's been keeping away?"

"Haven't heard from him or seen him since that night," I confirm.

Joe nods. "Good." He eyes Jax in the back, who just knocked Marco on his ass. "He's got good hands. Very good hands. Caden's my nephew, but his ego gets the best of him sometimes. Thinks he's better than he is. The only way he stands a chance against Jackson is if his crazy comes out and fuels a fire of adrenaline." Great. Just great.

A few minutes later Joe comes back to the front desk, boxes in hand. "I'm going to head out, run uptown to drop off the new gloves that just came in. I almost forgot…" He hands me an oversized cream envelope with beautifully scribed calligraphy on the front. "That was delivered for Jackson this morning before he came in. Messenger brought it."

"Thanks Joe. I'll see that he gets it. Have a good afternoon."

After Jax finishes up his training, he comes to the front desk. He's sweaty and his muscles are pumped up from a vigorous workout. My eyes roam his chest, the way his t-shirt clings to his pecs is a feast for the eyes. Unconsciously, I lick my lips.

"I thought you asked me to keep things low in here."

"I did." I snap out of my worship trance.

"Then stop looking at me like that."

"Like what?"

"Like you need to be bent over this counter."

I stare down at the counter, visions of our encounter in the closet flood my mind.

Jax chuckles. He hooks one arm around my neck and pulls me in for a kiss. "Going to shower. You're locking up tonight, right?"

I nod.

A dirty grin on his face, Jax looks at the counter and then back to me, arching an eyebrow. My cheeks start to pink just from the thought he puts in my head.

We're back in my apartment before I realize I've forgotten to give Jax the envelope that came today. It's odd that someone would deliver what appears to be a wedding invitation to the gym. His hotel would have made more sense, someone apparently knows Jax's routine.

"Sorry. I almost forgot. A messenger brought this for you today. Joe gave it to me and I put it in my bag. I got busy and it slipped my mind till now." I hand Jax the envelope and he furrows his brow.

"What is it?"

"I don't know. I didn't open it."

Jax opens the envelope and glances at the first few lines, he quickly discards it on the table.

"A wedding invite you weren't expecting?" I ask curiously.

"No. An invitation to a birthday party." He doesn't add more, his unhappy face relaying the surprise of the invite wasn't a good surprise.

He's quiet the rest of the evening. We're getting into bed before he shares what upset him. "My father is throwing a birthday party for my mother."

"Oh." I'm not quite sure how to respond.

He stays silent as we get comfortable and I snuggle into him. His voice is quiet when he eventually begins to speak again. "My mother's best and worst quality is the same. She's loyal to a fault." Jax says as he rubs my bare shoulder. Head on his chest, I trace the outline of a figure eight between the bulk of his pectoral muscle in the dark. My fingernail scrapes lightly in the plain between the ridges as I respond.

"I think loyalty is always a good quality. It's our choice of where to place it that can be a fault."

He nods and kisses the top of my forehead. "You're right. I just don't know how she stays with him after everything he's done to her. Why didn't she walk away?"

"Love isn't something you can turn off. When it happens, it takes a little piece of who you are. I think sometimes people keep fighting because they're more afraid to lose that piece of them, rather than lose the person they love."

Jax exhales deeply. "Jesus, Lily. You may not know her, but you couldn't be more right."

We're both quiet for a few minutes. "Have you ever been in love?" Quietly, I ask, tilting my head up to look at him even though it's dark.

His hand rubbing my shoulder freezes. "You first."

"Why me first?"

"Because now you have me thinking that you're lying there thinking about another man."

I laugh. "I'm not."

"Good because I don't think I could handle that." He rolls us so I'm lying on my back. "So have you?"

"I thought I was once. But I realize now that I wasn't

really."

He kisses my lips gently.

"Have you?" I ask again.

"I think so." He kisses the corner of my mouth, then the other corner, before softly kissing the center of my mouth again. "Every day I become more sure."

Chapter 22

Jax

After a night of tossing and turning, I've finally made up my mind. "I'm going to go back to D.C. for my mother's birthday party. I need to spend a few hours with Brady anyway. He's trying not to let on he needs me, but I know spending an afternoon in the office would give him a little relief."

Lily nods and smiles politely. "Okay."

"It's about my mother. Not him. Or me. I'm going to go for her. She had a breakdown after the news of my father's endless string of affairs hit. I've been holding a grudge against her for too long. Taking it out on her for loving him, because he doesn't deserve her love or loyalty."

She refills my mug of coffee and sets it in front of me. I catch her hand as she begins to walk away and pull her down on my lap. "I'll fly up tonight. Come back the day after the party." That will still give me a few days to rest before the fight with

Caden, although I don't mention that part to Lily. I've learned it's a topic we're never going to agree upon, so it's best to avoid it.

"You're coming back?" she asks, surprised.

"Of course I'm coming back." My brows draw together. "Did you think I was going to pack my stuff and say goodbye. It's been fun, nice to meet you?" The more I think about it, the angrier it makes me she would even consider I'd disappear after the last few weeks.

"I. We. I…it's just…we never spoke about the future…after your business is done here."

"My business is far from done here, Angel."

She looks up at me. Her freshly showered face free of makeup, she's even more beautiful than usual. There's something so vulnerable about her, yet strong at the same time. "I thought you said the bank was almost done and everything was almost wrapped up for the investors."

"It is." I kiss her shoulder blade. "That's not the business I was referring to. There's other, more important things, I need to take care of here."

The corners of her mouth twitch upwards with hope. She wraps her arms around my neck. "What other things do you need to take care of?" she asks coyly.

I trail one finger across her shoulder, my pointer finger slipping off the spaghetti strap of her tank top. Following the delicate curve of her collarbone, I reach across to the other shoulder and slip the other strap off too. The thin fabric of her night shirt falls, revealing her perfect breasts. I'm mesmerized as I watch her nipples harden before my eyes.

"There's lots of business here I need to take care of. Important business." My mouth drops to her nipple and I suck it in deeply, tugging a bit with my teeth as I release it pulling my head back. "I'm going to tell you all about it as I take care of it now." I lift her from my lap and scoop her into my arms. She squeals a bit, the sound makes me smile even more. "You ready for the play by play?"

She nods and bites her bottom lip, her eyes going from playful to hooded.

"I can't hear you." I begin to walk toward the bedroom.

"Yes." The single word comes out breathless. It makes my cock harden in my pants just knowing I can make her that way.

"Yes, what?"

"I want to hear the play by play."

And so I do. I tell her about each important thing I need to take care of right before I do it. Sucking her tits. Licking her sweet pussy. Making her scream my name as she comes.

My parent's home, the one I've lived in since the day I was born, sits atop a tall hill overlooking downtown D.C. Grand gates block the passage to strangers, leaving them only to imagine the characters in the storybook that is on display for the world to see. Punching in the code, I look up at the main house. Soaring white pillars frame the strikingly tall double front doors to the stately home. Strategically placed lights illuminate the finer points of architecture, leading your eyes to see what is on display, instead of the darkness that truly looms inside. It's a home very much like the man that lives inside. Perfect on the outside, standing tall, defying anyone to question its place in the community. But the inside is cold and filled with lies.

Three years ago I moved out of the main house and into the small guest cottage. I'd wanted to get my own apartment downtown, but my mother talked me into a compromise. Parking in the driveway of a place that once felt like home, I realize I feel more like an intruder than someone that belongs.

A large pile of mail waits for me on the dining room table, an announcement rests on top. Thick card stock and calligraphy proclaim the birthday party will take place at eight sharp. No doubt hundreds were hand delivered all across town, an invite for every dignitary. I wonder again if my decision to come was right.

A family portrait hangs on the wall in the living room, compliments of my mother when I moved in. I was only about five or six, dressed in a suit with suspenders, I stood proudly between them. Both of them smile widely for the camera, I step closer to study their faces. My father's smile is the same one I've seen a million times, he's perfected it over the years. Sadly, I'm not sure I can even remember what the natural one looks like anymore. But it's my mother's face that I examine for the longest time. I search her eyes, wondering if she was covering her sadness even back then, or if it developed in the years after.

Was there ever anything real in my life? Or did the lies and secrets surround me from the day I was born so I didn't know anything different.

Startled by the sound but not faintly surprised at the visit, my father's voice breaks into my thoughts as I stand staring at the picture. "You're liquidating a substantial amount of investments. What's going on Jackson?"

I shake my head and laugh out loud, even though I find nothing really funny. I make a mental note to change bankers. Come to think of it, there are probably a dozen changes I need to make in my life to rid myself of the old boys club that my father gets his information from. So much for damn privacy laws. "It's none of your business what I do with *my* money. But don't worry, I'm not paying off a madam that's blackmailing me or investing in heroin." I walk to the bar in the living room and pour myself a drink, not extending a courtesy to my unwelcomed guest. "You don't have to concern yourself about a looming scandal, if that's what you're worried about." I take a sip of the amber liquid, it burns as it slides down my throat. "Don't you have plenty of your own scandals to worry about anyway?"

"I know you're upset, but I won't tolerate being disrespected in my own home," he says with disdain.

I toss the rest of the liquid back and turn to face my father with a smile laced with venom. "That won't be a problem. I won't be staying long."

"And where will you go? Back to New York to waste your time hanging around a bunch of losers who think beating each other is a sport? And this Lily...she isn't the type of woman you need."

"You don't know anything about Lily," I spit. "In fact, you don't really know anything about me either."

"I know her kind. Enjoy yourself, sow your wild oats. But marry a well-bred woman."

"I'd fucking lay you out right now, if I didn't find you so pathetic." Looking at my father for the first time I see tired and worn.

"Lay me out? You sound like an animal. Like that half-breed brother of yours. That's what you'll wind up being spending your days in a place like you've been."

I laugh humorlessly. "Who would have thought the Senator's prodigal son would be envious of the illegitimate child?"

"Jealous?" he utters. "What on earth could you be jealous of that man for?"

I stare at him, incredulous. "He grew up without you."

I don't know why I expected my mother's birthday party to be anything less than a show. A venue for the world to glimpse the happy couple, an attempt at restoring the Senator's tarnished image. For the most part, I'd played the role I was expected to fill. It was just easier to go through the motions on autopilot than try to prove a point to my father. Although I did note his jaw clench when I decided to sit on the other side of the room with Lourdes, the woman who took care of me from the time I was a baby, rather than at his table, the one that was assigned to me. He didn't really care where I sat, but the whispers started immediately and we both knew it.

I ignore my father's act when I approach his table to ask my mother for a dance. "Well there's my son who's too busy running an empire to visit with his old man these days." He says while holding court to two fellow Senators at his table, one of whom is being groomed for a potential Vice Presidential run.

"Mom, would you like to dance?" Her face lights up when I ask. It makes the torture of spending time in the same room as my father worth it to see her happy, even if it's only for a moment.

"Thank you for coming," she says quietly when we make our way to the dance floor.

I nod.

"Are you back for good now?" she asks.

"No. I'm honestly not sure where I'll end up anymore, Mom."

She looks at me nervously. "But your business is here."

"And I have a good man running it. I spent the day with Brady. He's got things under control."

It looks like she wants to add something, but then she thinks better of it and simply nods. We're both quiet for a minute, before I tell her what I've only just realized to be true. "I'm sorry if I've been hard on you, Mom. I was taking out how I feel about him on you."

Her face saddens.

"I didn't understand why you stayed with him. It made me angry that you let him walk all over you."

190

"I love your father, Jackson," she says almost regretfully.

"I know. But that doesn't mean you have to let him destroy you. I feel like I lost *you*, Mom."

"I've always been right here, Jackson."

"I don't mean physically. I mean who are you, Mom? You're his wife, his partner, the woman who stands by his side in the photo shoots...but does any of that make you happy?"

A tear falls from her eye, yet she smiles.

"I'm sorry, I didn't mean to upset you. It's your birthday."

"You didn't upset me, son. I just realized what a fine man you've grown into. You see things clearly. Some woman is going to be very lucky to catch you some day."

I smile. Accepting her compliment. "I don't know what I can do to help, but I'm here if you need me."

"Thank you. That means the world to me."

I nod and lean down to kiss her cheek, pulling her close against me until we finish the dance. Feeling like I accomplished what I came here to do, I slip out early not long after.

Chapter 23

Lily

It had been a while since Reed and I had a Friday night movie slumber party night. Donning a sweatshirt two sizes too big and making two bowls of Moose Tracks ice cream, I settled into my worn couch, handing the one with three cherries to Reed.

"Nice sweatshirt." My best friend grins widely knowing full well it's Jax's. He'd worn it for a few hours before bed the other night and it had that Jax smell on it. It isn't cologne or soapy, it's just his manly, delicious natural smell.

"Thanks." I smirk, shoveling a heaping spoon of ice cream into my mouth. "So what did you bring to watch?"

"Ocean's Eleven, Fight Club, and Mr. & Mrs. Smith."

"Still on the Brad Pitt kick, I see?"

"I don't have a Jackson Knight to keep me warm at night, so Brad fills in."

I reach into his bowl and steal one of his cherries, popping it into my mouth before he can protest. "So how is Mr. Tall, Rich, and Lickable?"

"He's ridiculously perfect," I answer, catching sight of Reed's boyishly beautiful smile. He's almost as excited as I am that Jax and I have become so close. I wish he'd meet someone too. Someone he wants to spend more than one night with, that is.

"Do you think he'll move to New York or will you move to D.C?"

"I don't think we're really up to that point yet."

"I see the way you look at him. The way he looks at you. You're up to that point." He shovels a spoonful of ice cream into his mouth and then a shiver runs through him.

"Brain freeze?"

He nods.

"Just because it's only been a few weeks doesn't mean you're not in love."

"Who said I was in love?"

Reed looks at me, as if to say it's painfully obviously written on my face. "How are things in your love life?" I ask. "Delivery boy still around?"

"Who?" Guess not.

"When are you going to find someone to actually have a relationship with?"

"I have lots of relationships," Reed says matter-of-factly.

"You know what I mean," I warn.

"When a Jackson Knight walks into my life," he shrugs as if the answer was so simple.

"I'm not sure there are two of them," I say jokingly, although I'm pretty sure it might be true.

Reed drops his spoon into his quickly emptied bowl with a loud clank. "Do. Not. Even. Say. That."

"Caden's available if you're interested," I tease, bumping shoulders with him.

"Thank you for waiting until *after* I finished my ice cream to say that. My stomach sours just thinking about that man." Reed stands and takes my dish, even though I still have ice cream left.

"Hey, I'm not done!" I whine.

Shoveling the last few spoonfuls into his mouth, he says, "Sure you are," and winks as he walks our dishes to the kitchen sink.

"Fight Club?" he asks, picking up the DVDs.

"You hate fighting."

"Not as much since I saw Jax sparring with Marco the other day." He sighs. "Plus Brad Pitt can do no wrong."

I smile. "Fight Club it is."

We settle in our usual position on the couch. Him sitting up with his legs sprawled out across the coffee table and me with my head on his lap and the blanket pulled up to my nose. Advertisements for movies we've both already seen play on the TV.

"So what's going on with the sale of Joe's half of the gym?"

"It looks good. Everything seems to be going smoothly. The bank that the investors are using for their financing is the same as our bank, so it saves us some time in doing verifications, Jax said."

"And Ape boy has been keeping away still?"

"Haven't seen him. Although his fight with Jax is this Wednesday. I feel sick even thinking about it."

Reed sighs loudly. At first I think it's his response to my mention of the looming fight between Caden and Jax. But then I realize the movie has started and Brad Pitt's face on the screen has stolen his attention away from our conversation. Reed's eyes stay glued to the shirtless fighters for most of the movie. I, on the other hand, find it hard to concentrate on a movie about fighting, it only reminds me of what is to come in four days.

I showered and changed into a different sweatshirt, the new one still plucked from Jax's pile he left at my place. Reed had just left a few minutes ago and I'd eyed the movies he'd left on the floor next to the DVD player just before the knock at the door came. Scooping them up, I unlock the top latch and swing the door open. "Forget something?"

Jax's mouth widens into a smile. "Nice sweatshirt."

"I didn't expect to see you so early," I stammer, taken aback momentarily by his appearance. And what an appearance it is. Dressed in a navy suit with a pale blue tie that brings out the color of his eyes to the point that they almost don't look real, he looks completely edible.

"So you answer the door like that for just anybody?" One eyebrow arched, there's a hint of what could be jealousy in his tone.

Forgetting I have no pants on, I look down to find his sweatshirt is barely covering my panties. "I thought you were Reed."

"Not even sure I like you answering the door for Reed like that." His eyes draw a slow sweep up and down my bare legs before he captures me by the back of the neck and kisses me senseless.

"Wow."

His mouth curves into a wicked smile. "You going to invite me in, or do I have to feel you up right here in the doorway."

We spend a few minutes just inside the door, with me pushed up against it. Breaking for air, I whisper, "This is a nice

196

surprise. You're back early. I didn't think you'd be back till late tonight."

Jax's hand travels under my sweatshirt, I haven't yet put on a bra after my shower. He groans finding my bare skin. "There was no reason to stay." He lifts the sweatshirt, exposing my swollen nipples and takes one between his teeth. "And every reason to come back."

My heart swells thinking I'm his reason to come back early. Pressing his body gruffly against mine, he pins me to the door with just his hips as he takes my mouth in another deep kiss. I quickly become lost in him. A loud knock quickly brings me back.

"Who is it?" I question, my legs not yet sure of themselves, I sway a tiny bit as Jax releases me from his grip.

"It's me," Reed says from the other side of the door. I reach for the lock and Jax puts his hand over mine stopping me.

"Go put pants on," he says sternly.

"But, it's just Reed."

"I don't care who it is. Go cover up."

Pouting, I stomp back to the bedroom to throw on some pants and come back.

"I forgot the DVDs," Reed says with a knowing grin on his face. He eyes Jax with delight, and I'm not sure if it's because he's happy for me or just likes what he sees. Either way, it warms me to see the approval on his face.

"I'll see you two Wednesday," he waves and practically runs out the door.

"Wednesday?" I crinkle my nose not remembering any plan I had made with Reed.

"I invited him to the fight," Jax says nonchalantly as he closes and locks the front door.

A nauseating feeling of dread consumes me. I'd managed to forget about the fight for a few hours this morning. The thought of watching Jax get hit in the ring with Caden sickens me.

It's not that I don't have confidence that he'll win, but the fight is essentially my fault and I know I'll be feeling guilty with every strike.

Attempting to put the thought out of my head, I change the subject. "How was the party?"

"A joke," Jax grumbles, raking his fingers through his hair.

"I'm sorry," I offer, not knowing what else to say.

"Me too. He couldn't even let her have a night without making it into a public relations event."

Lacing my fingers with his, I raise his hand to my mouth and kiss each finger tenderly. He takes my other hand, weaves our fingers and cradles it against his chest. The intimate exchange seems to soothe him, a small but real smile creeping onto his face.

"I missed you," I blurt out, offering the truth, even though admitting it makes me nervous.

"I missed you too." He grins, snaking his arms around my waist and pulling me closer. "I really do like you in my sweatshirt," he says in a throaty voice as he reaches for the hem and pulls it up over my head.

"I thought you said you liked me *in* it," I tease.

"I do." His head lowers, he buries his face in my neck and breathes in deeply. "You can wear it later."

"Later?" I repeat mindlessly, not really asking a question.

"Much later." He takes my mouth in a passionate kiss, our hunger quickly igniting. "Need you now," he growls, lifting me at the knees and carrying me to the bedroom.

Laying me down centered on the bed, my eyes hooded with lust, he hovers over me still fully dressed while I'm stripped to only my panties. I lean up and press a trail of kisses to his throat, feeling him swallow beneath my lips. My touch is gentle, but it elicits a response from him that is anything but. Groaning, he cups my head, holding me in place while he kisses me mercilessly.

"Your shirt. Please take off your shirt," I tug desperately at the tails freeing them from his slacks, but I can't open the buttons from my position. I need to feel him without a barrier. Now.

Nimbly undoing the buttons, Jax bares his perfect chest and presses it against me. We both groan at the sensation of skin against skin. It's been only a few days yet my body is starved for him.

"Jesus," he murmurs in a sexy voice thick with need as he reaches down and grasps my butt in one hand, squeezing hard, using the other to guide my legs to wrap around his waist. "You feel so good, I missed this."

My fingers twine into his hair as he slides down my body, nuzzling between my breasts. "I missed it too. Missed you," I say breathlessly, pouring meaning into each word.

Jax's mouth moves to my nipple, it's already swollen and needy. I gasp as he sucks hard, feeling the sensation shoot through every nerve of my body. The intensity of his desire pouring out consumes me…my body, my thoughts, my heart. He moves to the other breast, his hand reaching down between my legs. I arch into him as he slides lower, leaving a trail of wetness as he alternates sucking and biting.

Reaching my sensitive flesh, he purrs with raw male satisfaction finding how ready I already am for him. "So wet and eager, my Angel," he feathers his tongue over my swollen clit. "I love how ready your pussy is for me."

Tremors run through my limbs as the vigor of his licks increase. His tongue moves expertly, he's gotten to know my body so well, so quickly. My hands clutch the sheets beneath me, gripping them as my orgasm quickly takes hold of me. Jax growls as I reach down and grab his hair, pushing him further into me if it's even possible.

"Jax," I cry out as I feel the waves begin to grip me. My fingers tug harshly at his hair. Repeating his name over and over as my body begins to tremble, he sucks down hungrily on my clit once more, pushing me over the edge. My body convulses on its own, a steady stream of moans thrumming through the air between us.

Before I can come back down from the brink of ecstasy, he licks his way back up my body. Hovering over me, he pauses, his breathing as labored as mine. His eyes roam my face, my body, the moment becoming intensely intimate. "You're so beautiful," he whispers. His pale blue eyes are filled with a mesmerizing mix of emotions that bring a well of happy tears to my eyes. I see truth, desire, need and something I've never seen from him before...vulnerability.

Kissing my lips softly, he slows down our once frenzied pace to languid and leisurely. The hunger is still in his eyes, but it's mixed with powerful emotions that course between us.

Eyes locked, he enters me unhurriedly. His jaw clenches and body trembles as he struggles to go slow, pushing his thick, hard cock inside of me inch by inch. A moan drops from my lips when he finally fills me. Every inch of me feeling stretched and gloriously full.

Steadying as he seats himself to the hilt, he threads his fingers with mine and lifts my hands over my head, restraining me. His muscular body controlling mine makes me feel defenseless, yet heightens my arousal to a level that intensely consumes me.

He claims my mouth again and begins to move, his tongue leading mine as he glides in and out smoothly. Each stroke is tender yet powerful as my body swells, enveloping him deeper. I wrap my legs around his waist and we move in unison to a dance without music, yet we're perfectly in time.

He tells me how beautiful I am, how incredible I feel, how my body takes him in as if we were made for each other. I feel completely and totally possessed by him, his tender words, his eyes

watching me, his cock inside of me…I close my eyes as ecstasy begins to wash over me.

His grip on my hands tightens, my knuckles white as he clenches down. I gasp as his pace quickens, his hips changing from rhythmic thrusting to forceful, deep pounding. My orgasm hits me with the same intensity as his need to claim my body. Moaning, I arch my back and chant his name over and over, riding each wave of pleasure until he joins me with a hiss of my name and I feel his heat pour into me.

The man who less than half an hour ago planted my hands firmly against the shower wall as he commanded my body and took me from behind, now pours my coffee and pulls out a chair for me as I walk into the kitchen. He's such a contradiction in so many ways.

"I have class today. But how about I make you dinner later?"

"We can stay at the hotel tonight. Have dinner there. You don't have to cook."

I smile. "I want to." I love doing everyday things with him. It just feels so right, so normal, so comforting. He feels like coming home to me.

He studies me for a moment. "Okay. I have to do some work and then I have Marco from four to six. I'll come by after that."

"I hope you shower first?" I tease.

"After this morning, I think all my showers are going to be here." He grins a cocky boyish smile. I have a feeling we're both going to be very clean.

Chapter 24

Lily

Jax has a business meeting across town this morning, so we say goodbye outside my building and I walk to Ralley's alone. It's a route I've walked since I was ten years old by myself. It's a good neighborhood. I've always felt safe. Yet again today, I can't shake the feeling of someone watching me. It's broad daylight, but my own paranoia has me practically power walking the short distance to the gym.

The busy morning of paperwork helps me to relax and I'm lost in my own thoughts when the bells on the front door jolt me even though I'm staring right at it. A man enters wearing a suit, he looks out of place. Handsome, I'd guess mid-fifties, but wears it well. Distinguished, one look and I know he's wealthy.

"Can I help you?" I ask, at first sure that he's made a wrong turn. But then he smiles and I watch as his eyes roam my body. It's not the subtle and elusive glance of a gentleman, even though he looks like one from the outside. No. It's the pointed ego blaring leer of a man who has little respect for a woman. The kind of vulgar ogle that makes me want to put on a sweater. Perhaps he's in the right place after all.

"I bet you can," he responds confidently. I'm met by stunning blue eyes that no doubt have captured the attention of droves of women over the years.

I smile politely. "Are you looking for Joe Ralley?" He's probably here for a business meeting. I size him up quickly. Someone who makes more money in an hour than I net in a month, giving him the false sense of self-worth that often comes from having too much money. It's a shame too, he really is handsome.

"Actually I'm looking for Caden Ralley," he says with a practiced smile that reminds me of a Cheshire cat. I shouldn't be surprised when he asks for Caden, this guy seems right up Caden's alley, yet I don't expect the name to drop from his mouth.

"He doesn't work..." I begin to respond, but I'm interrupted by the bells on the door as it's whipped open. Caden. My hand automatically feels for the taser we keep under the counter. "Caden, you aren't supposed to be here," I warn.

The visitor turns and looks at Caden, then back to me. I've backed up toward the gym, ready to scream if Caden takes one step toward me. Wisely, the visitor assesses my face and swiftly says, "Mr. Ralley, perhaps we should take our business elsewhere. Why don't we go have some lunch?"

Caden glares at me for a moment and then turns his attention to his visitor. He nods and the two men disappear without another word.

Chapter 25

Jax

A serene feeling cloaks me as I make my way through the chaotic city. Overflowing traffic bustles through the streets, taxi's honk and weave in and out, a barrage of people shuffle all around me, eager to get to their destination. Taking it all in as I walk leisurely to my hotel after my meeting, it dawns on me I was one of them not too long ago. Running in place, conducting my life on the go, yet never really knowing where I was heading. But something's changed.

The doors open to my suite and I stop to look around. Really look around. It's ornate and grand, and completely unnecessary. I smile thinking of Lily's comment the first time she saw it, "Why does one person need three bathrooms?" I'll be damned if I know. Just like so many other things in my life, I didn't stop to consider what I was doing. Rather, I acted as I was taught. As I was expected to act. Even the ostentatious hotel room, I could afford the best, so why would I expect anything less? Totally my father, a man I loathe to find any comparisons to, yet each time I act without thinking I find my actions resemble his.

I call guest services and tell them I'll be checking out of the suite today and checking into a regular room. It takes me five minutes to convince them nothing is wrong, it's just unnecessary to occupy it anymore.

I make a few business calls and catch up with Brady again on the state of Knight Investments. The office has been busy the last day, a barrage of new clients. My mother's birthday party likely a factor. The news ran a picture of her and I dancing that I didn't even know was snapped. *Forgiveness* was the title of the story. A shot captured from a private moment in time, a trait of humanity that my father undoubtedly has plans to exploit.

Packing up the few things I've brought before heading to the gym, I look around one last time as I wait for the elevator. How can I have thought this life was normal…what I was cut out to be?

My newfound peace quickly dissipates, replaced by fury and tension the minute I walk through the door at Ralley's Gym.

"What are you doing here?" I scowl, demanding through clenched teeth.

"Is that any way to greet your father?" Dressed in a three piece custom tailored suit, his perfectly poised consummate politician smile slithers over me like a snake coiling as it waits patiently to find the best place to sink its venomous teeth.

"What. Do. You. Want." I grumble. Anger radiates from my every word. I'm not yelling, but heads turn to watch. These men can smell a fight brewing.

A minute later, Lily walks from the back office to the reception desk where we're standing. At first, oblivious to the standoff, she approaches smiling. "Hey. How was your meeting?" She sees my face, notices the visitor, and turns to my father, her face faltering. "You're back?"

"Yes. I just can't seem to keep away," he responds sarcastically.

"My father's been here before?" I ask Lily.

"Your father?" Lily's eyes go wide. She looks to him and then to me, perhaps searching for the resemblance. It's not hard to find. "He was here earlier today." She looks confused.

"What are you doing here?" I repeat through gritted teeth.

"I think I should be asking you the same thing, Jackson."

"What I do is none of your business. I thought we cleared that up already."

My father clears his throat and straightens his spine, standing taller. "I need to speak to you in private. You haven't returned my calls."

"Then you've wasted a trip. We have nothing to talk about…on the phone or in person."

"Your business is dwindling. Clients need to be put at ease that you're at the helm. Apparently, I'm not the only call you aren't returning."

"My business is just fine. And none of *your* business."

"People talk. Let's not forget that many of your biggest clients are my associates. Fellow Senators, Congressmen, wealthy supporters."

"Yes. And those were the first ones to pull their business when the news broke you didn't practice the good Christian values you preach."

"Nonsense. You still have many clients from my blood, sweat and tears. Some of who are concerned you aren't steering the ship back to calm waters. Every business goes through rocky times, you need to hang on tight and work through them, Jackson."

"Is that why you came? To give me business help. I think you've done enough."

My father smiles. He turns his head to Lily and then back to me as if to make a point. "We're a lot more alike than you may care to admit, son."

"We're *nothing* alike," I snarl vehemently.

"I know what you're doing. I will not stand by idly as you destroy your life. While you destroy the family name by spending your days in a place like this."

"Get out! And don't come back." Rage pours from my body, trembling to find an outlet for my anger.

My father leisurely buttons his jacket and smooths it down, "That's okay, my business is done here." He looks around the room with disdain. "I've raised you better than this. You'll come around to your senses soon enough. You'll bore of being surrounded by ignorance and vulgarity."

The door opens to frantic clicks of the cameras from the few photographers that are still hanging around. Senator Knight puts on the smile of a trained actor and walks out.

After a moment, I turn to Lily. "I'm sorry about that."

"There's nothing to be sorry about."

"I don't know why he came here. What he was even trying to accomplish. We said everything we needed to say at the house, before my mother's party."

"Jax." Lily's face looks nervous and stressed. "He was here with Caden earlier."

"What are you talking about?"

"He came in and asked for Caden. I was about to tell him Caden didn't work here, when the door opened and Caden walked in. They left together right after."

"Did Caden touch you?"

"No. They were only here for a minute. What do you think the two of them have to talk about? It makes no sense."

"I have no idea."

"Sparring is about practicing, firming up your technique, not actually knocking your partner out," Marco says as he lifts himself from the floor for the third time this session.

"Sorry. Guess my adrenaline is still flowing." Raging might be a better word, flowing would imply smooth sailing, but the torrent that courses through my veins is more like a lethal tsunami threating to surge.

He raises the oversized sparring pads one more time. I hit him with a quick left jab and then the power of my right. He takes two steps back. "Caden's fucked in the ring with you," he smiles at the thought. We've never spoken about it, but I get the feeling most of the guys in the gym aren't Caden fans. He's arrogant and overconfident, traits other fighters detest, unless it's found in their opponent in the ring.

We train for longer than scheduled, but nowhere near what it takes to release the years of pent up anger that my father's visit bubbled to the surface. Marco throws a towel at me and shakes his head, smiling. "I'm going to need a good soak tonight. Haven't had that good a workout in a while."

Sweat drips from every pore of my body. I wipe my face and grab a water, chugging half in one long gulp and pouring the rest over my head. "You coming to watch?"

Marco grins. "Wouldn't miss it for the world. You come in one tenth as ready as you were today, Caden won't make thirty seconds." He grabs his gym bag and climbs out of the sparring ring. "Think I might run a pool. Find a picture of you from the paper dressed in your fancy suit and tie and post it next to the sign up sheet. Boys in here that haven't watched you train will underestimate your pretty face."

"You think I'm pretty?" I tease as Marco walks away. He gives me the finger and shakes his head without looking back.

Not yet ready to call it a day, I run for close to an hour, my feet pounding the deck of the treadmill as I go over my father's visit again in my head. What is he really after? And what could he possibly want with Caden?

The only thoughts able to shed light on the darkness overshadowing my mind are those of Lily. The way she lights up the entire room for me when she walks in the door. Her smile, her face, her body…the way she loves so deeply that she can't even let go after the person is gone. She's dedicating so much of her life to carrying out her father's dream, even after he's not here to share it with her anymore. I didn't even know what true love was until I saw the love for her father in her eyes. It makes me sad to know what I've missed out on in life, but inspires me to work to be lucky enough to have her feel that way about me someday.

I hit cool down on the treadmill, finally burning away enough of the bad energy to be able to stop running in place. I've spent six months harboring so much anger and resentment that it left no room for anything else. But now I'm ready to make way, to find a way to channel those feelings in the ring, but leave them behind at the end of the day. Because at the end of the day, all I want is to go home with Lily.

Chapter 26

Lily

Tension hangs heavily in the warm late summer night air. We've been together every night for the last week. There was never a question we were spending the night, the only unclear fact at the end of each evening seemed to be where...my apartment or his hotel suite. Yet tonight as I lock up the door to the gym after closing, there's an awkwardness. Jax's father's visit obviously still weighs heavily on him. We walk a block in silence, until we reach a fictional fork in the road...my apartment is to the left and his hotel is to the right.

"Can we stay at my hotel tonight? I have my laptop there and I need to send a few emails in the morning," Jax asks.

"Ummm...sure."

"What's wrong?" He stops in his tracks and turns to me.

"Nothing. It's just. I wasn't sure if we were going to stay together tonight."

"Why wouldn't we?"

I shrug. There is no real answer. It was more of a feeling.

"I don't know."

Jax's eyes search mine and he's quiet for a moment. He takes my face into his hands and focuses on nothing but our connection. There's an unmistakable intensity in his eyes, but there's something more. Something hidden beneath the surface. Hurt? Sadness? Worry? "I'm nothing like him."

At first the statement is so seemingly out of place, I'm not sure what he's even talking about. Then realization dawns on me. He's concerned I might believe what his father said. That he's like his father. "I know you're not," I whisper, my eyes locked to his.

He closes his eyes and nods. When he reopens them, there's still hurt and pain, but some of the tension seems to be relieved.

Jax was quiet all night and this morning he had to head out for a day of meetings he had planned. He says he's fine, but I can tell his dad's visit is still bothering him. So I leave Ralley's a little earlier than usual and stop at LaPerla on my way home to buy something I think will cheer him up. Spending a few hundred dollars on sexy lingerie isn't something I do on a regular basis. But I'm excited to see his face when I describe what I have on underneath my clothes during dinner tonight.

I'm just about to hop in the shower when my cell phone buzzes. The name on the screen surprises me and I almost hit REJECT. But in a moment of weakness I answer the call from Caden.

I regret answering it as my trembling finger disconnects the call. My eyes sting as I fight back tears, throwing the phone on the table harshly. The screen shatters but it's the least of my problems. I stand staring out the bedroom window for a long time, the tumultuous grey sky opening up with a crack of thunder making way for the pelt of heavy rain that follows.

I shouldn't have answered the phone. I'm not even sure why I did. Maybe because some part of me feels badly for hurting Caden, he wasn't always a jerk. It was all I could do to breathe after the death of my father, until Caden swooped in to take care of me.

I know what he did to me is wrong, a good man never puts his hands on a woman…no matter what. One of the many life lessons my father taught me growing up surrounded by men who use their hands to survive. There's no excuse for what he did, yet a pang of guilt still keeps me connected to him somehow. Guilt for not loving him back the way he loved me. So I answered the phone, even though I knew no good would come from it. And I wasn't wrong. I can only hope he was spewing lies, but there's a gnawing feeling in the pit of my stomach that won't go away no matter how hard I try to tell myself nothing he said was true.

I've gone through half a dozen emotions in an hour. Each one changing the speed of my frenzied pacing. I feel nauseous. Anxious. Angry. Confused. Betrayed. But above all I'm scared to death that everything Caden said could possibly be true. I pace faster and faster through my small apartment, checking the clock frantically every thirty seconds.

The sound of the doorbell jolts me still. I've been desperate for answers, yet now I'm terrified to ask the questions. It takes every bit of my strength to simply open the door. My heart lurches into my throat when I see him standing before me. He lowers his head to kiss me on the lips, but I don't kiss him back.

"You okay?" Jax asks, concerned as he takes in the blank look on my face.

I nod. I'm not, but I'm hoping I will be in a few minutes, so I stand to the side offering him entry.

"Am I early?" Jax looks at his watch and then to me. He's here to pick me up for dinner, yet I'm still wearing the jeans and ponytail I had on this morning. I don't respond.

Brow furrowed, he reaches down and takes both of my hands into his, pulling one to his mouth. "Hey."

I don't look up.

"Look at me, Lily," he demands quietly.

I look up, his eyes capturing my gaze. "What's going on? You okay?" There's a softness to his voice that I long to hear. Something about it reminds me of my dad. The way he was so tough on the exterior, yet I always knew the interior was filled with a tenderness that held my heart.

Panic dawns on me as I realize for the first time that it may be too late. Too late not to give this man my heart if what I dread being true turns out to be a reality I can't escape. I close my eyes for a long moment, hating to ask, but needing to hear that it's a lie.

Forcing myself to keep eye contact, I ask, my voice barely more than a whisper, "Are you the investor buying Joe's half of Ralley's Gyms?"

We look at each other for the longest time. It's so quiet in the room, I can hear my heart pounding in my chest. Each beat gets louder and louder with anticipation. Regret shadows over his beautiful blue eyes and I watch in despair as they close, taking the last bit of my hopes away. My stomach twists. Heart clenches. Sadness rips through me.

I slip my hands from his. A lone tear falls from my eye just as he opens his. "Yes. I'm sorry. I know I should've told you sooner. I was waiting until after the deal went through to tell you. I didn't want our relationship to influence yours and Joe's decision."

"You really thought we'd have a relationship after you destroy everything my father worked for by forcing me into bankruptcy?"

"What are you talking about? I'm not destroying anything or forcing you into bankruptcy."

I laugh. "What did you think having the bank cut off our line of credit without warning would do? You know our cash is tight!"

"The bank cut your line of credit?" he asks, having the audacity to look shocked.

"You know they did!" I scream, feeling the room grow smaller.

"I didn't have the bank do anything."

"Caden told me everything, Jax."

"Caden?" he questions, his jaw clenching. "What are you talking about?"

"You invest in Ralley's just as the bank cuts off our line of credit. You're the financial wizard, you know how it works. Without that line, we'll be out of cash in less than two months. Then you swoop in and buy the rest for pennies on the dollar."

He closes his eyes. His hands rake through his hair, tugging harshly. Stress creases his forehead and he has the gall to sound appalled when he speaks. "I didn't have anything to do with the bank cutting…"

I interrupt his lies. "So they just decided to pull my line of credit on their own?" I laughingly suggest.

"I had nothing to do with it."

"You're a liar!"

"I've never lied to you."

"No?" I laugh sardonically. "You just don't offer the truth."

At least he has the decency to flinch. "I'm sorry. I should have told you I was the investor sooner." He bows his head. "But

I would never do anything to ruin your business." He reaches for my hand. I pull it away as if he's the hot coil on the top of the stove that just burned my skin.

"Get out," I say eerily calm.

"Lily, you need to believe me. I'm crazy about you. I had nothing to do with the bank pulling your line of credit," He takes a step closer to me, I take two steps back.

"Just get out." My voice grows louder.

Jax searches my eyes, neither of us saying anything for a long moment. "I..," he begins to say something, but I've lost my mind.

"Get out!" This time I scream. Jax closes his eyes and nods. He opens the door and is half way through when I add my final thoughts. He turns looking hopeful when he hears me speak calmly again. "Tell me, Jackson. Do you specifically target businesses that were built by the blood and sweat of fathers, since you hate your own so much?"

His jaw flexes. I know deep down it's a low blow, but I don't give a shit. I want to hurt him as much as he hurt me. He turns back and walks out the door without another word.

There's a strong urge inside of me to go after him and comfort him. How messed up is that? I walk to the door and lean my forehead against it. My apartment is so quiet. I hold in my tears until I hear the door to the stairwell close behind him. Then they come, uncontrollable sobs and tears bleed from a cut so deep in my heart, I feel as though I might drown. I cry for hours. Eventually, emotionally exhausted, every ounce of energy depleted from my wrenched body, I cry myself to sleep.

I've been wearing the same clothes for two days. For two days, I alternated between feeling sorry for myself that Dad's dream was about to be sucked down the drain and feeling the hollow in my chest from missing Jax. Sure, I could have just picked up the phone on one of the dozen occasions it rang and I found Jax's name flashing on the screen, but that wouldn't have helped matters at all. No, it would only have made things worse. Aside from grieving my double loss, I'm also struggling with guilt because I feel worse about losing what I thought I had with Jax than possibly losing the business.

When Reed let himself in I was still lying in the bed, curled into the fetal position.

"Rise and shine, my little princess," Reed says in a happy voice that only makes me dig in deeper, clinging to my own sadness. I pull my legs tighter to my chest and try to ignore him.

He rips the blanket from my body. "I just want to be left alone!" I yell, selfishly uncaring I'm taking it out on my best friend.

"Not happening."

"Ugh," I groan, knowing exactly how Reed can be when he decides he knows best.

"Can't I just stay in bed?"

"Nope."

"Why not?"

"For starters, you look like hell."

"Great. Thanks."

"And we have plans."

"No plans."

"Yes, plans."

"Why? Why can't I just be left alone?"

"Because I love you."

Digging my face in the pillow, I attempt to protest, "Can't we have movie day and eat buckets of ice cream and stay in bed for two days?"

"You already stayed in bed for two days?"

"So."

"Two days is the limit to stay in bed."

"Who says?"

"I just did. Now get in the shower before I carry you in." He reaches over to the bed and swats my ass playfully, although I'm in no mood.

I groan as I get out of bed, knowing Reed totally would throw me in if I didn't do it myself. Dragging my feet, I pad to the bathroom and turn, sticking my tongue out at him before slamming the door shut.

How, in such a short period of time has my world become so small that I can't seem to escape thoughts of Jax everywhere I go. Everything reminds me of him. Closing my eyes to allow myself to relax into the pulsating shower stream, I remember the last time I was in the shower with him. My hands pushed up against the cold tile as the warm water washed over the small of my back and Jax pounded into my relentlessly from behind. The sound he made as he emptied himself into me, a primal raw growl that was just so ferociously male. Maybe that was all it ever was…sex. I wouldn't be the first woman to confuse love with lust from a man. But I was just so damn sure he was feeling the same way about me that I was for him.

Reed dragged me to lunch at our favorite little restaurant in Chinatown and then he took me to the best bakery in the City. He ordered us the warm molten lava cake with a side of vanilla bean ice cream and we sat at a table by the window so we could people watch. It hasn't stopped raining in two days and the weather has definitely taken its toll on my fellow tiny apartment dwellers. New York City people aren't meant to stay indoors.

Closing my eyes as the rich oozing chocolate meets my tongue, a small moan escapes as my lips.

"Really?" Reed grins wickedly. "Is that what you're like when you come?" He digs a heaping spoon into the tower of chocolate heaven sitting between us and shovels it between his lips, the fact that his mouth is full doesn't stop him from speaking. "I never saw the appeal of a vagina. But if it makes you feel like that, I might give it a whirl someday."

"You need help," I tease, feeling the most lighthearted I have in days.

"Wanna see my come face?" Reed offers. I'm positive I should say no, but of course I don't.

"I know I should say no. But sadly, I really do."

Reed closes his eyes and takes another spoonful of the molten chocolate lava cake. I watch both riveted and repulsed as his jaw goes slack and his breathing begins to speed up. He finishes with a giant moan. Meg Ryan has nothing on Reed Baxter.

He opens his eyes, arches his eyebrows, and scoops just the whip cream off with a wicked grin.

I can't help but laugh.

"There it is," Reed says.

"What?"

"The sound I knew was buried somewhere deep."

I take a cleansing breathe in and exhale out deeply. "I think I was a little in love with him," I admit without needing to tell him we've changed topics.

Reed sighs. "Me too."

I chuckle. "I'm being serious."

"Me too." He grins and consumes another mouthful of cake.

"Tonight is the fight between them you know?"

"It was."

"Was?"

"Cancelled," Reed says, offering no more.

"Why?" My brows furrow. "And how do you know."

"Jax called me."

"He called you?"

"Yep. Think he'll go out with me now that you kicked him to the curb?"

"What did he want?" I ignore his question.

"You won't take his calls. Wanted to make sure you were okay."

"Why does he care?"

"Because he loves you, that's why."

"Did he say that?" I hate myself for feeling hopeful as I ask.

"Not in so many words. But he does and we both know it."

"He betrayed me."

"Maybe he wasn't honest about why he came to New York, but that doesn't make what happened between the two of you any less real."

"He could have told me for weeks. He was using me to get to the gym."

"I think you're wrong," Reed warns in a tone that pisses me off.

"Whose side are you on?"

"Yours always. You know that."

"So why is the fight cancelled?"

"Joe said if Caden fought tonight, he wouldn't be in any shape to fight in two weeks at the Open and he needed him to show well for business at the Open."

My eyes go wide. "Caden showing well at the Open has no effect on our business."

Reed shrugs. "That's what Jax said Joe said."

Chapter 27

Jax

Sitting idly has never been something I was capable of. I've sent flowers, called, even wrote her a hand written letter and slipped it under her door when she didn't answer. I'm beginning to feel stalkerish. I walk circles in my small hotel room and bark at the Vice President of City Bank yet again.

"Bullshit. I'm not playing these games anymore. It was either you or Theodore. Committee my ass. One of you is behind it, and I want to know which one. Theodore golfs with my father. You're on the Senate campaign expense panel. Which one of you does he have something on?"

It's my third threatening call to Theodore Wells in the last forty-eight hours. The President of the bank was the lucky recipient of four calls. He again denies having anything to do with my father. Blaming the Ralley's line being pulled on a routine quarterly review. A total load of crap, it's not even the end of a quarter.

"When I find out which one of you assholes is behind this, you'll pay for it. And I *will* find out." I slam the hotel phone down so hard it bounces out of the receiver and falls to the fall. I leave it there.

I'm positive my father is somehow behind getting the bank to close Ralley's line of credit. I just can't prove it. He probably used Caden for information on how to get between Lily and I. But as usual, he's covered his tracks well. I've tried everything, threatening to pull my business with the bank and blacklist them with all my clients, yet everyone still denies my father was involved. But I can smell his handy work a mile away. It was a double win for both Caden and my father. Joe Ralley called off the sale and Lily won't speak to me. Joe and I had a long talk the other day. On some level, I think he may even believe I had nothing to do with the bank, but it doesn't matter. He'd work until he was ninety if that's what it took to find a partner to make Lily happy.

Heavy clouds hang low in the sky as I make my way to Ralley's. It's been four days since I saw her. Four days since the sun has crossed the horizon, four days without seeing her smile, four days of darkness. This morning I woke up and it hit me. Like running into a wall of bricks full steam ahead. I'm absolutely, positively in love with this woman. And I'm totally fucked.

I've been putting in way too many hours training at the gym, hoping she would walk through the door. I fell asleep with my knuckles on ice last night again. My body is physically exhausted, yet I keep going back for her. Swinging the heavy front door open to the gym, I expect to see Joe at the front desk again, my heart races when I see Lily's face instead.

She's on the phone, looking down as she writes in the scheduling book when I walk in, so I have a chance to see her before she sees me. It looks like the last few days hasn't been easy on her either. Beneath her eyes is dark, her lids puffy and swollen, like she's spent time crying recently. I deserve a giant right hook to the gut for having anything to do with making her feel that way. Selfishly, it gives me hope that she's obviously having difficulty coping too.

Feeling eyes on her, she looks up at me with her big blue eyes, for a second I think I see longing and possibility, but the softness drains quickly as she forces her gaze back down. She rises from her chair behind the front desk and I think she may try to walk away from me. No way I'm not talking to her now that she's finally in front of me again. I walk to the counter quickly.

"Lily." She freezes in her tracks, although her head doesn't turn to look at me. I'll be damned if I'm not going to try my hardest. "Look at me." She does.

"What do you want, Jax?" Her voice is filled with sadness she tries to disguise as annoyance.

"I want to talk to you."

"I'm busy."

"When then?"

"I don't have anything more to say."

"Well I do. You can just listen."

"I don't think...," she's interrupted by a voice that makes my blood pressure rapidly rise. Fucking Caden.

"She has nothing to say to you." He folds his arms over his chest.

"Mind your fucking business," I seethe.

He grins. "Why don't we leave it up to Lily." He looks to Lily then back to me. His attention is locked on me, even though his words are directed at Lily. "You have anything you want to say to this joker?"

Lily looks up at me, her face filled with sadness. "No," she says, her voice laced with sorrow.

"Leave," Caden growls.

I look at Caden and then back to Lily. "Is that really what you want?"

She says nothing for a full minute, then nods without looking up. With a sadistic smile, Caden waves goodbye before I walk out the door.

Chapter 28

Jax

Every chair around the massive dark mahogany conference room table is filled. Floor to ceiling windows light the otherwise dark room, the last of the associates drones on while flashing slides on a PowerPoint presentation detailing all the potential deals he's working on. Peeling my gaze from the window overlooking bustling D.C., I look up seeing the presenter for the first time. He's full of himself. Young, nice enough looking, a suit that costs more than a week's salary, practically salivating at the thought of the commission he'll make if he's able to piece together the deals he's got in the pipeline.

He catches me staring, it throws his rhythm off, but I don't look away. He pulls at his collar slightly, trying to be discreet, but I can see him starting to squirm. For some reason watching his money driven ass pisses me off, even though I should be happy since I'll earn a hefty commission with each deal he closes.

"Does anyone have any questions?" The associate looks around the room avoiding contact with me.

"Yes," I clear my throat and speak loudly. "How many hours a week do you work, Mr....," I struggle to remember his name.

"Garrison."

"Excuse me?"

"My last name...it's Garrison," he clarifies.

"Is that the answer to the question I asked you?" Angrily, I counter, staring directly at him.

"No. But..."

"Do you have an answer then?" Losing patience, I interrupt.

"I don't know. Maybe eighty hours a week?"

"Why?"

"I'm sorry, Sir," he stammers. "I don't understand the question."

"Are you an idiot?"

"Jax," Brady, my CEO and sometimes best friend interrupts.

"What? I asked him a simple fucking question and he couldn't answer it. So he must be an idiot."

"Garrison, why don't we take a five minute break," Brady suggests staring in my direction.

"Don't bother. Go on without me." I stand abruptly, the chair I was sitting in falls over. I don't bother to pick it up as I storm out of the conference room, slamming the door behind me so hard the walls vibrate with the strength of my fury.

"Righteousness doesn't suit you," Brady says as he enters my office a little while later. He walks to the credenza that acts as a makeshift bar, lifts a crystal glass and pours two fingers of fifty-year-old scotch to match the glass I already have in my hand. Only it's my second.

Ignoring him, I continue to sit behind my desk, staring out the window, lost in my own self-pity. Brady parks himself across the modern, sleek glass desk and waits patiently sipping his drink.

"So you want to talk about it? Or should I get another associate for you to berate for no apparent reason?" he asks flatly.

"He's an idiot."

Brady chuckles. "He actually is an idiot. But that's beside the point. He's a rainmaker and he gave a good presentation. You attacked him because he didn't answer a pointless question fast enough."

"It wasn't pointless," I grumble through my teeth.

"Okay." He pulls one foot up and crosses it over his other knee in a relaxed stance, like he's getting ready for a long story. "So fill me in then. What was the point?"

I throw back the rest of the golden liquid in my crystal tumbler and slam it down against the glass desk. It clanks loud enough to crack, but doesn't. Annoyed at his persistent questioning, I scowl at him. But Brady Carlson has been my best friend for a long time, he doesn't scare easily. In fact, the fucker throws his head back and laughs.

"You got nothing, huh?" he says while chuckling.

"Shut the fuck up."

"Good come back." He grins knowingly.

I deliberate walking around the desk and kicking his ass for a half second, then I cave and give in. Raking my hands through my hair as I blow out a loud steady stream of air, I begin, "I blew it with Lily. She wants nothing to do with me."

"I figured that much." Brady stands and walks to the bar, refilling both our glasses. He sets mine in front of me and asks, "How do you fix it?"

"I can't."

"Sure you can. Where there's a will, there's a way."

"Says the divorced at twenty-eight reconciliation expert," I retort sarcastically as I sip my drink. It burns going down. Three double scotches for breakfast isn't really my thing.

"If I had tried, I might still be married." He shrugs.

"She won't answer my calls. She wouldn't talk to me in person. The last asshole she dated wouldn't take the hint, I don't want to be that asshole. But I can't let go either."

"Did you try flowers?"

I give him a look that unmistakably says 'of course I have you moron' and shake my head. He sips his drink.

"Okay. So flowers didn't work."

"She doesn't trust me. It's not as easy as an apology."

"So make her trust you."

"How? When she won't talk to me and lives four hours away."

"Stay in her life. Don't make it a short-term strategy if you're in it for the long haul. Find a way to stay in her life and earn back her trust. You've tried saying I'm sorry. Try showing her you're in it for real."

Brady's right. Perhaps I've been going about this all wrong. Standing around alike a wounded puppy and telling her I'm sorry doesn't mean shit to a smart woman like Lily. "Maybe you're not as stupid as you look after all." I crack a hint of a smile. It's the first one I've even come close to displaying in the week I've been back.

"They don't call me Dr. Goodlove for nothing," Brady says, grinning proudly.

"They don't call you Dr. Goodlove *at all,* asshole." I smile before kicking him out of my office.

The value of my business to City Bank is far more substantial than just the hefty sum in my accounts, even though I'd probably be a priority client just by my own balance, even without the 'extras' I bring to the table. But it's the extras that make them roll out the carpet for me. Being the financing arm for the majority of the deals we broker at my firm is a lucrative business for them. Not to mention the services they provide as my father's Senate campaign finance trustees.

Normally, I'd meet with the bank President or Vice President when I have an important deal, but today it isn't inadvertent that I'm sitting across from Gertrude Waters again.

"Jackson. What can I do for you today? Do you have a new potential acquisition you'd like us to examine for financing prospects?" She takes out her notebook and readies her pen.

"Actually, no. I wanted to talk to you about Ralley's Gyms."

"Oh. I'm sorry that didn't work out. Ms. St. Claire seemed like such a lovely woman." Gertrude looks pensive as she speaks, it makes me wonder if she knows it wasn't really a committee decision that got Ralley's line of credit pulled. But I don't ask. Instead, I'm focusing on what needs to be fixed instead of finding out who broke it.

"She is lovely." I smile.

"Well how can I help?"

"I'd like you to open back up her line of credit."

"I'm sorry," she hesitates, "I don't think that's possible, Jackson. Perhaps if over the next year their cash flow improves…"

"Gertrude," I interrupt her. She quiets and listens. "You reviewed the books in more detail than anyone. They run a very profitable business." I stop and catch her gaze, speaking pointedly. "We both know their cash flow being a little tight wasn't the reason the line was pulled. I trust you would have mentioned it when we were together."

Gertrude stares, deliberating her response. Finally glancing around the bank and finding no one within earshot, she still speaks quietly. "Perhaps if the loan had a co-signer, I wouldn't need to go back to the committee to re-open the line," she suggests.

"Where do I sign?"

Gertrude nods and prints some papers from her computer. She slides them over to my side of the desk. "This will make you personally liable for the loan. Are you sure you want to do this, Jackson?"

"If that's what it takes for you to open back up the line of credit. Yes."

"It won't seem unusual, since you're going to be part owner of the business soon." She says as I sign the paperwork. I don't mention the sale is off.

"Would you like me to call Ms. St. Claire and let her know we will be opening it back up as soon as the paperwork is notarized and filed?"

"No. Definitely not. She can't know I'm guaranteeing the loan." I lean forward in my chair and lower my voice as if I'm telling her a secret, although I'd scream it from the rooftops if I thought it would help. "I'm in love with Lily and I just want to help her."

Her eyebrows jump with surprise, but her face softens and a warm smile forms at her lips. "That's very noble of you, Jackson. But I'm not sure it's quite ethical to hide the source of the loan guarantee."

"Do you think what went on to get this loan pulled was ethical, Gertrude?" I ask not letting her eyes evade mine.

She takes a deep breath. "Ms. St. Claire put in an application to have the loan decision reconsidered. I'll call her and give her the good news I was able to approve the application on reconsideration." She smiles.

"You're the best, Gertrude." I stand and reach over the desk, planting a kiss on her cheek. She blushes and smiles as she picks up the phone to call Lily.

Chapter 29

Lily

Day fourteen post Jackson Knight and I'm no better off than I was two weeks ago. In fact, I think I might be worse. I find myself thinking about him all the time. The first week he was relentless in his pursuit to win me back. But his multiple calls and deliveries each day have slowed. And now I find myself wondering if I've lost my chance to change my mind when I don't hear from him for a full day. When I ended things, I was so angry to learn he hadn't been honest with me about his interest in Ralley's Gyms, I couldn't see past the cloud of infuriation that engulfed me.

But for two long weeks I've replayed our time together over and over in my head. Like a record stuck in a skip, I see his eyes as he hovers over me. I could swear they're filled with real emotions. Real feelings. Something so deep and intensely genuine, it couldn't possibly be an act. Or perhaps I'm projecting my own feelings onto what I thought I saw in him. Is it even possible that everything he said is true? That once he realized how he felt about me, he didn't want to cloud my and Joe's business judgment when it was time to decide on accepting the investors' offer? Is it possible the timing was really a coincidence and the bank deciding to pull our loan had nothing to do with him?

Even if I did forgive him, a relationship that starts on a lie is riddled for failure. My father taught me that since the day I was born. Trust was everything to him. Heck, the man didn't even believe in contracts. Everything was done on trust and handshake.

At least things seem to be looking a bit more hopeful at work. I appealed City Bank's decision to close our line of credit and was shocked they actually reconsidered. Their relenting makes me question if Jax was truly involved in the decision to pull the loan in the first place. I just don't know what to believe anymore.

Either way, it made me realize we needed to take a look at all of our expenses Our cash flow has all but dried up even though we're billing out more membership fees than ever. We never used to rely on the bank so heavily. It's time I pull back the reigns and figure out where we can cut costs.

Reed comes over after work and we settle in for another Haagen-Dazs and movie night. Our third one this week. He always suggests them, feigning an urgent need to see some movie, but I know it's his way of making sure I'm okay. I really don't want to be alone, although my ass is going to be twice the size if I don't find a way to kick this bad case of melancholy I've come down with.

He doles out a full pint of ice cream into two heaping bowls and sizes up the contents. "Here you take this one. It has less."

"What if I want the one with more?" I pout, teasing.

"I'm celebrating so I get the bigger one this time. Plus, I've given you the bigger one the last five times. You better cheer up or you're going to look like your stepfather is an Olympic track and field gold medalist." He grins.

I smack him playfully. "Hey, your ass is…wait, what are you celebrating?" I've been so selfishly consumed with sadness, for a moment I panic and think I may have forgotten his birthday. Luckily it's not for another three weeks.

"I got my sales statement and commission check today from my first gallery showing." He takes out a plain white envelope from his pocket and fans his face with it, showing off proudly.

"Oh my god! How many did you sell?" I ask excitedly. It's the first thing I'm genuinely happy about in weeks.

"All but one!" Reed exclaims obviously ecstatic with the results.

My eyes bulge. He would have been thrilled to sell one. But he had thirty one paintings on display. I'm not surprised though, he's extremely talented.

My face falters. "Oh my god. I'm so sorry. Am I the only one that didn't sell?"

"No! The one of Kane didn't sell."

"Is Kane the nineteen year old whose shoulder blades jutted from his skin?"

"Yes."

"It didn't sell because he looks like a skeleton and it's scary."

He shrugs smiling. "I don't care. I'll keep him. I think he's hot."

"You would." I crinkle up my nose.

"Sit," Reed orders. "I need to tell you something."

"What?"

"You're painting sold for the most."

"Really?"

"Yes." Hesitantly he adds, "You know sales were done through a silent auction. Each one had a reserve and as long as the reserve was met, the painting went to the highest bidder."

"Okay…"

"Your reserve was five hundred. But the bidder paid more."

"How much more?"

"A lot more."

"And that is…"

"The winning bid was twenty thousand dollars."

"Twenty thousand dollars?" I inhale sharply. "That's awesome, Reed! I'm so happy for you." I pause for a moment. "Although it's kind of weird to think my picture could be hanging in some rich serial killer's living room."

"It's not."

"How do you know?"

"Because the winning bidder was Jax Knight."

Luckily there is a week's worth of work to be done in the two days before we leave for the MMA Open, otherwise the tremendous yearning I feel thinking about Jax would have me rocking back and forth in a corner somewhere.

"I spoke to our advertising rep, they have some open air space on channel seven they can give us on short notice if we have a winner at the Open. Capitalize on the publicity of a weight class champ to increase membership. Might help cash flow." Joe informs me as he walks out the front door carrying boxes we need to ship to Las Vegas for the Open.

"Great idea, Joe. Now we just need to win fights at the Open."

"I'll take care of that for you," Caden's voice surprises me, but it's the arm he wraps around my waist that brings me to an abrupt halt.

"Caden," I admonish.

"What? You don't think I'll win?"

"That's not what I meant." I peal his fingers from my waist and level him with an icy stare.

"You can't still be mad at me for what happened. I thought we moved past that." He forces the hand I'd just removed back around my waist and tugs me to him.

"Get off of me, Caden."

He ignores me and keeps going. "You just made me so mad, letting that asshole touch you."

"You're not listening to me, Caden. Get off of me."

He leans down and whispers in my ear. "You'll be begging for me to stick my dick inside you when I win." Revulsion courses through my veins.

"Don't hold your breath." I wiggle from his hold. "Finish what you need to do with Joe and go back up to 59th Street. I don't want you down here anymore." I walk away.

Chapter 30

Jax

I answer a few emails and decide to send Lily flowers. I know her and Joe will be leaving for Vegas today or tomorrow with the fighters, so I use it as an excuse to send something and wish her luck. The thought of her being anywhere near Caden makes my blood boil. I'm feeling so frustrated it's making me crazy, but I keep some semblance of control, reminding myself I have no right to feel the way that I do. It's my own fault I don't have a right anymore. I had it once and I have no one to blame but myself for losing it.

My cell phone rings and I hit REJECT, seeing my father's name flash on the screen. He thinks now that I'm back in D.C., things will eventually go back to the way they were. But things will never go back. I hate hotel living, but I'd rather be here than living on *his* property.

I shower and throw a few things in my gym bag, not bothering to pack a suit for after my workout. It's Saturday and the office will be scarce anyway. I'm just about to walk out the door when my cell goes off again. My finger hovers over the button to send the call to voicemail, assuming it's my father calling again. Instead City Bank appears on my screen.

"Hello, Mr. Knight?"

"Yes."

"This is Gertrude Waters."

"Hi Gertrude. How are you?"

"I'm good. But I wanted to discuss something with you. Do you have a minute?"

"Sure. What's up?"

"Well. I had to finish my report on the Ralley's Gym financing…" Gertrude trails off. I never withdrew my financing application, even though the sale wasn't happening anymore. I was afraid the bank might use it as another reason to pull Lily's line of credit. I expect Gertrude to tell me she knows what I've done, but she doesn't.

"I took a little extra time going through the reports I took back with me. Hoping maybe I could find some redundancies between all the gyms that I could suggest to Ms. St. Claire to consolidate for savings considering their cash flow was a bit tight."

"That's great, Gertrude. Thank you."

"Well. The problem is I did find some things. But they weren't the type of things I had expected to find."

"What do you mean?"

"I downloaded the vendor payments from all sixty two stores into one file and sorted them by name. I thought perhaps I'd find duplicate insurance policies or memberships that could be eliminated. Since the gyms all have their own set of books, it would be hard to see redundant expenses unless they were all merged together."

"Okay."

"I did find one expense that seemed to be recurring throughout all the locations. It wasn't huge individually, a thousand dollars per location, but when you add them up…and sixty one of the sixty two locations were paying this vendor for almost the last year, it amounted to roughly three quarters of a million dollars."

"What was the expense for?"

"That's what I wasn't sure of. So I called one of the locations and they told me it was a management fee they were instructed to pay monthly from the main office."

"Who is it to?"

"Ralley Training, Inc."

"Maybe it's a loan that Joe gave to the business at one time?"

"I thought that at first too. But there wasn't a loan on the Ralley's balance sheet. So then I looked up Ralley Training and it's not owned by Joe Ralley.

"Who is it owned by?"

"It's owned by Caden Ralley."

Rage travels through my veins like electricity through a two hundred and twenty volt live wire. "Are you sure?"

"I am, Jackson."

"Did you tell Lily?"

"Not yet."

"Don't."

"But…"

"I'll take care of it."

"Are you sure?"

"I'm absolutely positive."

"Anyone can enter the MMA Open, right?" I say to Mario, my trainer at the D.C. Ralley's Gym, without offering an explanation as I put on my sparring gloves.

"Yep."

"How are the matchups chosen?"

"Sealed gym ranking. The trainers rank the fighters they put in and they match up within weight class based on the ranking."

"How do you rank a fighter who has never fought in a professional fight?"

"You thinking about entering?" Mario smiles.

"Not thinking about it. Doing it."

"It's about fucking time."

"Can you rank me so I get matched up with someone specifically?"

"Has the guy fought in a sanctioned fight before?"

"Yes."

"Then no."

"Why not?"

"Max someone can rank an inexperienced fighter is a level five. Most fighters that have won a few fights will be a six or better."

Fuck.

I blow through two sparring partners in ten minutes, feeling more angry than when I started. Fighting usually helps me blow off steam. But this morning the more I hit, the more enraged I become. The third one gives me more of a challenge, catching me off guard with a strike that's more powerful than a usual sparring partner gives and we go at it full force.

I hit him with a series of quick strikes and he stumbles back, his back arching against the ropes. He grins at me, seemingly delighted at finding a worthy opponent. If this were a real fight, I'd not have let him regroup. Instead, I would have followed up with a leg strike hoping to double him over and bring him down with a knee to the back.

Mario reminds us we're practicing and we take turns maneuvering take downs on each other until we're both drenched in sweat. A crowd forms around the ring, some of the regulars stopping to watch our show.

"Boys!" Mario yells, grabbing our attention. "You want one minute full strength to have at it. I'll climb in and ref." We both nod.

Mario calls the start of the fight and I waste no time. Instead of dancing around the ring, showing off some meaningless fancy footwork and wasting my energy, I attack with all my might. A strong right makes my opponent wobble, but he quickly regains his footing. So I throw a roundhouse kick that lands square on his chest and it takes him off guard, knocking the wind out of him. I use the element of surprise to my advantage and easily take him to the ground. Mario gave us a minute, but I had him down and out in thirty seconds.

I shower and walk to Mario on the way out. "You look really good in there. You know who that guy you just put to shame is?"

I shake my head.

"Your weight class, won six out of eight. Ranked a nine." He shakes his head and chuckles. "Did you think I was blowing smoke up your ass every day telling you that you were good enough to make it?"

I force a smile, still feeling defeated even though I just won. "Yeah, but I need a fight against a guy who's probably ranked like that guy."

"Can't help you there," he pauses, "but you got an inside connection."

I furrow my brow.

"The guy running the fight," he reminds me, "Vince Stone. I seem to remember seeing a small mention in the paper once that you were related to him," he adds sarcastically, considering it was the headline for weeks.

Chapter 31

Jax

*T*hunder crashes in the sky, echoing through dark, ominous clouds. The plane shakes and bounces through the turbulent late night sky, reminding us of who's really in control. Mother Nature. And she's one pissed off woman right now.

The flight attendants sit strapped in their jump seats looking haggard from the weary day of travel. The dimmed cabin lights that are supposed to help passengers relax on the evening flight only serve to help bring attention to the flashes of lightening that explode in the sky.

Eventually we land in Vegas after what seems like the longest four hours in history. I'm about ready to hop over the seats to get past the twenty passengers standing in the aisle trying to pull their luggage out of the overhead compartments. I need out of this god damn tin can!

Fights start tomorrow, but my weight class pre-qualifiers aren't until the day after, so I have some time to rest and try to get myself matched up with Caden. I deliberated for hours over asking anything from the brother I've barely even met and hated since I found out he existed. But eventually, my need to beat the shit out of Caden and settle Lily's score once and for all outweighed my own animosity and hang-ups with my half-brother. In the end, all he did was be born anyway. It was our asshole father that set all the destruction that would come later in life into action.

I check into Caesar's Palace, the place is crawling with jacked guys obviously here as contestants or devout fans. Sleep comes easily for the first night in a long time, exhaustion finally kicking in. The time change west works for me, I sleep later than I normally would, yet I'm up an hour before I'd ever get out of bed back in D.C. Throwing on some sweats, I decide to go for a run, beat the rise of the Nevada heat.

Walking through the quiet lobby, I catch sight of a woman from the side. Long wavy auburn hair, a straight nose and high cheekbones. My suspicion becomes abundantly clear as I move closer.

"Liv?"

She turns, a look of shock on her face at seeing me quickly turns to confusion. "Jax? What are you doing here?"

"I came for the fight. Guess I don't have to ask what you're doing hanging around near a fight anymore."

She smiles. "Are you fighting?"

"That depends."

She furrows her brow, "On what?"

"On you talking your boyfriend into helping me." I grin mischievously.

"Oh no." She holds up her hands, gesturing there's no way in hell she wants any part of whatever it is I'm talking about. "Last time I got between the two of you, it didn't turn out too well."

"Well that's because he thought I was trying to hit on you."

"And you weren't?" She arches an eyebrow.

I chuckle because she has me dead on. "Okay. So maybe I was. But I'm a one woman man and my heart belongs to another woman." I smirk and wink. "Try not to be too devastated. You had your chance."

She shakes her head. "You're going to cause me trouble aren't you?" She asks wearily, although there's a smile on her face.

"Probably. But you'll help me anyway."

She sighs loudly. "Come, sit and have coffee with me and I'll see what I can do."

It's almost eight at night before my cell phone rings. When I didn't hear from Liv all day, I figured Vince had no interest in helping me and I'd already decided what I was going to do in my head. I'm entering the Open no matter what. Brady's right, I need to work on things I want to change in my life as a long-term strategy. Winning back Lily is important, but so is fighting. I've wasted so much time already, I'm going to really go for it. Gone are the days of living a life that makes me feel dead inside. I've got enough money to live for a long time, I'm about to start really living.

"Hey," Liv says when I answer. "Sorry it took me so long. Vince was busy all day doing press work and I didn't get to speak to him alone until tonight."

"How did it go?"

"Well…," she trails off.

"He's sitting right there, isn't he?"

"Yes."

"He won't help me?"

"Vince would like to talk to you himself."

"Let me guess, he's not happy I approached you?"

"Very good," she says cryptically. I picture Vince sitting right near her while she's talking, steam billowing from his ears.

"When can I talk to him? Qualifiers start in the morning."

"Can you come up to room 3200?"

"I'm walking out the door right now." I waste no time grabbing my keycard and heading up.

The irony doesn't escape me as the elevator climbs its way to the top level of the building. I've cut out the excesses in my life, checking into a regular room, yet my brother has the entire top floor penthouse suite. The same brother who didn't grow up with any excess…whose mother struggled while things were handed to me on a silver platter by our father. The heavy pendulum finally swings the other way.

Liv greets me at the door and leads me into the sunken living room. The room is spacious and doused in heavy plush fabrics. A large sectional takes up half the room. Typical Vegas overindulgence, a place where they put the celebrities or high rollers.

Vince stands, as do two other men. One looks familiar, the other I don't think I've ever seen before. I extend my hand to Vince first, he hesitates but shakes my hand with a firm grip. "Vince." I nod. "Thanks for seeing me."

He looks me in the eye when he responds, making sure he gets the point across. "Don't work me through Liv ever again."

"I…," I think about trying to explain that isn't what I intended to do, but really it's what I did. So I go for humble instead. "Point taken. Won't happen again."

He nods and then makes introductions. "This is my trainer, Nico Hunter." I shake his hand, the name finally making the connection as to why the enormous guy looks so familiar to me. He's a legend. Killed a guy in the ring early on in his career and dropped out of the circuit for a while. Came back and took the title, one of the few undefeated heavyweights ever to retire from the sport. "Nice to meet you. Big fan. I grew up watching you. Hell, I wanted to *be* you."

The big guy smiles and shakes my hand, but says nothing. Next Vince introduces an older gentleman. "This old bastard is Preach. Don't let him get your ear. He'll spend an hour trying to convince you he's the reason both me and Nico have belts."

Preach mutters something under his breath and extends his hand, "I *am* the only reason, they're both just too full of themselves to admit it out loud. But they know it where it counts." He pats his hand on his chest over his heart.

The spirited banter between the obviously close men breaks the ice and I relax a bit, taking in a hopeful breath.

"So Liv tells me you want to fight in the Open."

"I'm already registered. But I'd like to match up to a certain fighter."

"Because he is your girlfriend's ex?" Vince prompts.

"She's not my girlfriend anymore." My heart wrenches in my chest admitting it. "But I just found out he's been stealing from her for a year."

"And the woman is The Saint's daughter?" Preach whistles. "Boy's lucky The Saint passed on. Me and The Saint go way back, that little girl was the light of his eye."

I nod. "I bet she was. She's incredible."

Nico interrupts. "But you've never fought in a pro match before, so you can't rank at the level of the guy you want to fight? That's your problem."

"That's right."

"So you want me to screw with the rating card, put my reputation on the line, so you can get revenge on some asshole who is a thief?" Vince asks.

When you put it that way, it sounds like I'm asking for a lot. I feel whatever hope I'd felt momentarily slip through my fingers. "It's more than that. He took advantage of her after her father passed away. Started skimming the week he passed away and then snaked himself into her bed when she was vulnerable. Guy's more than a thief, he's abusive."

"Abusive? How?" My statement perks up the attention of Nico.

"He wasn't happy when we got together, even though she had already broken things off with him. Caught him with his forearm pressed up against her throat one night." Nico's jaw flexes and there's a silent exchange between him and Vince. Something I've said has hit a sore spot with these men, so I keep going. "Her entire neck was purple from the hold he had her in. I'm afraid to think of what the crazy asshole would have done to her had I not come in when I did." I pause. "Look, I love Lily, but I fucked things up between us myself. I hate it, but I accept she doesn't want to be with me. I'd be lying to you all if I said I wasn't motivated by wanting to dish out revenge. But the asshole deserves a good beating. If you don't want to help me, at least match him up with someone who is going to teach him a lesson."

The men stare at me in silence for a moment. "Preach, you keep your refs license current?" Vince questions.

"Sure do." Preach nods.

"You willing to fight Nico to earn the points you need to get in the ring with the guy?"

I look to Nico and back. The guy is gargantuan, but it doesn't even matter to me at this point.

I stand tall and look Vince straight in the eye. "Yes."

Vince holds my gaze in silence for a long moment, assessing my sincerity. "I'll bump up your rating and see you get matched up with the asshole."

Confused, I furrow my brow. "So I don't have to fight Nico first?"

Vince smiles. "Nah, he's got fifty pounds on you and still trains like he's got the fight of his life coming up. He'd annihilate you."

The three men have a good laugh at my expense and I stick around for another half an hour, even sharing a beer.

"Good luck," Vince says opening the door as I'm leaving.

"Thanks. I appreciate everything."

"No problem. I'm glad to find out you're not an asshole like that father of ours."

"That he is." I smile, shake Vince's hand and walk out the door of my brother's penthouse suite.

Chapter 32

Lily

I wake early to go check on the Ralley's banners and sign placement. We paid a fortune for the advertising, I can't afford not to have it seen on TV as much as possible. Once I shower, I flip on the local news, not surprisingly the Open is the hot topic for the Vegas headlines. A picture of Vince Stone flashes on the screen. It's from his championship fight and the ref is holding up his hand in victory. There's a smile on his face and his eyes are shining brightly, a hint of his brother gleams from beneath his piercing baby blues. It's more than just the color, there's a passion, a determination, something that makes me think the two men have more in common than meets the eye.

The familiar ache in my chest rises to my throat. I swallow the pain down, there's too much I need to focus on today to let thoughts of Jax consume me yet again. The TV screen splits from a picture of Vince to the two brothers side by side. I flick the switch on the remote to turn it off, my heart wrenching at the longing I feel from just seeing Jax's picture. The attention of the Open and Vince Stone likely brought the old headlines back into the limelight. The media just can't resist when it comes to three strikingly handsome, yet vastly different, men with an easily sensationalized story. The gritty and sexy Vince the fighter, the handsome and confident successful businessman Jackson, and their dapper Senator father who kept the relationship between the three a secret for almost twenty-five years. It's a ratings dream for the newscasters just from showing pictures of three irresistible men.

A knock at the door I expect to be room service breaks my thoughts. My hand on the knob, I peer through the peephole and find Caden on the other side of the door. There's no way I'm letting him in my hotel room. I've accepted his apology because he's Joe's nephew, but it doesn't come close to trusting him enough to be alone in a hotel room. We both made mistakes, I don't plan to repeat mine.

"Who is it?" I ask fully knowing.

"Caden."

"Oh. Caden, I'm not dressed yet," I lie.

"So?" He's offended, I can tell by his tone.

"Did you need something? I'm running late."

"Open the door, Lily," he says with impatience.

"No, Caden. I'm not dressed. What can I do for you?"

He hits the door. I jump, not expecting the bang. "Open the door, Lily," he warns.

"I'm going to call security if you don't leave, Caden."

"Don't bother." It's quiet for a minute and I think he might have left, so I look through the peephole. I know he can't see me, yet he looks right at the door, a sadistic smile on his face, holding a paper in his head. "They posted the matches. Just wanted to tell you to enjoy the fight today." He turns and walks away.

I spend the morning running around, checking in with the Ralley's managers that have come out for the Open, bringing their best fighters. We have five fighters in the Open, including two first timers with great potential and Caden. Joe and I meet at the sponsor check in desk, as usual, we're last in line, checking in at the last minute. I'm distracted by the man sitting at the end of the long table. Vince Stone. The line to have him sign an autograph is longer than the line for the check in. Joe and I chat while we wait our turn for our passes and tickets, but I'm constantly drawn to steal glances at Vince. He catches me a few times and smiles. By the time we make our way to the table, Vince is done and walks over. I suck in a breath and try to keep myself from overtly staring, though it's no use. He probably thinks I'm star struck, but I'm struck by the resemblance. It's not something you see easily, rather it's the mannerisms, the slight uptick on the side of his mouth when he's amused but trying to hide it. The sexy confidence that draws a crowd without so much as a word.

My words stuck in my throat, Joe steps forward and introduces himself. "Vince. How are ya? Joe Ralley from Ralley's Gyms." Vince shakes his hand and nods and looks to me. Awkwardly, I say nothing, so Joe does the formality. "This is my partner, Lily St. Claire, she's the daughter of…"

"The Saint," Vince Stone finishes Joe's sentence and extends his hand. "Nice to meet you Lily. I've heard a lot about you."

You have? I smile and shake his hand, words finally coming from my moving mouth. "Nice to meet you, Vince." Curiosity gets the best of me and I can't help but ask. "Were you a friend of my fathers?"

"No. I didn't know him. But my trainers said he was a great guy. I'm sorry for your loss," he says sincerely.

"Thank you." I furrow my brow.

"My brother," he says, seeing the confusion on my face.

"I didn't realize you two…," I trail off, not quite sure how to finish the sentence.

Vince smirks. "We didn't. Until last night." He leans down and kisses me sweetly on the cheek. "Go easy on him. He's not such an asshole after all." He winks and then disappears.

My dad never missed going to the locker room to wish his fighters luck before a match. My gut tells me I should skip going to see Caden, but I'm with Joe, so I feel safe. Marco is wrapping his hands when we enter. I try to keep distance between us but Caden jumps from the table he's sitting on and comes right to me. He hooks his big hand around my neck and pulls me for a kiss. It happens so fast, I barely have time to turn my head to give him my cheek.

"You're not even gonna give me a nice good luck kiss?" he grumbles, annoyed at my response to his unwelcomed advance.

"I came to wish you luck, I see it was a mistake."

"Oh, come on, Lil." Completely ignoring my resistance, he wraps an arm around my waist. "Since when are you such a prude?"

"Caden, keep your hands to yourself," Joe warns.

"Guess I should be thankful you're here in my corner and not rooting for that pretty boy," Caden mumbles jumping back up on the table for Marco to continue with his hands.

"What pretty boy? Who did you match against?"

Caden smirks a sinister smile. "You don't know?"

"Why would I be asking if I knew?"

Marco hands me the fight card without a word. *Jackson Knight, Washington D.C.*

My eyes bulge. "Did you know about this?" I ask Joe.

"Don't look at me, I've been with you all day." Joe takes the card and reads it for himself.

"Three minutes till call." A guy wearing a headphone pops in the room. "Let's go."

Vicious doesn't even begin to describe the grin plastered on Caden's face. It's so evil and vindictive, it sends a chill up my spine and I'm not the one getting in the ring.

The arena is jam packed, the crowd loud with excitement. The usher explains that the last fight went the full three rounds and was the closest fight he's seen in years. "Both bloodied. You missed a good one," he says excitedly as he points out our seats in the dimly lit arena.

We're four rows back from the octagon, I've felt numb since I read the card. I feel like I should do *something*. Not sit around and watch like I'm a bystander. I feel way too involved in whatever is about to happen in the ring to do *nothing*. Although I have no idea what that something would be.

Dad fought from the time I was a baby until I was sixteen. Yet I never watched a single fight. I was always there, but never in the arena. At first I was too young to watch, Dad said I wouldn't have understood and watching him get into a fight would have upset me. By the time I was old enough to understand that it wasn't a fight, it was a sport, a profession, I'd already gotten into the habit of watching the fight *after* the fight, on replay. I always felt it was my job to wait in Dad's locker room anyway. I thought it brought him good luck since he won every time I did it. Sitting here now, I realize waiting in the locker room probably wasn't good luck for Dad, but I'd give anything in the world to be in Jax's locker room waiting for him at this moment.

Unlike title fights or main bouts, qualifying rounds are short. Three, three minute rounds with a minute rest between each. Winners move on to the finals, where rounds become longer and strike strength commonly leads to concussions for those that aren't properly trained.

The lights flicker and a few seconds later the music comes on overhead. The entrances into the ring are a blur, I try to see Jax but I'm too short and can't see over the crowd from the position of the door. Luckily, qualifying rounds don't have much pomp and circumstance, and I'm grateful when the announcer starts in quickly after they reach the Octagon.

"Ladies and Gentlemen, in the red corner, standing six-feet-two-inches tall, weighing in at two hundred and one pounds, with a record of four and one…I give you Caden 'The Barbarian' Catone. The crowd goes crazy, I'm positive most people in the room have no idea who Caden is, but the adrenaline in the room is running high for any fight. Joe looks at me and nods, just like Dad it's his way of telling me it will all be okay. Then he takes my hand.

"Ladies and Gentlemen, in the blue corner, standing six-feet-two-inches tall, weighing in at two hundred and three pounds, with a record of one and zero…I give you Jackson 'Pretty Boy' Knight." The crowd goes crazy again, even though they've never even heard his name before. Heck, I'm not even sure when he could have possibly won his first fight.

The announcer speeds through a list of rules and rattles off some information about disciplines I can't make out between his mumble and the swiftness of his words. The two men turn to make their way to their respective corners and Jax is facing my direction for the first time since he entered the arena. My heart flutters seeing him again, being so near. He is undeniably gorgeous, every woman's fantasy, only he's real, in the flesh and my pulse races at the sight of it all. He's tall and strikingly handsome with a stubbled masculine jaw and eyes the color of the sky on a perfect cloudless day. And his body, oh that body. The muscles in my thighs tighten remembering tracing the valleys that define his muscles with my tongue. I'm not the only one to take notice either. You'd have to be blind not to find something to catch your attention and leave your mouth hanging open staring at Jackson Knight shirtless and ready for a fight. Women whistle and catcall to him like construction workers when a pretty girl with big boobs passes by in the heat of summer. Jax either doesn't care or he's so focused he doesn't let outside interference in. The women sitting behind me describe, in detail, the things they'd like to do to him. Joe squeezes my hand as I'm just about to turn and give them a piece of my mind.

Caden has only Marco in his corner, but Jax has a small team. Marco's cousin Mario, who trains Jax in the D.C. Ralley's Gym, is standing in front of him giving him a prefight talk. Flanking Marco to the left is Vince Stone, to the right the legendary Nico Hunter. A third, older man stands behind the cage as the men all huddle in the final moment before the fight begins. Jax nods his head and puts in his mouthpiece and the men take turns wishing him good luck before stepping out of the cage. Vince is the last one in the cage and my heart swells watching the two brothers share a moment. Something happened in the last few weeks to bring the men together, whatever it was, it appears to have been the beginning of a bond. With no trainers left in the cage, Jax takes a moment and scans the crowd. At first I think he's taking the moment in, searing a picture into his memory. But then his eyes find mine through the crowd and I realize he was looking for me. There's probably five thousand screaming spectators in the arena, but for one second in time everything else fades away and there's only me and Jax. He doesn't smile or acknowledge me outwardly, but the look in his eyes says it all and I know there's still unfinished business between us.

The first round is only three minutes long, but it feels more like three days. I quickly learn why my dad had always insisted that I stay behind in the locker room, rather than watching ringside. I've been to thousands of fights, but it's way more difficult to watch a fight when you're in love with the person inside the cage. I may not have spoken to him in weeks, but my feelings haven't quelled one bit. Seeing Jax so close again only reminds me I'm far from over him.

I suck in a deep breath as the bell rings and squeeze Joe's hand so hard my knuckles turn white. There's no fancy footwork and dancing around foreplay in this fight. Boldly, Jax strikes first. Lightning fast and powerful, the rapidness of his moves catches Caden off guard and he stumbles back a step as he lands a blow to the chest. Caden's face changes, dark fury and anger rising to the surface and he retaliates just as quickly as Jax made the first strike, only he retaliates with a roundhouse kick followed by a strong right elbow to the shoulder. And then it only escalates. Blow after blow, landing strike after strike, the two men literally beat each other breathless by the time the bell dings. The referee has to pull them apart, I'm not even sure either man actually heard the call for the end of the round, they're both so laser focused on pulverizing each other.

I let out a breath I quite possibly have been holding since the round started and my head is dizzy for air. The trainers rush in to treat the fighters, both already bloodied, skin splitting from brutal fists to the face.

"You okay?" Joe asks pensively, catching sight of my face.

"No."

"Can't remember the last time I saw a fight like this. There's a lot of heart up on that mat today, that's for damn sure.

Neither one of those boys is going to stop until one of them can't move a muscle anymore."

That's completely what I'm afraid of. The two men are back at it after a rest that was too short for me to catch my breath, no less a fighter. Again, there's no jumping around or warm ups, the blows starting almost immediately. Caden lands a strike connecting directly to the right side of Jax's jaw and I watch in slow motion as Jax's head flails back from the sheer momentum of the blow. A real wave of nausea rolls over me and I worry I might be physically sick. Jax stumbles but remains on his feet. Taking full advantage of his opponent's unsteady stance, Caden follows up with a leg kick from his rear leg that lands on Jax's inner upper thigh, frighteningly close to the groin. The ref steps in and gives Caden a warning. Groin strikes are illegal and inside leg kicks are the easiest place to slip up with an accidental groin strike. Although with Caden, it wouldn't be an accident, he's known for fighting dirty and I'm glad the ref either sees it or knows of his reputation.

Jax backpedals in a subtle manner, then stops and sets his feet. He quickly swivels his hips thrusting his rear left leg forward and lands a low strike on Caden just below the knee. Catching Caden in a moment of unbalance forces him to retreat from his attack and reset himself. Not many fighters would have taken two strong hits and have been able to turn it around so quickly like Jax just did. Whereas Caden's strength is in his offense, Jax is equally strong both offensively and defensively and seems to have picked up on Caden's weaknesses quickly.

Jax plants his feet again and prepares to unload another kick. This time Caden sees it coming, however, he assumes it will be another attack to his leg. Defensively, Caden drops his posture preparing to catch the kick and turns, leaving his head unprotected. Jax strikes, landing a powerful kick flush to Caden's face and stumbles him backwards again. Before Caden can reset,

Jax capitalizes with a combination of punches. Round two may have started off strong for Caden, but by the time the bell dings, Jax has turned things around and clearly taken the points.

Round three opens no different than the two before, with the two men delivering blow after blow. Jax takes each hit in stride, without as much as a waiver of his balance. Frustrated, and the effects of the relentless pummeling beginning to show on Caden, Jax lunges, forcing him to the ground and the two men grapple for dominant positioning.

Jax moves fast, and within seconds he has Caden in some convoluted hold that looks like if Caden moves a fraction of an inch, his arm might snap in two. But Caden is way too stubborn to give. He'd sooner have his arm shattered and be forced out on a stretcher than concede anything in this fight. Jax twists his body again to add pressure, there is no possible way Caden isn't in excruciating pain, yet an eerily sadistic smile crosses Caden's face. Right before he delivers a heal strike from the guard directly to the kidney. A completely illegal move for a reason.

The referee calls a timeout, scolding Caden as he sends him to his corner for committing the foul and checks on Jax who is writhing in pain on the mat.

"There's an ugly streak in that boy. I know he's my nephew, but god damn him, if he can't win a fight fair and square, he tries to steal it," Joe grumbles, as we both look on at the ref attending to Jax.

Jax motions he wants to continue, the ref forcing him to take another minute before bringing the two back to the center of the ring. The ref spends a minute dishing a stern warning to Caden and then the two are back at it. Unfortunately, the foul accomplished what Caden set out to do, allow him time to reset and catch his breath again. With less than ninety seconds left on the clock, the blows start back up again right away. Jax just needs to keep things at bay and he'll win by decision. Even if the judges weighed the first round as even, Jax dominated the second and this one is weighing heavily in his favor.

With an easy leg sweep, Jax takes Caden to the ground again and the two men roll around. Jax captures Caden in a scarf hold, but his grip slips and Caden escapes. It would have been easy for Caden to assume the dominating position, and score points with the judges, but instead he pops to his feet unexpectedly and rears his leg up high, stomping heavily on Jax who's still grounded. The force of his illegal stomp from the upright position to Jax's exposed torso, likely breaking at least one rib.

The ref jumps between the men before Caden can stomp again, but like a starving wild animal ready to attack anything in the way of its weakened prey, Caden throws a punch at the ref. And then the cage fills…security, trainers, judges, Vince Stone and Nico Hunter even flanking to stop the ensuing mayhem.

The crowd roars to a frenzied level, people standing on their seats and filling the aisles. Luckily, the organizers know how easily things can go from bad to worse in a room filled with raging testosterone, and they are prepared. Thank god. A few minutes later the cage is empty except for Jax, his trainer, and Vince Stone, and the crowd is back under control. The referee raises Jax's arm, declaring him the winner by disqualification and he winces at the pain in his ribs as his arm is lifted.

Chapter 33

Jax

"At least everything underneath is clear," the ER Doctor turns the portable cart to face me and the large screen lights up with x-rays. He points to an area of my ribcage. "You have a fracture here, but the lungs and spleen are intact. It's probably going to feel like you were trampled by a herd of elephants for a while with the looks of that bruise already forming, but it's a clean break and will heal."

"What's the treatment for it?"

"Not much. We used to wrap patients in a rib belt, but a while back they did a study and found it didn't provide any benefit. It'll heal on its own, with plenty of rest and pain killers." The doctor takes out his prescription pad. "Ice for twenty minutes of every hour when you're awake for the next two days. I'm going to prescribe you a week of Vicodin to start out. Did you drive?" he asks Vince.

Vince nods.

"Good I'm going to give you a loading dose now to get you more comfortable and hopefully you can get some rest tonight." The doctor looks over my face, turning it to the right and then the left, examining the lacerations. "Hate to see what the other guy looks like if you won." He shakes his head. "You staying with him tonight?" again he addresses Vince, but this time I respond.

"I'm alone, but I'm fine," my voice trails off, breathing hurts, but speaking is even worse.

"You're fine now. Can't always see everything on an x-ray though. If your breathing gets too shallow tonight could indicate a small puncture we can't see. You shouldn't be alone." The Doctor looks at me and then Vince and back to me.

Vince speaks up. "He'll stay with us tonight."

"I'm…," I begin to object but Vince talks right over me.

"We're good. Suite has an extra bedroom." I look at him uneasily and he smiles and teases. "We'll make forts out of sheets and catch up for the shit we missed doing the first twenty years."

I wake confused, looking around at the room I'm in, nothing looks familiar. The heavy drapes are drawn but I can still see the glimmer of sunshine peering in through the small gap pulling them closed left behind. I cough, pain shoots in my chest and I groan from the grueling ache in my ribs. Someone cracks open the bedroom door and peaks in, but says nothing.

"Who's there?" I ask. Speaking increases the intensity of the pain and shortens each breath to the point where I feel like I'm drowning. It makes me gasp for air and I cough again.

"It's Liv," she whispers and opens the door wider. "I didn't want to wake you."

"I'm up."

"Are you in pain?"

"Yeah. It feels like I was run over by a Mac Truck. And then it backed up and did it again."

"You slept so long your pain meds probably wore off. I'll get your pills and some water."

"Wait."

"What?"

"Where am I?"

"In the Penthouse suite."

"I don't remember getting up here last night."

"You were pretty out of it. Vince said the Doctor gave you a double dose of meds before you left the hospital and you were out before you got back to the hotel. Took Vince, Nico, and Preach to get you up here."

Shit. I don't remember a thing. Last I remember, I was still sitting in the hospital with Vince and the doctor came in to tell me my rib was broken. Liv disappears and comes back a minute later with water and a pill. I sit up in the bed, the change in position is painful.

"Thanks." I gulp down the water and the pill.

"What time is it?"

"Four."

"In the afternoon?"

She giggles. "Yes, in the afternoon."

"Where's Vince?"

"He had to go down for some appearances and then to host the afternoon session."

I sit up a bit straighter, wincing when my chest muscles flex, but pull the covers off of me. "I should go."

"I think you should rest."

"I will. But I'm going to go back to my room."

"Ummm...," she hesitates. "I brought all your stuff up here. Vince gave me your key card and I checked you out of your room."

"Thanks. It's about time I head back to D.C. anyway. I'm good. I can get around. But I appreciate everything." I swing my legs to the side of the bed. Fuck, it hurts like hell when I move.

"I think you should stay," Liv says. "For Vince's benefit too."

"Why for Vince?"

"He was pretty riled up last night. Nico had to talk him down from hunting down the guy you fought. He takes the sport very seriously and says guys like that set back the advances of getting it accepted as a legitimate sport by ten years." She pauses. "Nico has to leave tonight. His wife is pregnant with their second child and they have a one year old. I'm surprised he even came."

"Not sure I'm in any condition to stop Vince from doing anything."

"Maybe not. But having you here is good for him too. He'll never admit it, but he's been curious about you since he found out you were related."

I smile because I've felt the same way.

"Will you stay?"

"Yeah." The truth is, I was only leaving because it seemed like the right thing to do. I have nowhere I need to be anyway. "Do you know where my phone is?"

"Sure, I'll get it for you."

Liv opens the curtains and brings me some fruit while I check my phone. There are hundreds of new texts. Brady, Marco, my father, business associates that saw the fight...but none from the one name I want to see flash on my phone. I didn't jump into the ring with the foolish notion that winning would mean I'd win Lily back, but seeing her face in the arena last night I thought maybe, just maybe, there was a chance in hell. I toss the phone on the end table feeling rejected all over again.

"She didn't call?" Liv asks reluctantly.

I shake my head no.

"I was on the other side of the arena with Vince during the fight, but Vince pointed out who she was. I watched her reactions as she watched the fight. She sat on the edge of her seat the entire time. Nervous. She was white as a ghost when Caden stomped you. I saw her run toward the cage. But then I lost her in the crowd. I think she still cares about you if that matters," she offers trying to make me feel better, but it feels more like pity.

I attempt a smile, she's sweet for trying to help. "Thanks, I'm going to take a shower."

"Jax?"

I turn back.

"It's her loss if she doesn't forgive you, because you're totally worth forgiving."

Chapter 34

Lily

I barely slept last night thinking about Jax. Wondering if he's alright, how he's feeling after the fiasco in the ring. He walked away, but he's bound to be in pain today. The insanity of what Caden did yesterday still leaves me unsettled. Surely he'll be barred from ever competing again in the octagon. No organization accepts multiple intentional fouls.

Sitting at our table at the Sponsors' luncheon I know I should be networking, but I feel empty. Everything seems hollow and meaningless. Like there's a gaping hole in my heart that I'll walk around with for the rest of my life unable to be filled.

"You okay, dear?" An older women sitting at the table with white hair and deeply set wrinkles asks. Her smile is soft and her face warm and concerned.

"Yes, thank you." I smile politely.

"Man trouble?" she asks, leaning in.

I smile at her persistence. "Is it that obvious?"

She nods. "I was married for forty-one years. Lost my Gerald last year."

"I'm sorry to hear that."

"Want some advice?"

I haven't even told her the problem, so I'm not so sure how she could advise me to fix it. But I'm polite nonetheless because she seems sweet.

"Sure." I smile.

"There's only two choices with a man. Forgive him or forget him. If you can't do the latter, then you need to forgive him because he's already stolen your heart."

I have no idea what I expected her to say, but it certainly wasn't that. So simple. So poignant. So clear. Yet it takes a woman I've never met to point out the obvious. I stand and kiss her on the check. "Thank you."

She nods knowingly.

"Can you tell me what room Jackson Knight is in, please?" I ask the clerk at the front desk.

"I'm sorry, we can't give out that information."

I show her my sponsor badge, as if it carries some sort of authority. "I'm a sponsor here, I'm supposed to meet him this evening, but I'm going to be a little late and I just want to let him know," I lie. "Do you think maybe you could help me? My boss will kill me if I blow this deal."

The woman hesitates, assessing me briefly, but then punches a few keystrokes on her computer and looks up at me confused. "I'm sorry. Mr. Knight has already checked out."

"Do you know when?"

She punches a few more keys. "Last night. Looks like he checked out early." She shrugs. "Oh wait a minute. I remember Mr. Knight. I checked him out last night. He was the one that was injured during the fight, right?"

"Yes, that's him."

"Right. He didn't leave actually. His girlfriend brought back his key. She said he was going to be staying in her room so he didn't need the room anymore." The woman whispers, "I'm not supposed to give out room information, but they're in the Penthouse if you want to reach them."

The sudden image of Jax and another woman makes my heart ache and my stomach revolt. Why hadn't it dawned on me that he would move on so quickly? I think deep down inside I believed he really cared about me. The realization I was so easily replaced rips open the wound created the day I found out he was planning on forcing Ralley's into bankruptcy. It stings with fresh pain.

A sinking feeling of despair hits me and I want nothing more than to go home. Get the hell out of the craziness that is Vegas, even though the fights aren't over yet. I walk to the elevator bank in a daze, feeling sad, the old woman's words coming back to haunt me. You either forgive or you forget. I guess I was easy to forget.

I pack up my things and call Joe to let him know I'm leaving a day ahead of schedule, but he doesn't respond. We have dinner planned with some potential vendors interested in stocking their lines in the gyms, I'm sure they'd rather talk to Joe than me anyway. But I don't want to leave without letting Joe know, so I go down to look for him.

Vince Stone is at the security desk. I smile politely and show my badge to the guard. "Lily," Vince calls from down the hall as I start to walk away.

"Everything okay?" Vince questions.

"I'm looking for Joe Ralley, have you seen him?"

He shakes his head. "Haven't seen him."

"Thanks." I take a step away and then something stops me. He may not be mine, but I can't help myself. I need to know he's okay. "Have you seen Jax? Is he okay?"

"Broken rib, pretty bruised. But he'll live," he says. "Liv said he woke up a little while ago, doc gave him pain killers so he was out like a light for half the day."

Liv. A lot has happened in the last few weeks. Jax is apparently close with a brother he despised only a few weeks ago and his new girlfriend has a name. Liv. Wonderful, how cheery, perhaps he's working his way through the alphabet, L-i-l, L-i-v.

I nod, wishing I'd never asked, and begin to walk away. Vince yells over his shoulder, "He's in the Penthouse if you want to visit."

Sure, I'd like nothing more than to spend some quality time with Jax and Liv.

Chapter 35

Jax – 2 days later

The hairs on the back of my neck rise before I see him. My body alert when he turns the corner into the hotel lobby where I'm standing. He grins, it's the face of a madman. I already know he doesn't play by the rules, the twisted fucker has balls of steal as he walks right up to me. I'm standing between Nico Hunter and Vince Stone, two of the most powerful fighters in the world, and he doesn't hesitate one bit.

Nico takes a step forward. "Give me one reason, you piece of shit."

Ignoring him completely, Caden focuses on me. "I'll be back inside that sweet pussy in a week," he leans forward and whispers. He must have a death wish. I grab him by the neck and warn, "You're out of your fucking mind, Ralley. I'll have the police waiting for you when you land in New York."

He doesn't flinch. Probably thinks I'm talking about the fight. "I know all about the money you stole. Told Joe about it this morning. Heading to talk to Lily about it now. Was going to let them decide what to do with you, but on second thought, your ass definitely needs to be locked up. So you step one foot in New York, I'll make sure you do five years for grand theft." His face is turning purple from my grip, yet he makes no attempt to break free. Twisted doesn't begin to describe how fucked up this guy is.

"He's not worth it," Vince warns.

I squeeze harder, knowing I could crush his windpipe right at this moment. I probably should, although the thought of sending this jacked up asshole with rage issues to prison is a lot more appealing than a death that comes quick and relatively pain free. I let go and he grins and walks away.

"That's one sick son of a bitch," Vince says as Caden walks away as calmly as he approached.

"No shit," Nico agrees.

My taxi pulls up out front and I say goodbye. "Thanks for everything."

"You got it." Nico says with a nod. "Take care of yourself, man. If you're ever in Chicago, stop by the gym."

I nod and turn to face my brother. "I can't thank you enough for everything. I owe you."

"You'll give Liv an exclusive when you win the title next time. Recover, get your girl back, then get back in the ring."

I smile. "Okay, but I'm going to lose a few pounds and drop down to your weight, so she has to write about how I kicked your ass."

He laughs. "In your dreams, brother. In your dreams."

At the airport, I change my ticket to D.C. in for a ticket to New York. Joe told me Lily left early. I need to tell her about Caden stealing and go to the police. If she doesn't want to be with me, I'll deal with it, but there's no way I'm letting that sick son of a bitch anywhere near her

.

Chapter 36

Lily

Not even Reed can get me to smile the last two days.

I go to work, spend twelve hours a day trying to get caught up, and come back home to share a quart of Ben and Jerry's with my best friend. I'm a ball of fun.

The last member exits, I lock the door and sit behind the reception desk to draw. It's the only thing that brings me any peace. Although it's probably not healthy because I have no desire to draw anything but Jax.

I lose myself in sketching the rigid lines of his jaw, drawing him from memory, I close my eyes and picture the stubble on his face. Remembering the way it felt under my fingers as I brushed my hand across his skin in the early morning after we spent all night exploring each other's bodies. A light tap on the door startles me from my daydream.

For a second I wonder if my memory is playing tricks on me. Because suddenly, standing a few feet on the other side of the glass, is the man in the flesh. My heart leaps in my chest and I feel more alive than I have in weeks. I take steps toward the door, but my feet feel weighed down and getting one foot in front of the other is like wading through a pool of neck high water.

I unlock the door and he opens it slowly. "Can I come in?"

I blink my eyes a few times to snap myself out of it. "Yes. Sure. Sorry, you just caught me by surprise."

I lock the door behind him and turn. He's right there, so close I could reach out and touch him. It's all I want to do, but I don't. My body is drawn to his with a pull that's surreal. It's a test of endurance just to keep my hands at my sides.

"How are you feeling?" I ask referring to his ribs.

"Better now." His eyes are such a beautiful shade of blue and so full of emotion, I almost believe that it's me that makes him feel better. Then I remember the girlfriend that was in his Penthouse taking care of him and I force down my own desires. I walk back around the counter to put a safe distance between us.

"I'm glad you had someone to take care of you."

He nods. "He turned out to be a pretty good guy."

"Your brother?"

"Yeah. Him and Liv took care of me for a few days. Doctor gave me painkillers that knocked me out pretty good."

Liv. Does he really need to bring her up? How insensitive can he be? "What can I do for you Jax?" My entire demeanor changes, my body might not know this man no longer belongs to me, but my brain sure does. I'm actually glad he brought her up, it has the effect of throwing a glass of cold water in my face. Waking me from my dreamy eyed stupor.

He furrows his brow, noticing the change. The temperature just dropped ten degrees, it would be hard not to. "Did I say something wrong?"

"No. Why would you think that?" I say, sarcasm unmistakable in my voice.

"What's going on, Lily?" he walks to the counter.

"Nothing Jax. What did you want? I'd prefer to discuss whatever it is you came here for. I really have no interest in discussing your Penthouse romp with your girlfriend."

"My girlfriend? What are you talking about?"

"Liv. I went to the front desk to see how you were feeling and they told me your girlfriend had checked you out and into her Penthouse."

"Is that what this is about?"

"No. It's about forgetting. I just need to move on with my life and you aren't helping every time you decide to pop back into it."

"You're jealous of Liv?"

"I'm not jealous of anyone!" I defend myself a little too vigorously.

"Liv is Vince's girlfriend. I was staying with Vince and Liv. In the second bedroom of the Penthouse they shared together." He crosses his arms tightly over his chest. His jaw tightens and I can't tell if it's from the argument or the touch so close to his ribs.

"Whatever. It doesn't matter. Just tell me what you're here for." My head feels so jumbled.

"You think so little of me that I would be over you so quickly? That I'd bring a woman to Vegas knowing you'd be there?"

Feeling painfully confused, I look at him, my emotions in turmoil, and he glares at me, waiting for a response. Only I have no idea what to say.

"I don't know what to say, Jax."

"You just said it all," he says quietly, his handsome face looking forlorn. "I need to tell you a few things and then I'll be gone. I won't interrupt your life anymore after that. I promise."

There's a somberness in his expression when he continues. "Caden has been stealing from you for a long time."

"What are you talking about?"

"Remember the auditor that came in? Mrs. Waters?"

"Yes."

"She consolidated the ledgers from all sixty-two of your gyms to see if she could find any redundancies when she was here. Sixty-one of the stores were paying a management fee of a thousand dollars a month to Ralley Management Inc. for the last nine months."

"Who is Ralley Management?"

"That's what she wasn't sure of. She thought maybe it was a note the gyms were paying back to Joe, so she didn't mention it at first. But the checks were cashed on a City Bank account so she was able to verify the account owner. There was only one. Caden Ralley. He's been syphoning sixty-one thousand dollars a month for close to a year. That's why your cash flow was tight. It was hard to see it since it wasn't a big amount for any one location."

A knot forms in my throat and I can barely breathe. "I don't understand."

"You said yourself you leaned on him after your father died. He took advantage. Probably set it up with the stores when you were going through a hard time, so none of the managers bothered to ask you about it."

The memory comes back to me. "I sent out an email telling the managers to work with Caden, that he would be helping keep the books organized while I was out for a while." I sit down, feeling suddenly dizzy and overwhelmed. "I'm such an idiot."

"You're not an idiot. You were devastated when your dad died and taking help was a smart decision. Caden took advantage of you."

I feel like such a fool. How could I have not noticed so much money disappearing. "What do I do now?"

"You need to report it. I'll go with you to the police if you want tomorrow. But he needs to be arrested. He's out of control and I know he's planning on coming back here. Thinks you two can get back together now that we're…" he trails off.

"Not together," I finish his sentence with a low shaky voice.

He nods.

"Okay. He should be punished for what he did to you anyway."

Jax attempts a smile. "You want me to pick you up in the morning and we can go together or you want me to meet you there?"

"I'll meet you there. The thirteenth precinct is just two blocks over."

He nods and turns toward the door. "One more thing."

"There's more?"

"I want to come clean about one thing too, Lily."

"What?" My head is spinning, I'm not sure how much more I can take.

"The bank line of credit? They didn't reconsider it and open it back up. I guaranteed it."

"I don't understand."

"I wanted to help. I can't prove it, but I have a feeling my father used his influence to hurt you and make it look like I did it. He didn't want me to invest in Ralley's. Didn't want me to stay in New York. I know you don't believe me, but I had nothing to do with the bank pulling your line of credit, Lily."

"So you guaranteed a half million dollar loan personally to fix it?"

"I'm sorry. I just didn't want any more secrets between us. I was only trying to help. Now that Caden won't be syphoning cash out, your cash flow will improve in no time and I'm sure the bank will really reconsider. Then they can cancel my guarantee and you can be totally free from me."

Nothing in the world hurts more than the thought of his last few words. Being totally free of him. But I'm so drained at this moment, I can't even think clearly.

"Thank you for doing that for me and Joe."

He looks down, seeing the drawing I'm working on for the first time and looks me in the eyes. Something clicks inside of me and I suddenly feel like I might break. Break into a million little pieces right in front of this man. He's so strong and balanced and I'm an emotional train wreck bearing down on a crash full speed ahead.

We both say nothing until he turns, grabbing the door and orders, "Lock the door behind me. Call a cab. Don't walk tonight."

Two hours later, my mind is still swirling but I know one thing. I'll never be able to forget this man. I'm not sure what I'm going to say, but when I see the towering lights of the San Marco Hotel up ahead, I tell the driver to go straight instead of turning toward my apartment.

The elevator climbs painstakingly slowly to the thirty-third floor. I smile when I realize he's staying in a regular room and not a suite. My knock on the door is so light, I'm surprised when the door opens.

Standing before me, a towel wrapped around his narrow waist, is the man I'm head over heels in love with. The one I have no choice but to forgive, because there's no chance in hell I'm ever going to be able to forget. I just hope he'll forgive me too.

We stand there staring for a long time, our eyes locked, my heart beating out of control, a connection sizzling between us more powerful than anything I've ever experienced with another human being. "I can't forget you," I whisper.

Not surprisingly, he seems confused with my comment. "Come in."

He closes the door behind him and turns to face me, goosebumps break out all over my body when he reaches his big hand down around my neck and takes a step closer to me. He squeezes my neck, forcing me to look up at him, and when I do he leans down and kisses my lips ever so gently. "I can't forget you either," he says, his nose just inches from mine.

"You were jealous of Liv? I was so pissed you thought so little of me that I would bring a woman to where I knew you'd be, I didn't even stop to realize what it meant. If you're jealous, it means you still have feelings for me. I was just showering and coming to you."

"You were?"

"Were you jealous, Lily?"

So much so that I couldn't even think straight. "Yes."

"Why?" he takes a step closer. His chest is heaving and his breathing is as labored as mine.

"Because."

"Because why, Lily?"

He wants to hear me say it. "Because the thought of you with anyone else causes me physical pain."

He takes my hand and lifts it to his mouth, kissing the palm and then every finger. "Why does it hurt?"

"You know why." My voice shakes out of me.

"No, I need you to tell me why. I need you to go first, because I've never been so sure about anything in my life and you keep running away from me."

"You hurt me."

"I know I did and I'm sorry. But I've never run away from what I feel about you. And I've been trying to show you for weeks, but you won't give me a chance. Are you really going to give me a chance this time, Angel?"

"Yes." I swallow the lump in my throat. I've been so self-consumed with how he hurt me, I never stopped to think about what I might be doing to him.

"I…" my words get stuck in my throat when I really see his chest for the first time. I've been standing here with him in a towel since he opened the door, how could I have not seen it sooner. It's huge. The bruise covers half of his rib cage and it's dark blue, almost black. Seeing it makes my heart feel like a huge hand has reached in and strangled it so tightly I can barely breathe. Remembering what he did the first time he saw the bruise on my neck Caden had left, I lean down and gently kiss it. First I trace every inch of the outline of it. Then I spend the next few minutes covering every inch of his beautiful skin that is blackened with whisper soft kisses. His chest tightens when I hit a certain spot and I know that must be where the break is. Tears burn my eyes thinking of the pain that Caden has caused him. Caused us. Physically and emotionally.

He looks down watching as I cover the last bit of bruised surface with kisses. His eyes are searching mine. He needs assurance as much as I do. This confident man, full of arrogance and sexy bravado, looks so vulnerable. So I open up my heart, taking a risk I know will crush me if it doesn't work out, but it's a risk I have no choice but to take. Taking a deep breath, I look up into his eyes as I finally confess, "I'm in love with you, Jax."

His eyes close, and when he opens them again, something is different. He stares at me so intensely, I'm sure he can see through to my soul. It should scare me, but instead my heart wants to open and sing. His eyes travel around my face and then lock to mine, everything else in the universe fades away when he speaks and it's only me and him. "I smell you when you're nowhere near me. I feel you, without touching. When you walk into a room, I know you're there even before I look up. Every time I see you smile, I smile. Your happiness has become my happiness. Either I'm in love with you, or you really are my very own angel. Either way, we were meant to be."

Tears threaten to spill as he speaks. I hold them back for as long as I can. The first one falls when his voice cracks. "I'm sorry, Angel. I never meant to hurt you." He wipes my tear with a soft brush of his thumb on my cheek. "Please give me a reason to wake up every morning and show you I'm worth forgiving."

I smile even though tears begin to stream down my face. "I hate waking up without you next to me. I sleep on my side of the bed when you're not there and every time I reach over, I'm reminded it's empty. And it makes me feel empty."

Jax smiles, his own eyes filling. He takes my face between his hands. "We'll have to do something about that." Softly, he kisses my lips. Pulling his head back to look at me, a devilish grin threatens at his serious face. "I can think of one way to make you feel less empty right now." He arches an eyebrow.

The thought of him filling me makes my body hum and my teary eyes glaze over.

"It drives me crazy when you look at me like that, you know," he growls.

"Like what?"

"Like you're picturing what I'm going to do to you before I even get your panties off."

I smirk. "I'm not wearing any. I took them off in the taxi on the way over here."

His eyes flash and he growls into my mouth as his hand goes under my skirt and up my thigh. My body tingles everywhere he touches, lord I missed this man. We both groan when his finger slides across my wetness. His eyes narrow. "You came over here without panties, Angel?" he says, a possessive warning in his voice, making me wetter. I close my eyes and squeal when he grabs a handful of my ass and pulls me tightly against him.

"I was hoping you'd like me without panties."

"I do, Angel. I do. But a little breeze hits this skirt and someone else might catch a glimpse of this perfect ass." He squeezes my bottom roughly.

"Now who's jealous?" I tease.

"Me. Always. Because this…" his finger reaches under my skirt and finds my clit immediately. His two fingers stroke me possessively, "…this belongs to me."

My gasp is stifled under his kiss. A kiss that's hungry, rough, assertive, but also filled with emotion, longing, forgiveness, and love. My legs are unsteady and head dizzy when we break for air.

"My ribs. Any movement hurts," he says with a devilish crooked smile as he walks backwards taking me with him toward the bed. "Doctor says I should lie flat on my back." He stops at the edge of the bed, his hand trailing back under my skirt. "So you know what that means?" I whimper as he slips a finger inside of me. "It means you're going to ride me. I'm going to lie on my back and watch you take my cock inside of you. All of it. I want to see you circle those hips with me so far inside of you, greedily pulling me until you're grinding your ass against my balls."

I groan. God I missed his mouth. The way he tells me exactly what he wants. His dirty words have my body throbbing just thinking about him being inside of me again.

I loosen the towel at his waist and it drops to the floor. He springs free, hard and ready. I lick my lips with anticipation. "Lay back," I breathe.

His eyes glued to me, I unbutton my shirt slowly. Reaching behind me I unhook my black lace bra, then slip down my skirt. I stand naked before him as he lies on the bed, his eyes raking over me with a hunger that fuels me.

Careful not to move him too much, I straddle him, gliding my wetness over the length of him. He groans. "Fuck, Angel, you're killing me." I smile, inwardly triumphing at the hunger he doesn't even try to disguise when he looks at me. "It's going to destroy me to not be able to move you around where I want you." His eyes devour me, I feel his words soak through me, penetrating deep into my bones. "Bring your pussy to me. I want to taste you before you take me." I bite my lip, hesitant at first. Then he licks his lips, salivating for me.

I crawl up the bed, positioning myself over him, slowly dropping down so he can reach me. He sucks my clit into his mouth, a moan I feel from the bottom of my toes to the tip of my head roars from my lips. "Ride me baby. Ride my mouth." His words vibrate against me. Fingers digging into my hips, he reaches up and moves my hips, rocking me back and forth. My throbbing clit pulses, making me lose all inhibition. I take over the rhythm he sets, gyrating my hips back and forth as he licks and sucks, his tongue burrowing inside of me as I grind down on his face, my orgasm hitting me quickly, almost violently. I moan his name breathlessly as I come, my entire body convulsing as his mouth keeps working, hungrily lapping at every last drop my body has to offer.

Somehow, broken rib and all, Jax finds a way to make love to me. Slow, passionate, raw, all consuming love making that connects us in way that I know deep down can never be broken again. True love making, because we both finally give in, letting what we feel show through in our emotions as we exchange the words.

Afterwards, when we finally still, I roll to the side not wanting to put any weight on his ribs.

"Jax."

"Yeah, Angel."

"You bought my painting."

"I know."

"Why? We'd just met."

"I just knew," he says so simply with a shrug.

"Knew what?"

"Knew I'd want to see your face every day. If I couldn't have you, I'd have the painting."

"And if this doesn't work out? What do you think your next girlfriend will think of a picture of a half-naked woman hanging around?"

He turns his head to face me. "There is no next girlfriend, Angel. Haven't you realized that yet?"

Epilogue

Lily – Six years later

"You have your own cinnamon bun, you know," I scold, but I'm not really mad. Besides, we need to be out the door in five minutes or we'll be late.

"Yours tastes better," Jackson grins, his lips lined with white frosting, the smile he gives me lets him get away with so much. Just like his father.

I playfully swat at his hand reaching to lick the icing from my plate with his finger. "Wash your hands when you're done, piggy." I stand. "We're out the door in five minutes. We don't want you to be late for your first day of kindergarten. I'm going to go grab my shoes. Put your plate in the sink when you are done eating *both* our breakfasts."

"I don't care if I'm late," Jackson whines a bit. He's been nervous about starting kindergarten the last few weeks, although he'll never admit it. The boy idolizes his father so much, he thinks he has to be fearless just because Jax is.

"Well I do. So put a move on it, brat," I tease over my shoulder as I run up the stairs to get my sandals.

My phone chimes before I can get back down the stairs. It's my tenth text from Jax this morning. He feels badly that he isn't going to be home to walk Jackson to his first day of school, but I'm glad he decided to fly out to Vegas for Vince's fight a few days ago. After a rocky start finding out about the existence of each other, Jax and Vince have found their way. Lately it seems like the two spend so much time talking, they're trying to make up for lost time. Although if you ask the two of them, they'd swear all of their talking is due to the new gyms Jax and I are opening with Vince, an extension of our Ralley's business out on the west coast. But if you ask me, the business venture was only a ruse to give them more reason to spend time together. Unconsciously, my hand goes to the small bump growing again in my belly. I hope it's another boy. I'd love to have mini Jax paired with a mini Vince. Although I'd venture to guess we'd have lots of broken furniture when the two tots discovered wrestling.

He's fine. Not nervous at all. I lie, texting back when he inquires again how Jackson is doing. Telling Jax his mini me is nervous will only make him feel guiltier.

How is Vince feeling this morning? Last night was Vince's fourth time defending his champion title. The fight was the shortest yet, lasted barely one minute before Vince won by TKO.

Still sleeping.

Hurt harder than it looked on TV?

He's hurting alright. Just not from the fight. Rough celebration afterward.

LOL. Okay, behave.

Always. Be home tonight, Angel. Take care of my boys.

You don't know this one is a boy yet. I rub my belly.

Sure I do. I smile, shake my head, and roll my eyes.

Jackson is standing at the door waiting anxiously for me when I get back downstairs. He looks up at me, his big blue eyes nervous behind a sea of dark lashes. It grips at my heartstrings, but I don't let on I know he's scared. The Knight boys are a prideful bunch, I wouldn't want to damage his ego.

Side by side, we walk the seven blocks to PS 199. The tension on his face increases as his new school comes into sight. I want so badly to reach down and grab his hand, squeeze hard, letting him know everything is going to be okay. But I don't. Aside from not wanting to shatter the fearless façade he works so hard to face me with, I remember back to my dad walking me to school. How I loved to hold his hand, he made me feel so safe – like everything in the world was going to be fine as long as he was near me. But kids could be so cruel. I don't want Jackson to be picked on like I was for holding my father's hand. I have to put my own hands into my pockets to restrain myself from not reaching for Jackson's, but I know it's for the best.

We arrive at the front door. Two boys linger at the top step, they spot Jackson and yell his name excitedly. His face lights up with relief and it makes me exhale the breath I'd been holding. My little boy turns to me, awkward with affection for the first time, and seems conflicted. Then he smiles and reaches out his little fist.

"Fist bump," he offers clearing his throat. I've watched Jax and Jackson do it a million times, but I'd always gotten a hug. With a mix of pride and reluctance, I tap my fist to his before he runs away – never looking back.

Jax

People turn their heads and whisper as we walk by. I'm not sure if they recognize Vince and Nico or if it's the sight of three oversized, muscular men shoving each other as we walk.

"What the fuck?" Nico growls, his lidded cup spilling as we clip him while walking. Vince and I have been wrestling since we got to the airport. This time, I barrel him into the wall, unfortunately shoving at Nico in the process. We're only fucking around, but people aren't sure and clear out of our path like we're royalty coming down the red carpet.

"You assholes make me spill one more time…," Nico trails off, blotting the top of his cup and the fluids dripping down the sides.

"Spill your decaffeinated green tea with honey? What kind of guy orders shit like that anyway?" Vince goads Nico. Nico's clean eating habits are a frequent topic of ball busting between the two men. It's in good fun, although it won't stop Nico from serving a bruise to Vince's chest if he continues. When men our size screw around, it always ends with bruises.

"The kind that's going to kick your ass in two minutes if you don't shut your trap," Nico warns.

"Old man, I'm the four time reigning Light Heavyweight Champion of the United State of America. I don't think you have a shot anymore." Vince holds his arms up victoriously as he concededly rattles off his title.

"You wanna go?" Nico dares.

"You bet, old man. You bet." Vince smiles.

Nico shakes his head. "Why don't you put some of your effort to get me into the ring into your brother," Nico deflects.

I quickly interject. "Been there, done that. Let's not go down that road again. Thought we finally put that debate to bed,"

I say. After my fight with Caden, I needed to know I could win and not just by default. So I got in the ring twice more for sanctioned fights. Won both times too. I don't regret a minute of it. If I hadn't done it, I would have wondered *what if* for the rest of my life. Instead, I learned I could win, I had what it took, but it wasn't what I really wanted to do. I love the sport, yet fighting for a living wasn't in me in the end. So I went out on top. Although my brother and Nico couldn't comprehend that my heart was somewhere else.

Caden was banned from fighting after his conviction for Grand Larceny. In the end, Lily decided it was Joe's decision what to do about the money Caden stole. I was surprised when Joe turned his nephew in, but relieved Lily and I didn't have to look over our shoulder for a while. Last I heard, his sentence was extended for fighting too many times in prison. Some people just never learn when to quit.

Lily and I grew Ralley's from sixty-two stores to nearly one hundred and fifty after I put a ring on her finger. And now with taking on my brother as a partner for the new stores, we'll be at two hundred by year end. I finally found a way to merge the three things in my life that I love - running our company, my wife, and fighting. I'd be hard pressed to find a happier man than me.

"Alright gentlemen. And I use the term very loosely." I grin as we arrive at my gate. We're all flying back home to our wives. Vince with another championship under his belt, and Nico and I proud. "I'll see you in a few weeks. When that lovely wife of yours delivers." Vince's wife Liv is pregnant too, our wives are excited the cousins will only be a few months apart. "Hope his head won't be as big as yours, little brother." I tousle the top of my brother's head and we hug, a one armed chest bump, guy style.

"Later, Spawn 1," Vince yells over his shoulder, walking down the terminal with Nico.

"Later, Spawn 2," I yell back.

Turned out my father, elected again despite being the biggest liar and user east of the Mississippi, gave me something that made my life complete after all – my brother.

Lily

Pregnancy definitely slows me down. It's nine at night, yet I'm ready for bed. Jax just landed and should be home within the hour, I hope I can stay awake that long to see him. I crack the door to check in on Jackson. His eyes are shut, but he stirs a bit when I turn off the TV. I smile at the poster of Vince "The Invincible" hanging over his bed and tiptoe over to collect the clothes he wore today lying in the middle of his bedroom floor.

I lift the shirt and shorts and something falls to the floor from his pocket. Leaning down in the dark, I can't make out what it is, till I pick it up. Jax's pocket watch. Jackson's groggy voice speaks, taking me by surprise. I'd thought he was sleeping.

"Can I have that?"

"This?" I hold up the pocket watch, confused at why he has it.

"Yeah."

"Sure." I walk to the bed. "But where did you get it from?"

Jackson shrugs his shoulder. "I don't know, it was in my pocket when I got dressed this morning. Maybe Dad put it in the wrong shorts. My favorite blue shorts are almost the same color as his."

I lean down and kiss him on the forehead, pulling the covers up.

"I was playing with it in my pocket at school today when the teacher was going around the room and making us stand up and say our name. I might have been a little nervous," he says, trying to come off casual. So Jax's son. He reaches up to take the pocket watch. "It's weird. But it made me feel better. It reminded me of dad and then I thought of watching Uncle Vince on the TV last night, and by the time they got to me, I'd forgotten all about being nervous."

I hand him the pocket watch and smile watching him fold it into his hand and snuggle back up on his side.

"Night, Baby."

"Night, Mom."

Leaning my back against my son's closed door, I smile and wonder how I ever got so lucky to have had two amazing men in my life. My Dad and Jax. I barely remember telling him the story about my dad and his pocket watch, yet it touched him so much, he remembered and gave that gift to our son. It's just the kind of man he is. Thoughtful, kind, protective, sexy, and beautiful. A man I took a chance on forgiving so long ago and never looked back. A man worth forgiving, because I could never forget.

Dear Readers,

Thank you so much for all of your support for my MMA Fighter series! Nico, Vince and Jax have consumed my life for such a long time, it was truly hard for me to move on. In fact, it was so difficult, that I decided to go a very different direction for my next book. VERY different! But I'm madly in love with Left Behind and I hope you will all take a chance with me on something new!

Please take a sneak peek at Left Behind, coming 10/16/14! This book has my heart and soul, and I hope it will steal a little piece of yours too!

Sign up for mailing list and receive Chapter 1 of 'Left Behind' as a free gift.

http://eepurl.com/0ABfr

And please add Left Behind to your reading list!

http://bit.ly/1rbXtmS

Other Books by Vi Keeland

Worth the Fight
amzn.com/B00FLG5B9S

Worth the Chance
Amzn.com/B00I2UKQOK

Belong to You
Amzn.com/B00BUTCXLE

Made for You
Amzn.com/B00DPWVKS6

First Thing I See
Amzn.com/B00AWXY3HG

Connect with Vi

http://fb.me/ViKeeland
http://on.fb.me/1uxLPTH
Twitter - @vikeeland
Instagram - @vi_keeland
http://www.vikeeland.com

Acknowledgements

Writing a book is emotionally and physically draining, yet beautiful and exhilarating at the same time. It's a roller coaster ride filled with many ups and downs. I'd like to acknowledge some of the people who put up with my down days, my neurosis, my unresponsiveness, and all around slacker behavior when I am engrossed in a book.

To my husband, for the support he gives me in…well…everything. For enduring my emotional mood swings and listening to me walk through plots he has no interest in – except that it's important to me.

To some very special women, Andrea, Carmen, Jen, Lisa, Beth, Dallison, & Nita - Thank you for everything! For beta reading, editing, making beautiful graphics and trailers, and always giving me your honest opinions. But most of all for your friendship and support.

Thank you so much to all of the bloggers that generously give their time to read and support Indie Authors! Without your support, many would not find our stories.

Finally, thank you so much to all the readers. I'm blessed to have amazing people read my books and fall in love with my characters. I find your enthusiasm inspiring and I do read every one of your emails! So keep your notes coming, I truly love hearing your thoughts!

All my best,